THE
TRANSLATION
OF
MAX

THE
TRANSLATION
OF
MAX

PAMELA DEANE

And now, a disclaimer:

Love writing, hate editing. I would be obliged if you could find it in your heart to forgive errors because, although I've done my best to catch them all, I'm sure there are still a few lurking between mundane words or behind seemingly correct punctuation and verbose sentences. Sneaky little sons-a-bitches.

DEDICATION

Although not strictly autobiographical, in essence *The Translation of Max* parallels my life and that of my older son during a perplexing and challenging eight-year stretch. I dedicate my attempt to coherently express that time, to my son Adam who lived it, and to my son Jason who was too often right there in the trenches with us.

I look at you and see all the ways
a soul can bruise, and I wish
I could sink my hands into your flesh
and light lanterns along your spine
so you know that there's nothing
but light
when I see you.

From the Poem: "I Love You the Distance Between Paris and New York," Shinji Moon

CHAPTER 1

Maxim slid his thumb over the jagged edges of the Lugar. It felt cold, weighty. I'll just wait for them to come to me, he thought. They don't think I can see them. If I sit here...don't move...don't blink, they won't know, will they? He could see them slithering up the lawn, their fat bodies moving with synchronized precision, the tails swaying back and forth to the cadence of legs crabbing rhythmically through the slick blades of grass. Closer...closer.

It was almost noon when Max exploded from his room. He strode down the hall, shirt unbuttoned, tails flapping behind him, and burst into the kitchen. "Let's go!" he screamed. "Now!"

Maggie jerked her head up from the raggedy assortment of washcloths she was folding. For a moment, she fumbled with a blue and white sackcloth towel. Her eyes widened, her heart fluttered in her throat, then she regained her composure.

Stay calm, Maggie. This isn't entirely new. Just a little more...volatile. Nothing to be afraid of.

To give herself a little time, she picked up her mug and walked over to the coffeepot. She turned to face her son, a cup of cold coffee in one hand, the carafe in the other. "Okay," she said. She didn't really know what she was agreeing to, but she did know that Maxim's behavior lately was not something she wanted to tackle head-on. She tried a nonchalant air. "Ya want a cup of coffee first?"

1

"Hell no, I don't want a cup of coffee! Let's go! Now, bitch!"
Keep your voice even. Composed.

"That's fine, Max. Why don't you get your shoes on while I find the keys?"

"I don't have any shoes!"

"Where are the Nikes we bought last week?" Maggie knew almost instantly she shouldn't have asked, but the shock of $100 down the drain caught her off guard.

"Forget the shoes! I threw them away on my way home last night. Let's go!" Maxim edged closer to her, chest inflated, fists clenched, eyebrows furrowed. The sable, shoulder-length hair he was once so proud of now hung in matted strands. His eyes narrowed to slits as thin and black as mechanical pencil leads, daring his mother to challenge him.

"Okay, let me find my keys. Why don't you wait for me in the car, Max? I'll be right out." The slight tremor in her hands belied her steady voice

To her relief, Max turned on his heels and marched out the door, slamming it behind him. A few seconds later, she heard the car door slam shut.

Maggie knew exactly where her keys were. Two months ago, as Max had become more and more erratic, she began hiding her keys and the keys to the old Studebaker Lark she had bought for $500 the week before Maxim's birthday. At that time she figured it was a way he could get himself to school or to appointments and basketball practice when she was working. But what seemed like a viable solution then became just one more headache, and now even restricting his driving did nothing to keep him home. Night after night she had heard the front door bang shut as he left the house. She tried yelling after him; she tried calling the police.

Neither had helped.

Occasionally, Max could still be calm and endearing. At these times she could see a trace of the child she had raised, but usually he was bizarre and terrifying. He seldom slept, seldom ate, and seldom went to school. At seventeen, Maxim Timothy Axline had become a lost soul.

Earlier that morning, when Maggie had rifled through the

Yellow Pages, she wasn't sure what she was looking for, all she knew was she needed help. She flipped through the "C"s, passed "Consultants" and "Contractors," to "Counselors-Marriage, Family, Child, & Individual." Her index finger hovered over "New Light Christian Counseling" and "Get Joe's Help Counseling for Men."

"Really?" she huffed as she turned the page. She paused on "Empowering Women" but quickly discounted it when a chorus of "I Am Woman, Hear Me Roar," flitted through her mind. So many choices. Too many.

"Drilling, Driving Instruction," she murmured as she thumbed through the "D"s. When her eyes locked on "Drug Abuse Information & Treatment," the telephone book slipped from her grasp and thudded against the white tile counter. She stared out the window at the blur of rain dripping metrically from the eaves, then shifted her eyes cautiously to the telephone book as if it was Norman Bates and she was getting ready to step into the shower. "I can do this," she told herself. She picked up her pen, squeaked a sigh, and resolutely circled "Awakening: Your Journey Begins Here," "Center for Dual Diagnosis," and "New Day Connections." All sounded expensive and foreign to her prosaic, raised-in-the-50s vocabulary.

Her fingers grazed past "Columbia River Center for Drug and Alcohol Abuse," then returned to it. "I can do this," she repeated.

The phone ticked against the stem of her reading glasses as she held it to her ear.

"892-" The room felt dank and closed in around her. Her finger trembled and slipped to the wrong number.

Damn!

She glanced at the listing again. "892-6—" She slammed the receiver back in the cradle. But not now," she whispered. "Not right now."

Maggie slid the phone book back in the drawer and turned to dirty dishes piled up from the night before. She needed to keep her hands and her muddled brain occupied. Maybe doing the dishes would give her a sense of routine, of normalcy. By rote, she squirted soap into the sink. The froth of green Palmolive, the smell, the scald of water were familiar and

3

calming, cleansing more than the spaghetti sauce that formed a stubborn crust on plates and forks. She took her time, in no hurry to face what she knew was coming.

By the time Maggie got her keys, Max was already in the car. She buckled her seatbelt and eased out of the driveway. "Now, where did you say we were going, Max?"

"You know where we're going. You know exactly where we're going, you stupid, fucking bitch!" Max screamed.

"Got it." Maggie didn't have the vaguest idea where she was headed, but she did know there was no point asking again. As she drove, she was bombarded with a steady stream of foul language. "You're an ugly whore, you know! You dumb, fucking bitch, you think you know everything!"

During the fourteen-mile trip to town, Maggie willed herself not to talk, not to cry, not to react. "Think!" she told herself. Should she drop him off where some of the kids hung out? It was hard to believe his friends hadn't noticed changes in him, but no one had said anything to her.

Were they all high?

She could drop him off at the mall, or a friend's house, but neither option sounded right. Mentally, Maggie scrolled through the listings in the Yellow Pages. Why hadn't she written down the addresses? There was one, though. She knew about where it was. She had driven past it many times on her way to work, but the exact location never really registered. It was a gamble. She didn't even know if it would be open on Sunday. She turned west on Fourth Plain Boulevard and headed in the direction of Columbia River Drug and Alcohol Center.

CHAPTER 2

As they approached The Center, Maggie risked a quick glimpse at Max. His expression was still dark and brooding, but he had become less explosive. She bit her lip and pulled into the parking lot. Before she could come to a full stop, the door-ajar alarm blared as Max bolted from the car and ran towards the main entrance.

Maggie parked and flew after him, hardly having time to process the absurdity of the situation. Neither she nor Max had really known where they were going, yet now they were there, Max seemed to accept it, almost as if he had planned it all along. By the time she got in the door, Max was already shouting at a man who appeared to be one of the counselors.

Maggie leaned against the counter. "This...is...Max," she panted. "I think...he needs...to talk to someone."

The counselor simply pointed and said, "Sure. Max, you can go down there to the second door on the left." Max turned abruptly and swaggered down the hall. The counselor shot Maggie a knowing glance and followed. She didn't know his name, but sent up a silent prayer of thanks and collapsed into an orange naugahyde chair.

It took only ten minutes for the drug and alcohol team to make an evaluation, which was actually no evaluation at all. Maggie had barely scanned a *People* magazine, when John, one of the team members, came out to the lobby and introduced himself. He told her there were two more D & A counselors

5

with Max, but they were sure that drugs or alcohol were not the problem. "We've sent for the people from the mental health staff next door," John explained. "We think they may be able to make a more accurate E-val."

Maggie's mouth dropped open. *Mental health?* She could barely wrap her mind around the words. Her mind raced, flitting among the possibilities. She knew very little about mental illness. In fact, other than a brief bout of depression when Max's father left them and moved to Arizona where there were warmer nights, warmer women, and an entire population of people who were naïve to his flaky schemes and harebrained business deals, she was oblivious to it. She couldn't even put an official name to what type it could be.

Maggie had heard the words "psychotic," "depression," "schizophrenia," and "bipolar" bantered around from time to time, but more often than not they were referred to in obscure slang terms or euphemisms. "He has a disorder" and "she has anger issues," or "your Aunt Liddy is just a little batty" and "the old man who runs the Keegler's Deli is nutty as a fruit cake." As a child she also remembered listening to covert quips and veiled jokes between her parents when they drove past Western State Hospital in Steilacoom. She always asked who lived there, but the answer she got was never more than a hazy, "Oh, just a bunch of crazies."

She sucked in a sharp breath. Now, could one of those "crazies" be her own son?

CHAPTER 3

The smiles are forced, Maggie thought. She'd flicked through the rest of last year's May, 1993, issue of *People*, and had picked up an even older one, when two men came out of the conference room. Maggie bowed her head pretending to read the article proclaiming Meg Ryan one of the year's "most beautiful people," but her eyes strained upwards to watch them. Both were young, slender, sported wire-rimmed glasses, and had an air of restraint about them. In fact, other than one wearing a green Izod shirt and the other a Madras plaid, they were two buttoned-down peas in a Freudian pod. They stood at the receptionist's counter and talked quietly and intently, stopping every once in a while to casually look in Maggie's direction and smile, before returning to a real head-bobbing conversation.

Eventually, they broke huddle. One went back down the hall, and the other strolled over to her. He held out his hand, "Hi. You must be Max's mom. Sorry, I wasn't able to get your name yet. I'm Jeffery."

She rose and took his hand. "Hi, I'm Maggie Axline. Yes, Max is my son."

Jeffery scanned the empty lobby. "Mind if we talk here for a few minutes?" he said as he sat down.

Maggie's eyes flashed, then closed momentarily. She felt haggard and drawn and hardly trusted her own ability to speak intelligently. She opened her eyes, and a weak, high-pitched, "hu" squeaked out as she dropped into the chair again.

"Mrs. Axline," he began, "we aren't sure yet, but we think Max may have a mental condition. More tests should be done. May I ask you a few questions?"

Maggie searched his face for clues. "But what do you think it is? I mean, do you have any idea? You don't think it's drugs?"

"Like I said, Mrs. Axline—"

"Maggie," she interjected.

"Like I said, Maggie, our evaluation was fairly cursory, but we don't think it's drugs. We think Max may have a disorder called schizophrenia." Jeffery paused to give that little tidbit of information time to trickle down. "But Max brought up a few things I'd like to ask you about."

Maggie stared at the floor, the nod almost imperceptible. She felt the earth shift beneath her, and she clutched at the arm of the chair.

"Max said there were alligators outside your house, and last night he saw them creeping up your lawn. I assume this was a delusion..." Pause. Smile. "But he also said he was going to shoot them if it happened again." Pause. No smile.

And the seconds tick, tick, ticked. Maggie's mind swirled. *Wait, what was he saying?*

"Mrs. Axline...Maggie...do you or anyone in your home own a gun?" he finally asked.

"A gun? What? No! We don't have any guns."

"He said it was a German Lugar. Is there any way he could have gotten hold of one?"

Maggie shook her head. "No. Wait! We have a toy one. I mean a toy Lugar. It's made out of pot metal, I think. I guess he could club an alligator to death, but he couldn't shoot one." Her eyes rose to meet Jeffery's. A tiny smile tugged at the corners of her mouth but was gone in a split second. "This whole thing is ludicrous," she finally managed. "How can something like this happen?"

"Yeah, well that's the sixty-four-thousand-dollar question. Wish I could give you a definitive answer, but I can't. No one can right now." Since the gun issue had been resolved, Jeffery's shoulders had relaxed some.

He was upbeat and positive, at least as much as he could be

under the circumstances, but the outcome was that since Max was not yet an adult, Maggie would be responsible for getting him to a psychiatrist for further assessment and treatment. "We deal mostly with adults or wards of the state and other...specialized population," he told her. "I think you should call a mental health doctor as soon as you can. We do have a list of people we've worked with to get you started if it would help."

"One more thing," Jeffery continued. "Does your insurance have mental health coverage?"

CHAPTER 4

Maggie scavenged through the "important papers" drawer in the kitchen. She tossed out appliance warranties, outdated license renewals, and dog-eared scraps of paper with telephone numbers that had long since lost meaning. At the bottom of the heap was a "Guide to Your Health Plan" booklet. She flipped it open to the table of contents and scrolled her finger down the list of benefits section to "Mental Health Coverage."

"Gotta be something...something ...something," she murmured as she fumbled through until she found page 87. Yes! There it was! "Mental Health Coverage," she read. Her mouth hung open. "There is no coverage for mental health in this plan."

Maggie slumped into a chair. Her mind was murky. She picked up the list Jeffery had given her and tried to concentrate.

While she had been talking to him, Max had stormed by. "You can wait in the car, Max," Maggie yelled after him, "I'll be out in a minute." But by the time she had the list of psychiatrists and got out to the car, Max was long gone. After driving around for a while, she gave up and went home. She had to get some sleep before work the next day, but that same feeling of being overwhelmed that had lurked in the corners of her mind for months, came once again to the forefront and jabbed at her nerves. If only she had more time to deal with it. Being a high school teacher had its advantages, but it demanded her full attention every day, and nights and weekends were jam-packed with lessons to plan and papers to grade. Bringing her private life to work added to her stress, but calling in sick only generated more work. And needless to say, personal calls from a loopy son during a class did little to bolster her credibility as a competent educator.

In a fog, Maggie flipped on a rerun of *The Flintstones* and dropped to the couch. Fortunately, her younger son Braxton was at a friend's house for the night. She always felt she had to act as a barrier between the two boys, but was never sure how to do it without causing a bigger rift. At least with Braxton gone, she felt a little flurry of relief. One less thing to worry about.

Maggie slept through *ER, Columbo,* and back-to-back episodes of *Rosanne.* At nine o'clock, she hauled herself from the couch, grabbed a stale maple bar, slumped to her bedroom, and flopped in a heap onto disheveled sheets. Five a.m. would come too quickly, and her required eight-hour day would probably stretch into ten at the least.

She had checked Max's room as she went by, already knowing it would be empty, and left the porch light on and the front door unlocked.

He didn't come home that night. Nor the next.

On the third evening, the phone was ringing as she came in the door about six. It was her neighbor.

"Hey, Maggie, how're ya doing?" Roger began.

He sounds casual, Maggie thought. Maybe a bit too casual. Her experience with the family on the two-acre parcel adjoining hers to the north had been cordial enough but always a bit staid. She had never really communicated with them other than an informal chat or perfunctory wave in passing. He was a minister at a rural parish. Maggie knew little about the family other than there was also a wife and two kids— a middle-school boy and a teenage daughter —and a Border Collie/mutt mix that snapped at her heels to herd her every time she walked the three-quarter-mile gravel road to get her mail.

"Roger?"

"Yeah. Listen," he said after a pause. "Is Max okay? I mean

11

how's he doing?"

"Well, to tell you the truth, Roger, he could be better. Why?" Maggie didn't know where this was going, but she waited for him to make the first move.

"Well, it's just that he came by our house about four thirty this morning."

"What?" She had checked his room when she first got up, but he could have come in right after that while she was in the shower. She hadn't thought to check again before she left for work.

"Yeah, and he didn't look so hot. I wanted to check to see if he was okay." Roger hesitated as if he was deciding whether or not to go on. Finally, he said, "It was kind of weird."

"Oh? How?" Maggie tried to match Roger's relaxed air, but she felt the throbbing against her chest wall.

Roger forced an awkward chuckle. "Seems he wants to marry Sarah."

"What?"

"He asked for Sarah's hand in marriage, Maggie. That's how he put it."

"Ah, shit!" The words exploded before she could check herself. She knew Max was acquainted with Roger's daughter but only on about the same level that Maggie knew her folks. Seemed like a nice enough girl—at least for a sixteen-year-old.

Roger was silent, but she sensed he wasn't done yet. "What else, Roger?"

"Oh, well, I'm sure it's nothing, but he said he was going to kill himself if I wouldn't let him marry Sarah."

Maggie plunked down on the counter stool. Suicide was something she'd never thought about before. Something Max had never even mentioned.

"Maggie? You there?"

"Oh, yeah, Roger, I'm here."

"I mean, I don't think he sounded real serious," Roger went on, "but I thought you should know. Now, if there's anything I can do to help you, anything at all..."

"Of course. Thanks, Roger. I'll let you know."

Maggie hung up and laid her head on the cool tile counter. She felt drained. Emotionally, mentally, and physically drained.

12

She heaved herself up and trudged down the hall to Max's room. Still gone.

Feeling completely helpless, not knowing where Max was, what he was doing, when he would be home, was taking its toll on her ability to concentrate at school, as well as her ability to sleep at night.

Maggie was sure—well, almost sure—he wouldn't actually try to kill himself. Surely he was not so far gone, so desperate he would do that. Still, the thought had been planted in her mind and she couldn't shake it.

Twice during the next week, there were signs he had come home during the day. There was spilled Coke on the floor, the toilet seat was up, and there were so many dirty dishes in the sink it looked like a whole army of his friends had been with him. Braxton would have been at school, or practice, or anywhere but home during this time. Besides, Braxton usually picked up after himself. Max, on the other hand, always seemed oblivious to the mess that followed him wherever he went.

Finally, on Friday evening as Maggie was sitting at the table correcting Act I précis of *Julius Caesar*, the phone rang. She leapt for it. "Hello? Hello?"

Dead silence on the other end. "Max? Max, if that's you, please say something."

Nothing.

"I'm worried about you, honey, where are..."

Click.

Whoever it was had hung up. If it was Max, was he trying to tell her something? Was he simply checking to see if she was home? She turned in that night with the queasy feeling that something unpleasant was lurking and about to rear its ugly head. She tossed most of the night before REM sleep mercifully kicked in.

CHAPTER 5

The blare jarred Maggie out of her sleep. Her hand flew up and slapped at the alarm clock, but the clamor continued. Her fingers fumbled for the telephone, knocked it off the cradle, and grasped at the cord, pulling the receiver toward her. "Max? That you?"

"Mrs. Axline?" The voice was firm, business-like, and anything but Max's.

"Yeah, this is Maggie Axline."

"Mrs. Axline, this is Southwest Washington Hospital calling."

Maggie squeezed her eyes tight and held her breath before she said, "Uh-huh?"

"First of all, Mrs. Axline, I want you to know that Maxim is going to be all right, but he's here because he's been in an automobile accident."

"I'll be right there," Maggie said, already halfway into her jeans and searching for her tennis shoes.

"Do you know where we are loc—"

Maggie was already slipping on a sweatshirt and grabbing the keys.

On her way out, she noticed the Lark was missing. Max must have found the keys earlier, or surely she would have heard him come in to find them. But right now she didn't have time to analyze it. She jumped in her car and made the twenty-five-minute trip to the hospital in eighteen.

14

She tried to will her heart to slow its rhythm and her mind to clear as she parked, but she couldn't control the feeling of impending doom. When she approached the entrance, massive glass doors whooshed open to a room of chaos. Police officers stood talking to each other, and people with furrowed brows sat around the waiting room keeping their eyes glued to nurses with clipboards flitting in and out of the patient treatment area.

She approached the check-in desk, and a receptionist slid back the glass window.

"Maxim Axline?" Maggie said. Was it her imagination, or did she actually "harrumph" her?

The thick-eyed girl yawned, then ran her finger down a sheet. "You a relative?" she finally said.

Well, of course I'm a relative, you insipid little twit! What came out was, "Yes."

As if she had read Maggie's thoughts, the girl glowered and pointed. "Through those doors and to the left. It's bed 7A."

The emergency room was lively that night. As she made her way to Max's cubicle, she sidestepped doctors, oxygen tanks, portable heart monitors, and patients on gurneys being whisked away. Don't make assumptions, Maggie told herself. "One thing at a time. One thing at a time. Deep breath," she whispered as she came to 7A and drew the partition curtain back.

Max thrashed on a gurney like a trout that had just been landed and still had the hook in its mouth. His legs flopped up and down, and he grasped at the IV while a male nurse tried in vain to hold both arms down.

"Max!" Maggie snapped in her best you'd-better-cut-that-out-right-now-or-you're-in-big trouble-mister tone. It triggered an automatic response and Max stopped wrestling with the nurse and stared at her.

"Oh, hi, Mom!" he said as if nothing out of the ordinary was going on.

Maggie walked over and took one of his hands in hers while the male nurse secured the other one with a strap then stepped aside for a moment so he could secure that one. Finally, he took an audible breath and said, "Hi, you must be Mrs. Axline."

15

Oh, how she wanted to say, "Nope, just someone passing by," but she nodded. "Do you know what happened? Is he going to be all right?"

"He doesn't appear to have any serious injuries, but the doctor will be in to talk to you in a minute. The only thing I know is that there was a car accident. I'll let an officer know you're here. Let me grab a chair for you." He tilted his head. "You want a cup of coffee? Looks like you could use one."

"Got anything stronger?..." Maggie glanced at the name tag pinned to his scrubs. "Neil."

The corner of Neil's mouth skewed upwards. "Sorry. But the coffee's strong enough to carry a warning label," he smirked and went out.

Before Neil came back, an officer stuck his head in. "Mrs. Axline?" He looked over at Max. "Hey, Max, how you doin'?" Then without waiting for an answer, asked her to step out to the nurses' station.

"You know anything yet about the accident?" he began

Maggie had the distinct feeling he was going to try to ease into this slowly and was choosing his words carefully.

"No. Was my son driving?" She always did have more of a stomp-on-my-toe, sock-me on-the-jaw, and-get-it-over-with mentality. There was no point dragging it out.

The officer got the message and dove right in. "Yes, he was, Mrs. Axline. He was going up the hill on Hyden Park Road and came around the corner on the wrong side. He hit the car coming down the hill head-on going about forty-five. The good news is, no one was killed, but unfortunately, there were five adults in the other car, and all of them are here in the hospital." He paused to let this much of the insanity soak in.

Maggie buried her head in her hands and felt the room swaying. A chair touched the back of her knees, and a hand took her elbow and guided her down. Her fingers slid from her face, and she looked up. "What else?"

The account of the accident didn't take as long as it felt, but her head was swimming and her thoughts were so tangled she asked questions she was pretty sure he had already answered.

When he was through there was no doubt as to whose fault it was. In one car, five responsible adults: an attorney, a CPA, a

16

contractor, a housewife, and a teacher, all wearing seatbelts, all sober, were coming home from a night out, when their lives were suddenly, drastically, and irrevocably altered. In the other car, three idiot teenagers with underdeveloped frontal lobes were on their way to another kegger. Not one was wearing a seatbelt.

Overwhelmed, Maggie could think to ask only one more question. "What do I do now?"

CHAPTER 6

They pulled back into her carport about six Saturday morning. The doctor had said Max had some internal bruising but no visible injuries. He would have preferred to keep him overnight for observation, but when Max kept pulling the IV out of his arm and became belligerent when the sedation wore off, he agreed, rather quickly Maggie thought, to discharge him. She had promised to keep an eye on him and call if he exhibited any behavior that seemed out of the ordinary. The irony of that one did not escape her, but she said she would and packed Max out to the car, hoping for the best. It was obvious he was sore when they got home. He asked for help getting out of the car, scuffed into his bedroom, and closed the door quietly behind him.

Maggie put on a pot of dark French roast and sat down to make a list of what she had to do that day and the week to follow. She wrote: "1. call wrecking yard – see about car," "2. call auto insurance people," "3. Max's psychiatrist appointment on Wednesday."

Was that all? She tap-tap-tapped her pencil against the tiles. The police had taken care of the accident report and said she would be hearing from them soon. Tap-tap-tap. There was something else swirling at the back of her mind. It was something about...tap-tap-tap...oh! Of course! She wrote down, "4. Attorney?" It was hard to even think about, but the acrid and undeniable truth was there would probably be lawsuits. She didn't know the extent of the injuries yet, but all the adults

18

and both boys with Max were still in the hospital. While she had been waiting, she picked up snippets of information, and although vague, it sounded like there were very serious, but not life-threatening, injuries. She had to assume they or their insurance companies would sue. Would her insurance cover all of it? Confronting the possibility finally sapped Maggie, and she lay her head on the cool counter and let the tears come.

Two hours later, she awoke in a puddle of slobber, her throat begging for a cool drink. Stiff from sleep, she hobbled to the sink. She turned on the faucet until the well water ran "as cold as a well digger's ankle," as her mother would have said. It had been years since she had died, yet time and again Maggie heard her mother's voice surface in her memory, sometimes in archaic whimsy, other times in prudent axioms. Both gave Maggie solace. When life overwhelmed, her mother's mantra, "one thing at a time and everything will get done," became her mantra.

And that was the catchphrase that was on automatic rerun as Maggie pulled out the telephone book to look up "AA Wrecking." As she waited while the phone rang ten times, she wondered if they realized the wry humor in their name. Finally, a gravelly, yet oddly chipper voice said, "AA Wrecking. If we can pull it out, you can put it in. Allen Appleton, proprietor here. What can I do you for?"

Of course. AA. "Hi, you towed my car in early this morning. It was in an accident." Maggie paused. "On Hyden Park Road?...White Studebaker Lark?" She waited for a hint of recognition. Nothing. "The police said to call you. It's registered to—"

"Oh, yeah!" the raspy voice interrupted. "You Axline?"

"Yes," she sighed. "Yes, I'm Maggie Axline. Shall I come down there to sign something? How bad is it? Do you think it can be salvaged?"

"Aw, hell no! There's no way this car's going anywhere. Complete total."

Appleton's abruptness didn't bother Maggie. Better that than coming at it from the back door.

"So, do I need to sign something?"

19

"Well, usually the insurance company takes care of all that. Have you talked to them yet?" He didn't wait for an answer. "You can come take a look at it if you want. `Course there's not much there that don't look like scrambled eggs." Appleton hesitated. "You driving it? Glad you're still around to call me if you was."

Maggie didn't want to get into details. "No," she said, "but I need to take care of the paperwork if there is any. Did you find the registration?"

Appleton snorted. "Oh yeah. Thought we was going to have to take a blowtorch to the glove box to get it open, but we did it with just a jimmy."

Maggie could tell that Allen Appleton, proprietor, was clearly proud of this handiwork. "Well, thank you for your help, Mr. Appleton," she said. "If you would hang on to that and anything else you find, I'll contact my insurance agent, and they can take it from there. Maybe you could jot down my number in case you need it?"

"Already got it! On the registration!"

Maggie could almost see his grease covered chest swell with pride at his resourcefulness.

Maggie punched the receiver button and cradled the phone between her shoulder and ear as she rummaged around the phonebook drawer until she found her insurance agent's card. Maybe she would have some advice about talking to an attorney. "One thing at a time and everything will get done," she chanted as she dialed the number.

CHAPTER 7

"Yes, Maggie, contact an attorney," was the advice she got from her insurance agent, her neighbor, a smattering of friends, and both of Max's grandfathers.

Her insurance policy had a maximum coverage of $300,000, which, according to her agent Leslie Stalls, would be spread pretty thin with that many injuries.

Maggie had not planned to tell people about Max's possible illness until she had seen the psychiatrist, but the accident forced the issue. By Sunday morning it was in *The Columbian, The Battleground Reflector, The Camas-Washougal Post,* and *The Oregonian.* With some people, she kept the details ambiguous, saying only he had not been "completely himself" lately. But the grandfathers were a bit trickier. Her father was the flamboyant, whistle-at-you-from-across-the-street-to-get-your-attention type. Her father-in-law was the quiet, stare-at-the-mashed-potatoes-until-someone-notices-and-passes-them-to-you type. She adored them both. She wasn't at all sure how they would take it but decided to come clean, beginning with her father.

She jotted down a couple of notes to help organize what she was going to say and called him. "Hey, Dad!" she began.

"Magpie! How's my third favorite daughter?" he quipped. Each of his three daughters was addressed in the same way. "Keeps 'em on their toes," he was fond of telling anyone who would listen. But since one of her sisters was living in Australia and the other in Texas, Maggie received the brunt of his humor.

"I'm okay. What cha doin'?" Maggie stalled as she checked

21

her notes again, still unsure of the best approach. Even though it was before noon, she knew he was already leaning back in his cracked white leather recliner watching the sailboats and pontoon floaters on the Willamette, a gin and tonic in one hand, binoculars in the other. Since his retirement, this had been his modus operandi every day of the week.

"Oh, just sitting here wondering what the poor folk are doing right now. What's up, sweetheart?"

"Listen, Dad, have you read *The Oregonian* yet today? I mean, other than the sports section?"

"Hey! Did I tell you the Trail Blazers played in that new Rose Garden last night? I gotta go to a game there."

Sidetracked!

"Yeah, I heard. How'd they do?"

"They won, but they were lucky! Damn it all, Maggie, if Strickland doesn't stop mouthing off to Carlesimo, he's going to get himself kicked off. They need Kersey back, anyone can—"

"Dad! Listen for a minute, will ya?" When the other end of the line went silent, she dove in. "It's just that Maxim was in a car accident Friday night. It's in the paper, Dad. It was pretty bad." She heard the familiar clink of ice and a quick slurp.

"Dad, you there?"

"Is he okay?"

"Yes, actually he is, but a lot of other people were hurt. Dad, it was his fault." Maggie gave a broad account of the accident and the injuries, ending with, "I think all of them are still in the hospital."

"Aw, damn it all. Sorry, honey. That's rough. You all right?"

"I'm okay, but, well, Max is having some other problems, too. I mean, he's been acting...strange...the last few months. I'm not sure yet what's wrong with him, but..."

"He's seventeen, Maggie; of course he's strange. He'll grow out of it. You did."

"This is different, Dad. It's not just normal teenage stuff. I'm taking him to a psychiatrist in a couple of days." Maggie waited for what she knew was coming next.

"He doesn't need a psychiatrist, Maggie. What that kid needs is a good swift kick in the behind. They all do at that age. Did I ever tell you about the time my brother and I rode the rails from Eureka to San Francisco?"

"Yeah, Dad, you did. But this is—"

"When we got home, I thought my Aunt Millie was going to kill us!" He chuckled at the fate that had awaited him dozens of times in the story telling.

"Dad!" Maggie interrupted again. "No, Dad. They think he might have...a mental illness." The word "schizophrenia" played on her tongue but wouldn't come out. It was too new, too unfamiliar, too harsh.

"Illness, schmillness," he scoffed. "He needs a firmer hand, for God's sake. It isn't like he's had a father around to straighten him out. Not that you haven't done a fine job of raising those two boys, Maggie, but..."

Maggie listened for the next ten minutes to her father's dos and don'ts of parenthood, the perils of drugs and alcohol for teenagers, quips about her own teen years, and his clichéd Dr. Spock approach to discipline. But when she broke in to ask him if he thought she needed to hire an attorney, his tone was sobering. "Well, I think it would be a good idea, honey."

When Maggie hung up, she was more confused than ever. A lot of what he said made sense, more sense than the bizarre world of a psychotic illness. A world that was as foreign to her as living on the Sahara would be to an Inuit.

She mulled over what her dad had said as she drove to her father-in-law's house on the other side of town. Maybe talking to someone face-to-face would help.

Maggie pulled alongside the chain-link fence and swung open a cock-eyed gate with a rusted sign on it that read *Caution! Guard Dog on Duty!* She started to holler "Coco," when a chocolate lab bounded around the corner of the house and ran toward her with pure, unbridled delight. Maggie started the expected scratching routine starting at the tail end and working her way across the back, shoulders, and neck, ending with a good ear workout.

"Some guard dog you are," she said as she nuzzled him. The very wet tongue that had been lolling, waiting for its chance to express itself, slurped indiscriminately at Maggie's cheek, neck, hands, arms, and finally, knees before the frenzy of fur

23

heard, "Coconut!" and ran off in the direction of the garden.

She took her time and followed the lab to where her father-in-law was jabbing at offending weeds that sprouted between rows of corn and end-of-the-season tomatoes, onions, zucchini, and kohlrabi. Coco ran over to him, still waggling, then ran back to Maggie as if to say, "See? See? We've got company."

Clive leaned on his hoe as Maggie approached. "Hey," he said, "you hungry?"

She strolled over to the small John Deere tractor and collapsed onto the flatbed trailer attached to it. She nodded, drew in a deep, therapeutic breath and released it. The dirt puffed up around Coco as he slumped to the ground next to her.

"Right back," Clive said and ambled toward the house.

Maggie looked around. Everything about that place was comforting. As she waited for Clive to return, she could feel the tension leave her shoulders. This simple little farm, this scruffy dog, and this dear man were her solace. Here, nothing was asked of her, nothing was expected of her, and nothing was beyond her comprehension.

Clive returned with a loaf of bread and shakers of salt and pepper. He picked Indian summer tomatoes as red as fire engines and pulled the last of the green onions from the rich, dark soil. He cleaned the onions on his trouser legs, sliced tomatoes with his Old Timer pocket knife until the juice ran down his arms, and the two of them sat in the garden and let the warmth of September wash over them as they ate simple sandwiches. Maggie talked about Max, the illness, the accident, and Clive listened.

The hour went quickly and did more for her than an entire day at a health spa. As Maggie walked back to the car, Clive and Coco walked with her. When she knelt down to scratch Coco in that delightful place on the back next to the tail, Clive said, "Want me to do anything?"

Maggie's shoulders sagged. "No. Wish you could, but...no." Then, with one foot in the door she paused. "Clive, do you think I need to talk to an attorney?"

"Yep," he said.

CHAPTER 8

First thing Monday morning Maggie thumbed through the phone book once again, this time searching for a lawyer. She had called in a substitute for the first two periods at school, which would give her two hours to line up an attorney while she kept an eye on Max a little longer. She had a couple of recommendations from friends, so she started with them. All were "out of the office," "in court," or "not accepting new clients at this time," according to their receptionists. She made one last attempt.

A chirpy voice picked up. "It's a good day at Crandall, Biggs, and Sweetwater."

"Hi, this is Maggie Axline. I'm looking for someone to represent me in the case of a...well, I guess in case of a law-suit...well, maybe a possible lawsuit...I'm really not sure--"

"One moment please. I'll put you through to Mr. Crandall."

Maggie breathed a heavy sigh of relief. She was thrilled to actually talk to someone, yet she couldn't help thinking it must be a pretty slow day at Crandall, Biggs, and Sweetwater if they could put her through to one of the partners. But their ad in the Yellow Pages had read, "We specialize in traffic violations: infractions and serious offenses. No charge for phone pre-consultations."

A deep, resonate voice answered. "This is Bernard Elroy Crandall."

"Yes, Mr. Crandall, this is Maggie Axline. My son Maxim was in an automobile accident, and I'm concerned there might

25

be lawsuits. I may need someone to represent me. Is that something you might be able to take on?"

Crandall's cavernous voice softened a little. "Axline? Didn't that just happen? Over on Hyden Park Road? Seems like I read about it in *The Columbian*."

"Yes, that's the one." Maggie felt heat rise to her cheeks.

"Sorry to hear about it, Mrs. Axline. Nasty business," Crandall said. "You haven't heard from the insurance companies yet, have you?"

"No, not yet," Maggie said, then she realized it was probably far too early to hire an attorney. In her usual proactive, take charge approach, she had once again jumped the gun. "But I was thinking maybe I should. What do you think?"

"Well, I do think I can represent you, but if you hire me right now we'd probably be spinning our wheels. Why don't you sit tight and see what develops? Who knows? Maybe you won't even need me." Crandall's demeanor seemed genuine and professional, yet casual enough to ease Maggie's trepidation.

"That sounds wonderful," Maggie said.

"I'm going to put my secretary on the phone right now, and you can give her your name and telephone number. We'll start a temporary file for you so if you have to call back you can make an appointment without going through the Spanish Inquisition. Would that be okay?"

"Sure, that would be wonderful." Maggie let out a long breath. One thing at a time, she said to herself as she crossed "4. Attorney?" off her list.

At least for the time being.

CHAPTER 9

The first two days of the week went fairly smoothly. While Maggie was at work, for the most part it seemed as if Max stayed in his room or lolled around the house nursing his bruises. Once in a while in the evening, he would fly into a tirade about an imagined injustice that had been done to him, but mostly he shambled about and watched TV until late into the night. He was restless and irritable but too sore to gallivant around town. This was one time Maggie was thankful they lived so far from the lure of the teenage hot spots. Maxim didn't have a car, and she figured he was too sore to walk or hitchhike to get to them. The appointment with the psychiatrist was on Wednesday, and knowing Max would be home when she came to take him to it was just one less thing to worry about.

He seemed to have forgotten all about alligators on the lawn, and even though he had not been leaving the house at night, he was still far from being in touch with reality. The night after he had come home from the hospital, she had heard an agonizing scream from his room. When she got there, he was writhing in pain.

"My legs are broken! I think they did it in the hospital! I can't get up!" he cried. "How am I going to go to the bathroom?"

"No, Max," Maggie soothed. "Look, I'll massage them. They'll feel better, you'll see."

But when she started to rub them he shrieked again. "Don't touch them! God, I can't even stand up. You gotta call an

27

ambulance!"

There was no way she could convince him he was all right, but after an hour of talking to him, he finally let her help him drag his legs to the bathroom. Back in his room, he lay back down and seemed to forget all about the ambulance.

As had become her habit, when Maggie went to work Wednesday morning she stuck her head in Max's bedroom. Sometime during the night he had hung his heavy comforter over his window and pulled the mattress off his bed. He lay curled up in the fetal position next to it. Maggie wondered what new torment had been going through his mind.

She hoped he would still be home when she got there.

And that is what was on her mind when a call came in during her fifth period class.

CHAPTER 10

"So. What does Caesar mean when he says, 'Yond Cassius has a lean and hungry look'?"

Maggie was in the "wait ten seconds for the answer" zone when the phone rang. It was not school policy to put calls through to teachers in classrooms unless it was an emergency. Maggie scowled and called, "Okay, be thinking about that," over her shoulder as she reached for the receiver.

"Maggie?" the school secretary began. "I'm sorry to interrupt your class, but I have a guy on the line that wants to talk to you. Something about your son. He didn't say which one. Shall I put him through?"

"That's okay, Carol Ann. Sure, put him through." She hung up the phone to wait for the call to be transferred and turned to the students. "Okay, get out a piece of paper and write your answers down. I have to take this call." A familiar groan rumbled through the class followed by a scuffle of notebooks and a few can-I borrow-a-piece-of-papers?

Even though she knew it was coming, Maggie jumped when she heard the ring, and snatched up the receiver. "This is Maggie Axline."

"Mrs. Axline, sorry to bother you at work."

"That's okay," she said, but all she could think was, *get to it, get to it, get to it.*

"This is Ken Simmons at EL America?" he said.

"Yes, Mr. Simmons." *Get to it, get to it.*

"Over on 123rd?"

29

"Yes?" *Get to it.*

"Mrs. Axline, is Maxim your son?"

"Yes. Is he all right?" *Dear God! GET TO IT!*

"Oh, yes. Oh, I'm sorry, Mrs. Axline. Yes, Maxim is okay, but he's here and...well, he's...distraught." Mr. Simmons' voice was gentle and concerned. "He came in here crying about an hour ago. He was yelling that his mother was dead, and they were keeping it from him. He said he was sure of it, but no one would tell him the truth."

Maggie quivered a sigh and shut her eyes. "How did you know where I was?"

"Maxim told us where you worked, so I took a chance and called. It all sounded so strange. I guess it didn't ring true. He was pretty hysterical when he came in, but he's calmed down some now. I was wondering..."

She forced her eyes open and twisted her head far enough to watch the students who, by this time, were mostly watching her. She lowered her voice. "What were you wondering, Mr. Simmons?"

"Well, do you think he could be drinking?" he asked. "I have a son who gets into it once in a while, and he can get pretty strange when he does."

"Yes. Well, that's a possibility," Maggie hedged. Mr. Simmons was empathetic, but she didn't see the point of telling the whole story. "Mr. Simmons, do you think you could keep him there for about half an hour? I'll come pick him up."

Maggie hung up, forced a smile, and turned back to the class. Before anyone could ask questions, she chirped, "Okay, I need to go handle some business, so I'm going to have someone come in for the rest of the period, and..." Maggie thought quickly. "...we're going to pick up reading where we left off yesterday. Do you remember your parts? Open your books to page fifty-three, Act II, scene 1. And guards, *please* remember it's, 'Stand *ho!*' not '*Stand,* ho!'" A knowing snicker floated among them as they found the right page.

Fortunately, sixth period was her prep time. She could pick up Max and stall until it was time to see the psychiatrist. She) let him out of her sight before then.

CHAPTER 11

The first thing that surprised Maggie when they stepped into the homey but dated office, was that Dr. Carlos Canseco had fiery red hair that stuck out in all directions. The second thing that surprised her was that he did not have an accent.

"Hello," he said as he extended a hand towards Max. "You must be Max. I'm so glad you could make it today."

"Yeah," Max said, "I was wonderin' how you been. You still riding that Harley, man?"

"Well, let's talk about that. Why don't you come on in to my office? More comfortable there," Dr. Canseco said and acknowledged Maggie with a quick smile and tacit nod as he ushered Max into his office and closed the door.

Maggie settled herself on a green velour sofa and picked up the latest copy of *Psychiatry Today*. She ran her finger down the table of contents. It stopped on "Grieving in parents who have a child with a psychotic disorder." She opened to page sixty-three and scanned the article. "Parental loss of a child through schizophrenia usually mirrors the loss of a child through death, although it often develops into a longer pattern of chronic grief."

The magazine dropped to her lap. She tilted her head back and closed her eyes. How in the hell did this happen? She searched her memory trying to figure out when it had all started. It was true Max had been a handful growing up. Maggie always figured she had earned a "Mother's Badge of Honor" raising that one. He'd had his share of tantrums and more than

31

his share of getting into mischief, but mostly he was a normal child with a lighthearted, curious disposition.

Fragments of Max as a child played in her mind. She saw him laughing as he swished his arms and legs to make snow angels. She saw him practicing heroic Evel Knievel stunts on his BMX bike until the summer sun dropped behind the tall cedars. Had it already started then?

He had teased his brother relentlessly but only until Braxton was in trouble. Once when Braxton had taken a nasty tumble off a concrete wall they were "tightrope walking," both had come home crying, Max consoling his little brother, reassuring him. Surely he couldn't have had it then.

It was forty-five minutes before Dr. Canseco came out and closed the door behind him, leaving Max in his office. "Well," he said, as he pulled an oak captain's chair close to the sofa, "I believe I know a little more about Max now. You said on the phone that the folks at CRMH thought he may have schizophrenia, and from what I can tell after talking to him, I think they may be correct."

Maggie choked back tears. This isn't the time to go to pieces, she thought. You knew it could be this. One thing at a time. One thing at a time. "So, can it be cured, Doctor? Or at least treated?"

"Oh, yes, there's plenty we can do to help Max, but I believe he has chronic schizophrenia rather than acute schizophrenia. It's still a little early to tell, but if I am correct, it means he may have it for the rest of his life." Dr. Canseco paused and leaned back in his chair. "But," he went on, "with medication and treatment, many people have learned to cope with it, so there's certainly a chance that Max could live a decent life."

Maggie noticed the doctor did not say he would live "a normal life," or a "productive life." Was that an unintentional omission rather than a skirting?

"But what about right now?" she asked, and heard herself sound every bit as desperate as she felt. "I mean, shouldn't he go to a hospital, or something?"

"I'm afraid they won't admit anyone to a psych ward unless they exhibit a threat to themselves or someone else, and from what you and Max have told me, that isn't the case. I know you gave me a lot of information on the phone, but is there anything else you can tell me that might help?"

"A threat?"

"It means has he tried to harm himself or anyone else."

Maggie's head inclined, and she stared at the stack of magazines on the Formica coffee table, trying to remember.

"Mrs. Axline?" Dr. Canseco said after a while.

"Oh. Well..." she raised her eyes. "The last few months he's gone out at night a lot. Sometimes all night. I always figured he was drinking or doing drugs. Do you think he is? A time or two I thought I smelled whiskey or something."

Doctor Canseco's head bobbed up and down several times before he answered. "There's a chance of it. Many of my younger patients who have schizophrenia do," he said. "From the studies they've done, most researchers agree that either drinking or drugs, sometimes both, can be brought on by a need to self-medicate. They don't know they're sick, but feel an uncontrollable urge to try to help themselves."

The doctor watched Maggie with genuine interest. "How are you doing, Mrs. Axline?"

Maggie shrugged. "Okay, I think."

The doctor patted her hand. "I know it's a lot to take in all at once," he said, "but more recent studies show that schizophrenia is quite often hereditary. Do you know of anyone in your family or in his dad's family that had mental problems?"

The corner of Maggie's' mouth tugged upwards. She was picturing Aunt Lillian with the doll she pretended was her baby and Uncle Cornelius who hijacked an airplane from a local airport and tried to fly it blindfolded. Then there was her father who slid into a bottle after her mother died and never come back out. "Well," she said, "none that have been diagnosed, anyway."

Suddenly her face sobered, and she stared at him.

"Yes, Mrs. Axline?"

"I was wondering if... I mean, my other son Braxton. Will he...? Do I need to watch...?" She couldn't finish the thought. It was too horrifying to put into words.

"Well," Dr. Canseco seemed to weigh his words carefully. "I wouldn't be too concerned about that, Mrs. Axline. Chances are

33

you'll never have to face that problem. No, I wouldn't lose any sleep over it." The doctor smiled. "Maxim's brother's name is Braxton?"

"I'm afraid so," she said. She appreciated the break in tension. People had questioned her choice of names before. And with the last name of Axline, what *was* she thinking? But in her defense, her decisions were made when she had a different last name and during extremely stressful times. In a frantic rush to the hospital, between excruciating labor pains, Maggie had blurted out her choices. "Maxim! It's going to be Maxim!" and "Braxton! It's a family name, damn it!"

Her husband, not used to seeing his wife in crazed hysteria, didn't dare argue. And both times, when she was in less agony and more coherent, she rationalized her decision by saying they were strong, uncompromising names that would serve them well in life.

Then, when their father had skedaddled to greener pastures, she changed their last names to her mother's maiden name, Axline. Now every time she called one of them, it was "Maxim! I mean Braxton! I mean Maxim! ...Oh shit!"

But despite the assonance of their names, they were as different as chalk and chewing gum. Where Maxim was spontaneous and volatile, Braxton was reticent and calm. When caught red-handed getting into mischief, Max would spill his guts, but Braxton would clam up like a cloistered monk in a Carthusian monastery. Even now, although he wouldn't talk about it, Maggie discerned an uneasiness and growing anger in Braxton.

And it was no wonder, Maggie thought. How could not only a psychotic brother's actions, but a distressed mother's as well, not affect a fourteen-year-old? He spent more and more time at friends' houses, and Maggie didn't blame him one bit. When he was home, she could talk to Braxton but not with him. He would listen and nod but never tell her what he thought about all this craziness going on right in front of his nose. Like her, Braxton would go about his day-to-day business of going to school, doing his homework, eating dinner. But he talked little, seldom smiled, and never laughed. And like her, Maggie decided, he was simply trying to get through life the best he

34

could.

Dr. Canseco brought Max out, gave her his prescriptions, made their next appointment, and shook hands with Maggie. "And, Mrs. Axline, here's my card. I've jotted down my home number on it, as well." He made direct eye contact with her and said, "If you have any problems, any problems at all, you are to call me any time of the day or night. Do you understand?"

And that was the third thing about Dr. Canseco that surprised Maggie.

CHAPTER 12

Maggie started Max on his meds as soon as they got home from seeing Doctor Canseco. The list of side effects was extensive, from dry mouth and slurred speech to spasms and tongue protrusion, but at this point she would have given him rat poison if she thought it would make him better mentally. After a few days, he did seem a bit improved. He went out less and slept more.

A few times she came home in the evenings to dirty dishes strewn about and the lingering stench of cigarettes and pizza; sure signs that Max had friends over during the day. She assumed one of them was Jonathan, his crony and cohort in all mischievous deeds since grade school. He was rebellious, lived his life recklessly, and was not, Maggie felt, a stabilizing factor in Maxim's life. "Borrowing" his father's Porsche, and driving eighty-five on a country road before flipping it five times when he hit a deer (so the story went), was not exactly conducive to good mental health, as far as she could see. It was pure luck both he and Max had walked away from that one.

Nevertheless, she rather liked Jonathan. He was quirky, but could be quite charming when he felt like it. Was he aware of Max's eccentric behavior, or was he too high to notice how Max had changed?

She was uneasy about any of his friends being there, but was relieved Max was at his own house rather than theirs. But two days before his next appointment he left the house and didn't come home until the next evening.

Maggie knew something was wrong the moment he

stormed in the door. She was in the kitchen stir-frying dinner, and Braxton was watching television but retreated to his room when he heard Max come in.

"Where is he?" Max bellowed.

Maggie slid the pan off the burner and turned from the stove. "Where's who?"

"That man who was here," he fired back. "He can get the hell out of my house!"

"There's no one here, Max. Just Braxton in his room." Maggie tried to keep her voice steady. Where was that number Doctor Canseco had given her?

"Don't lie to me! I saw him through the window!" Max shrieked.

Maggie glance down the hall as Braxton came out to the kitchen. "Mom?" he said.

"It's all right, Braxton. Why don't you go outside for a while?" she told him as she shuffled through her purse for the telephone number.

Braxton started to turn, but before he could go, Max yelled at him, "I knew you were here! Where the fuck do you think you're going?" Max was in a fighting stance, slightly crouched, with one hand behind his back, and the other swinging back and forth by his side, fist clenched.

Braxton started to leave again, but Max sidled closer until he was within two feet. "Come back here, you fucking coward!"

Braxton paused, spun around, and looked at Maggie, eyes wide, bewildered. And in that split second, it happened.

Max's arm drew back and uncoiled. His fist hit Braxton directly in the left jaw. Braxton reeled backward a few feet, thudded against the wall, and dropped.

"Oh my God!" Maggie screamed and jumped in front of Max.

Braxton got up and stumbled to the door.

Max held his stance, his arm once again swinging freely by his side, ready for another wallop. His eyes were black with anger, and he breathed and snorted through his nose.

Maggie steered Max to a barstool and pushed him down. He immediately got up, and she pushed him down again. This time, he stayed.

With her hand still on his shoulder, she pulled out Doctor Canseco's number and dialed.

After several rings, he picked up. She tried to talk quietly, but the tremors she felt rippling through her body, transferred to her voice. "Dr. Canseco, this is Maggie Axline," she said. "Max punched Braxton in the jaw."

"Are you alone?" Doctor Canseco said.

"Yes, at least in the house. Braxton is outside."

"And Max?"

"Right here in front of me."

As Maggie talked, she kept her eyes on Max. In front of her she no longer saw the the troubled teenager, she no longer saw her son. In his place she saw a stranger who had injured her younger son and could, in a heartbeat, do the same, or worse, to her.

"You need to get out of the house now!" the doctor said.

"What about Max?"

"I'm going to call the police. I have your address. You must leave the house immediately, and don't come back until you see the police. Are there any weapons in the house?"

All the things that Max could use to do damage flashed through her mind. She turned her head to the side and lowered her voice. "No. I mean there are knives in the kitchen, but that's all."

While she was on the phone, Max stood up, pushed her hand away, and swaggered down the hall. Maggie hung up and ran outside where she found Braxton in the detached workshop, the lock that might afford some defense long since broken. She scanned the workbench. Wrenches, screwdrivers, duct tape, and an odd assortment of nails, screws, and hardware was strewn about. She finally picked up a tire iron. There were plenty of tools in there that could do harm, too many to hide. Maggie could only hope Max wouldn't think of them.

It was only then she really saw Braxton. Even with the light out, she could see the glint of the moon in his stunned and sober eyes. Her breathing came in abbreviated puffs, she grasped his hand, and there in the dark, they kept their eyes chained to the front door. But Maxim did not come out. About twenty minutes later, the police turned into the circular driveway and parked in the porte-cochere attached to the house.

"Thank God," Maggie croaked. "Stay here, Braxton," she said and went out to meet two policemen.

"You Mrs. Axline?" the larger of the two officers asked.

Maggie nodded. "Max is my son. He's still in the house. In his bedroom, I think. It's down the hall on the left."

"Are there any weapons in the house?"

"Huh-uh, I don't think so. Shall I take you in?"

The officer shook his head. "We can handle it, ma'am."

She sucked in a frayed breath as the two officers cautiously opened the door, leaving it ajar, and stepped into the unknown. A moment later, she heard the husky voice of one of them talking to Max. Then, through the open door, she saw them bring Max to the entry, but before they could get him outside, he broke loose and backed up, his fists once again balled, his eyes hot coals.

"Come on, Max," one of them coaxed. "We aren't going to hurt you."

The other officer circled around behind Max, while the one talking to him stepped forward. In a flash, Max's fist made contact with his face. Maggie grimaced.

There was a scuffle.

Most of what followed was a blur of flailing legs, blue uniforms, handcuffs, and white rope. In less than a minute they had Max on the floor, hog-tied. Together, they picked him up by the ropes, carried him out to the patrol car, and hoisted him into the back seat.

The policeman that Max had hit gulped air and turned to Maggie. He exhaled in a loud, slow gust that made Maggie think of the wind that whistled through the cedars. It was a desolate sound, perhaps made more so coming from a policeman. At least he'll have something to talk about back at the precinct, she told herself.

Maggie looked at his weary face. "I'm so sorry."

Why do mothers always feel responsible for their children's actions?

"I'll be fine," he said. "This guy who called us, was that his

39

doctor, did they say?"

Maggie nodded. "Where are you taking him?"

"The doc wants us to take him to the psych ward at Vancouver Memorial. You know where that is?"

Maggie did know where it was. Ironically, it was in the same hospital where she had delivered both her sons. Now, it housed a rehabilitation center and, as she had just learned, a psychiatric ward.

As the police car pulled away, Braxton came out of the workshop. He winced when she started to hug him. Her eyes flicked to his jaw. It was already beginning to swell.

So, while one of her sons was being driven to one hospital, Maggie was driving her other son to a different hospital.

CHAPTER 13

In came the tide
In came the tide
Then what did happen?
The sea monsters died.
In came the tide
In came the tide.

Max had been four-years-old when he dictated that poem to Maggie. Now it ran through her mind as she sat in the ER lobby waiting for Braxton. He was going to be sore for a while, but at least a cracked mandible was not the end of the world.

They wired his jaw shut and sent him home with Vicodin and strict, but superfluous, instructions to take in only food he could suck through a straw. At least he had fared better than the sea monsters. Or was that the beginning of more "monsters"?

Max, on the other hand, was physically none the worse for wear, even after he had been trussed up like a pig about to be put on a spit to roast. Mentally, it was another story. He was admitted to the psychiatric ward. Maggie called at four in the morning, as soon as she got home with Braxton.

A muted night-shift voice answered. "Ward B. This is Jennifer."

Maggie hesitated. It still seemed so surreal she wasn't even sure what to ask.

Only one way to find out.

41

"This is Maggie Axline. My son was brought in last night about nine? His name is Maxim. Maxim Axline? I was wondering..."

What was she wondering? Was he okay? Was he crazy? Were they going to help him? Or keep him? Her mind was still so muddled, for the life of her she couldn't figure out what to ask.

"Oh, sure," Jennifer jumped in. "Yes, Maxim is sleeping right now. They didn't bring him up here until about two. They do the evals downstairs in the ER."

Maggie listened while Jennifer went through the admitting process and what would happen next, adding only an "uh-huh" or "okay" once in a while.

"So," Jennifer finished, "it's probably not a good idea to come see him today, Mrs. Axline, but I'm sure the doctor on duty will want to talk to you. Do you have a number where he can reach you?"

Maggie had already decided to get a substitute for the day, so she let Jennifer know she would wait at home for the doctor to call. "As soon as he is able to. Please."

She scrambled some eggs for herself and made a milkshake laced with eggs for Braxton, then gave him a Vicodin, put a cool washcloth on his jaw, and sat with him until he fell asleep. In the living room, she put the telephone on the end table next to the couch, turned on the early news, plunked down, and pulled a throw over her. She fell asleep during the challenges facing Woodland's new mayor, and was awakened by the phone during a promo for "Beyond Cherry Garcia: Cooking for the Dead." She reached for it as she glanced at her watch. It was 9:15 a.m.

"I'm calling for Maggie Axline. This is Dr. Friedman at Vancouver Memorial?"

Doctor Friedman sounded exhausted, like he had been worn down by life. He spoke precisely and in a monotone, measuring his words and pausing often, as if he were explaining the Pythagorean Theorem to a small child. Maggie didn't mind. She was, after all, still floundering in uncharted waters. Maybe more knowledge would rescue her.

"So, is he going to get over it?" Maggie asked during one of

42

his pauses.

"We can't say definitely," Dr. Friedman hedged. "But we can say he can get better. I've spoken with Dr. Canseco, and I'm going to keep Max on the same medication. For now, Maxim needs to stay here so we can monitor him to see if he stabilizes."

Maggie was torn. She felt both helpless and relieved. Quite frankly, she thought, if he was there, it would give her and Braxton a chance to catch their breaths. "Do you have any idea how long that will be?"

Dr. Friedman detailed the legality of involuntary commitment. They could keep him at Vancouver Memorial for seventy-two hours without consent. "After that," he said, "he will do another evaluation to see if he can go home, or if we need to," pause, "make other plans for him."

"Like what?" Maggie asked. "What other plans?"

"Here at Vancouver Memorial," the doctor explained, "we can keep patients for up to two weeks. But, in severe cases," pause, "if they need intense therapy," pause, "we are authorized to transfer them before the two weeks are up to a facility that is," pause, "better equipped to treat them."

"A facility? In Vancouver?" she asked.

"It would be to another hospital, but not here in Vancouver," he said. "There are several options, but for now, we need to see what we can do here."

Yes, Maggie thought, one thing at a time.

Dr. Friedman said she needed to sign some papers, but she could do it the next day when she came to the hospital if she wanted to visit Max.

Did she? She wasn't at all sure.

But the next day after school, she bucked up her courage, and found herself squaring her shoulders and climbing the concrete stairs to the psych ward on the second floor. The sign above a button outside the locked ward read, "For assistance, push." Under it, someone had scrawled "ONCE" in bold letters.

She pictured nurses and orderlies scurrying about as psychotic patients demanded their attention and doctors barked orders, all the while trying to get to that damn buzzer someone was pushing ten times. She carefully gave it one firm push. She heard nothing and understood how a person could

43

get trigger-finger. She splayed her finger by her side and waited. Several minutes went by. She was weighing the consequences of pushing it again, when the speaker above it crackled.

"Yes?" a voice rasped.

"I'm here to see Maxim Axline?" Maggie said.

"You related?"

"I'm his mother." No response. Did they need more? She was about to tell them her name, when the heavy metal doors slowly swung open.

On the other side there was no chaos, no harried nurses, no eccentric patients. In fact, it was surprisingly serene. A burly orderly stood half-way down a beige and bare hall, waiting for her. "You Maxim's mom?" he asked as she came closer. "I'm Dave. You'll need to sign in. Let me show you."

Maggie wrote her name on the daily visitor's register and signed the papers Dr. Friedman had told her about while Dave waited to show her where she could talk to Max. "We encourage families to visit," he said as they walked toward the cafeteria. "But that first day, when a client is being admitted and getting used to the place, it's kind of hard to have people come to see them."

"Can you tell me how he's doing?" Maggie asked.

"Well, 'course I'm not his doctor, but he seems to be settling in pretty well. Yesterday he was real jumpy and he talked a lot, but today he's better. Calmer anyway." He unlocked the cafeteria door. "Want some coffee while I get Max for you?" he asked.

"That'd be great." Maggie's shoulders loosened a little as she pulled a brown folding chair up to one of the metal tables. Dave went to the coffee pot at one end of the room and brought back a thick, white mug with tendrils of steam rising from a liquid as black as a coal mine at night, then left to get Max. Maggie blew on her coffee and let her gaze skim the dining room. It was small and efficient with no adornment on the walls. At one end there was a pass-through window and at the other end two vending machines. It was strictly institutional.

Five minutes later Max ambled in followed by Dave who headed for the kitchen. "Hey, Max, ya want some tapioca

44

pudding?"

When Max scowled at him, Dave said, "I'll take that as a yes." He unlocked the door, but turned before he went in. "Mrs. Axline?"

"Oh, no thanks, Dave. And call me Maggie...please."

Dave put the pudding and a spoon in front of Max. "Well, I'll leave you two to visit for a while. I'll check back in an hour."

Max's eyes tracked Dave out the door, then he shoved the pudding away. "You can't trust 'em." He checked behind him. "Any of 'em."

"You sure, Max? I thought Dave seemed pretty nice. Here," she pulled the tapioca over to her and reached for the spoon. I'll try it first. I'll bet it's okay."

Max's eyes slid over to her as she ate a spoonful. "Mmmmmmm, it's good, Max. Why don't you try some? See? I'm still here." She pushed it back.

He picked up the spoon and tapped it on the bowl a couple of times. "This is the worst hell-hole I've been in yet," he grumbled. "Worse than Attica." He put the spoon down and smirked at some imagined, private joke.

Where was he? Where had his twisted, tormented mind taken him?

This was Max's reality. As real to him as the ache in her heart was to her. "What do you call this place, Max?"

Max ignored her question. He lowered his voice and bent toward her. "The screws here will kill ya if they get a chance. Watch your back." Max jerked his head toward the door, "I heard 'em last night. They were beating up some poor bastard in the next cell."

Maggie could swear she'd heard James Cagney say the same thing in an old gangster movie. Or was it Bogart? If Max thought he was in prison, it would account for the tough veneer.

Maggie tried several times to change the subject to cars, girls...what he would do when he got out of the slammer, but it was no use. In less than thirty minutes she was exhausted and ready to leave.

They sauntered down the hall, the silence between them deafening.

Dave saw them and came out of the nurses' glassed-in

45

cubical. "Through already?" he said and started to pat Max on the shoulder.

Max winced and shrank back. "Don't touch me, screw!" he growled.

"Okay, okay," Dave held his palms out in front of him. "Come on, Max's Mom, I'll let you out. Max, why don't you go back to your room, now?"

Without even a goodbye, Max turned and strutted down the hall. The cocky gangster, Maggie thought as she turned in the other direction.

CHAPTER 14

"Dr. Friedberg is still with a client. Do you want to continue to hold?"

She had twenty-five minutes for lunch, and Maggie had been waiting for almost fifteen of those. The students would start trickling in shortly. "Yes, I can hold for a few more minutes," she told the nurse.

Six minutes later she was still on hold and trying to keep a lid on the early birds. "Lindsay! You don't need to slap Mathew because he won't give you a pencil. And Matt...Matt! Would it kill you to give her a pencil? You have three in your hand, for crying out loud! No! Don't throw—" A pencil ricocheted off a desk and thwacked against the bulletin board. *Freshmen,* she thought, and rolled her eyes.

"Sure, Rachel, put your assignment in the basket."

"Yes, Pedro, put it in the basket with the others."

Then, as they came forward, fluttering their papers in her direction, she repeated, "In the basket...In the basket."

The bell rang, but she stayed on the phone for five more minutes, now just pointing at the incoming basket. Most had taken their seats; a few were still working the room. Her eyebrows puckered, she sighed, and hung up.

Three hours later, she was back on hold. Finally, "This is Dr. Friedberg. Thank you for waiting, Mrs. Axline."

"Thanks for taking my call, Dr. Friedberg. How's Max doing? Shall I come see him today?"

"Certainly. That would be fine, but I don't think you'll see a

47

lot of change in Max. We've had him on 25 milligrams of Thorazine, but," pause, "we're increasing it this afternoon. Hopefully, we'll see some changes by tomorrow morning."

"And if you don't?"

"If we don't," pause, "if he is still the same when he has his seventy-two hour evaluation," pause, "we will recommend that he be transferred to another facility."

"What facility?" Maggie snapped. "I mean, do you know where that would be?"

Her heart was doing its own version of a drum line. She put her hand on her chest and forced a deep breath. "Sorry," she said, "do you have any idea yet where he would be going?"

"We've contacted one place." The monotone of Dr. Friedberg's voice calm Maggie. The pauses made her listen more closely. "It's a very reputable hospital...They are better equipped to handle longer-term care...It's St. Peter...in Olympia."

Maggie's mind raced.

How's he going to get there? Am I going to have to take him? How long will he be there? How in the hell am I going to pay for it?

As if he had read her mind, Dr. Friedberg said, "We would send him in an ambulance. How long they keep him will depend on how the treatment goes, of course."

"My insurance doesn't cover this." Maggie knew she sounded pathetic, but she had to ask. "Will they still take him?"

"Well," Dr. Friedberg paused a particularly long time, then said, "I wouldn't worry too much about it. They will have payment plans, I'm sure."

Maggie watched as they hefted Max onto a gurney and strapped his hands down. He wasn't fighting them. In fact, from the struggle Dave and another muscular orderly were having, he must have been all dead weight.

Sedated?

"We do this for his own good," Dave told her. "And ours," he added with an impish grin as he secured a strap over Max's chest. "He started behaving himself when you got here, but he was putting on quite a show before that. Isn't that right, Max?"

48

She rode the elevator down with them and tagged behind as they wheeled him to the ambulance waiting outside the emergency room.

"Say goodbye to your mom," Dave said and stepped aside for Maggie.

Max's vacant stare tore into her. She doubted he could fully understand what she was saying, but she said it anyway, maybe more for her own good than his. "Bye, sweetie," she said, taking his hand in hers. "They're going to take you to a real nice place, now. They're going to help you get well. I'll come see you as soon as I can."

Maggie bent over him and kissed a stubbled cheek, then stepped back and watched them load her son into the ambulance.

Her stomach lurched and tumbled as her heart plummeted to her feet. The air around her was thick with sadness, and the gloom enveloped her.

Maggie stood on her tiptoes to make eye contact as long as possible.

"Love you," she called as they closed the doors.

CHAPTER 15

Patience. It was not Maggie's strong suit. She did have fortitude, grit—whatever you wanted to call it—but she was sorely lacking in patience. Dr. Friedberg had said someone from St. Peter would be in touch with her in a day or two, as soon as they had done an intake evaluation. But for Maggie, waiting for someone to call was like waiting for a turtle to cross a finish line. On the third, she simply had to nudge it.

She bowed out of the faculty meeting, telling them she had an urgent appointment—more a "bending of the truth" as she saw it rather than an out-and-out lie—and went home early to call the hospital. Her fingers fumbled as she dialed, then redialed, the number.

"St. Peter Hospital, how may I direct your call?"

"The psychiatric ward?" she said. It was a question, but it must have been the right one because she was transferred immediately. Then she was transferred again...and again...and a fourth time, until she was talking directly to the doctor who was seeing Max.

"'Mornin'!" he picked up, and with that one word, Maggie could tell he was going to be a far cry from Dr. Friedberg. "This is Eli Moon. How may I help you this extraordinary day?" he bubbled.

Dr. Moon sounded young, effervescent, and far too positive to have been dealing with psychotic patients and their exhausted families. She liked him immediately.

"Well, good morning to you, too!" His enthusiasm was

catching. "This is Maggie Axline, Maxim's mom?" she said and waited for the recognition.

"Oh, glad you called, Mrs. Axline. Saves me a call this afternoon, and anytime someone can save me some work, they're okay with me," he teased. "I'll bet you want to know how your son is."

"Exactly," Maggie said. "And maybe you can tell me how long he's going to be there?"

"Well, you know, I think Max is pretty darned confused right now. He's been extremely agitated the last two days, but if he's not better tomorrow morning, I'm going to gradually increase his dosage of Thorazine to 200 milligrams a day."

"Again?" Maggie said, hearing the whine in her voice. "I'm sorry. Of course you know what you're doing, I was just hoping..." She remembered reading that the side effects—the twitching, the uncontrollable movement of the arms and legs, the drooling—could all increase as the dosage was increased. And then there was the even more worrisome possibility: seizures.

"Of course you were. That's a mother's job," he said. "I promise we will increase it slowly in small increments until we get Max back on his feet. That's kinda what we do here."

"That sounds really...good," Maggie said and relaxed a little. She liked Dr. Moon, and not only for what he was doing for Max. "Do you know when I can see him?" she asked, feeling a little more sure of herself.

They talked for another ten minutes. She made plans to meet with the doctor when she visited Max in two weeks.

"But," Dr. Moon said, "it may be a month or longer before he will be ready to face the real world again. But I'll bet you could use a little rest for a while."

And right then, Maggie decided she would just have to adopt that man.

Doctor Moon transferred her to the bookkeeping department so she could get an idea of what this little trip into *The Twilight Zone* was going to cost her. As she had guessed, they couldn't give her a finite answer, but if he stayed for one month, it would probably be between $15,000 and $20,000. They would, however, discuss a payment plan with her when

Max was discharged.

Maggie had to chuckle at the ludicrousness of the situation. It seemed like she was   treading water just to make ends meet and now this? She needed a new roof, a new car, and some underwear and socks without holes would be nice. She felt the knots tighten again in her shoulders and neck as she hung up.

Two weeks. At least it would be enough time for her to recuperate a little. She hoped it would be for Braxton, too. Maggie couldn't remember the last time she had a full night's sleep. The last time she and Braxton had a relaxing meal. The last time she didn't jump every time the phone rang.

Two weeks. Enough time to go out to dinner, take in a movie, stroll through the grocery store without the worry of what waited for her at home.

She hadn't realized until then how much Max's behavior had controlled her. In her mind Maggie could not reconcile her private battle. She could not ignore that maternal impulse. She wanted Max with her to nurture, to make chocolate frosted graham crackers for, to read storybooks to like he was two years old again.

How much more can I take before I end up in an institution myself? That'd be one for the books now wouldn't it? Reader's Digest human interest article. Mother in loony-bin feeds chocolate-covered graham crackers to her also-crazy son.

But now, at least for now, she would try to mend.

So, for fourteen days, Maggie wallowed in the humdrum of her routine. She went to school, came home, whipped up dozens of chocolate milkshakes laced with protein powder for Braxton to suck through straws as they lolled about watching Johnny Carson or reruns of *M.A.S.H.* late into the night, and slept in until an unheard of 9:00 a.m. on the weekends. But all the while Maggie knew this was only a stop-gap in her life, a temporary situation that would soon change. This was simply her respite from her "real life."

She called the hospital every two days to ask how Max was doing. The first week she got the same answer in different words: "not much change, Mrs. Axline," "hasn't really improved much, Mrs. Axline." But the second week, there was a glimmer of light, "Well, he seems a little better today, Mrs. Axline," and, "I think he's eating better today, Mrs. Axline." It gave her hope. Her stomach flip-flopped when she thought of him being home. But she wasn't sure if it was a positive or a negative flip-flop.

She'd find out soon enough.

CHAPTER 16

The gentle Indian summer sun gave way to October's rambunctious celebration of fall. A bitter wind blew impressive gusts across I-5 as Maggie made the one-hundred-six-mile trip to Olympia to see Max. Her Toyota quivered when the wind bullied it sideways then eased up for a few minutes before the next taunt.

By the time she reached St. Peter Hospital, her resolve to remain unfrazzled had blown away with the wind. She got out of the car, gulped in a breath, repeated her mantra, and marched toward the brick and glass building.

The process of getting into the psych ward was the same as at Vancouver Memorial, but that was about the only thing that was the same. Everything at St. Peter was on a grander scale: the lobby, the nurses' station, the dining room. It was obviously geared to helping more people and, Maggie thought, in a more expensive way. But she didn't care; anything to get Max "back on his feet," as Dr. Moon had euphemistically put it.

It was nine o'clock when she arrived. That gave her enough time to talk to Max for a while before her ten-thirty appointment with the doctor. An amicable nurse showed her to the dining room where Max was already waiting. She had lived this moment in her head many times on the drive there, creating as many scenarios as she could imagine to prepare herself: Max being unresponsive, Max being angry, Max being cocky.

She fixed a smile and stepped through the door.

Her smile vanished.
Nothing she had anticipated prepared her for this.

The cafeteria was a yawning void. Void of color, void of personality, void of people. No tantalizing smells wafted from the kitchen, no cheery clank of pots and pans interrupted the hush. At the far end of one of the grey Formica tables, Max sat bent over, his arm skewed, his head buried in the crook of his elbow.

Maggie stopped in the doorway, and Max raised his head. Slowly, he stood and elevated his fist high above his head like the sign of Black Panther solidarity. He rocked back and forth, shuffling from one foot to another, and as she got closer, she could see the tears brim, then make runnels down his cheeks.

Maggie swallowed hard, forcing her eyes wide open to will her own tears to stay put. It almost worked. But as she stepped around the table, Max came to her and she wrapped him in her arms. He buried his face in her neck, and she could no longer hold it back. The grief, the regret, the guilt spilled out of her in complete silence.

Neither sobbed aloud. Neither said a word. But in that few minutes of holding each other, Maggie knew they both acknowledged their lives would never again be the same.

CHAPTER 17

"Well now," Maggie began as she sat down, swiping at her face with the sleeve of her sweatshirt, "how've they been treating you, honey?"

"Okay." He lowered his eyes and stared at the table.

And so the conversation went. Maggie asked all the questions and tried to think of things that had happened at home she thought Max would be interested in: the fire truck that had responded to a false alarm next door, the honey bees that had swarmed out of the big cedar tree and practically scared her to death, the new Grandfield's store that had opened about eight miles away.

"You can buy everything there, Max. Yesterday, I got groceries, then went over and got some socks, and then went to the gardening section and picked up some of those spigot covers for the winter, all in the same store. They even have a section where you can rent videos," she rambled, grasping for something to say.

She told him she got a new burgundy comforter for his bed so it would be all ready for him when he came home and that Jonathan had called to see where he was. Between sentences, she would pause for a response. Max seemed to listen, but he offered only one or two words.

"What's your room like here, Max?" she asked.

"It's okay."

"Do you have a roommate?"

"Yes."

"Do you like him?"

Shrug.

"What's his name?"

Shrug.

After about half an hour of a one-sided exchange, Maggie glanced at her watch. "I have an appointment to see your doctor now, Max. Dr. Moon? Do you remember Dr. Moon?"

Max said nothing, but as she crossed what seemed like a mile trek to the other end of the dining room, Maggie could feel his eyes on her. Before she went out, she turned and said, "I'll find you and say goodbye before I go, Max." When there was still no response, Maggie said, "I love you, darling," and went in search of Dr. Moon's office.

"I don't think he's ready to go home quite yet. Right now he's still on Thorazine," Dr. Moon said as he jumped up to get a paper off his desk.

When Maggie had come in, he had gotten up to shake hands with her and gracefully moved to the couch where they "would be more comfortable." He was a cheerful, husky, spontaneous doctor. No formalities, no lab coat, no pretenses. In fact, it looked like he was wearing golf togs. His smile was expansive and inviting, his manner was open and comforting, and Maggie took to him straightaway.

"What I'd like to do is get Max on Prolixin injections before we let him go home," he said as he sat back down. He handed her a paper explaining the medication and its side effects. "You'd have to take him in for a shot once a week, but at least he wouldn't be able to skip a dose." He paused and cocked his head. "Oral meds often do the trick all right, but the problem comes when patients stop taking them because they feel so much better." An impish grin tried to surface before he went on. "If fact, sometimes they feel so 'normal' they think they don't need medication anymore, so they...," he shrugged, "stop taking it." He paused again, crinkled his chin and raised his eyebrows, as if he was trying to gauge Maggie's comprehension level. "'Course there are no guarantees," he finally added.

Too much information. Overload! Overload!

"So," Maggie grasped at straws, "you think for sure it's

57

schizophrenia then?" The word still burned on her tongue. "I don't really know too much about it yet, but a friend of mine is bipolar. Is it kind of like that?"

"Not really," he said and grinned broadly.

But not offensively, Maggie thought. She detected a bit of twinkle in his eye that said, as serious as it was, this was not the end of the world.

"Bipolar disorder is fairly common. Schizophrenia? Mmmmmm...that's a whole different game of golf. But," he added, "to answer your question, yeah, I do think that's Max's condition."

Dr. Moon must have noticed the muddled expression on Maggie's face. "It's a common confusion," he went on, "but in truth they're worlds apart...other than they're both stigmatized by society."

Maggie just stared at him and he continued. "Okay," he said, bouncing once, shifting his position on the couch, and raising his hands to emphasize his points. "See...a person with bipolar disorder can alternate between very high moods and very low moods." His hands went up and then back down. "Now those can be hard to deal with, but usually treatment can help. These people can continue working at least most of the time and carry on pretty normal activities."

"Now," he held his hands parallel in front of his chest and moved them up and down in unison as he explained, "schizophrenia is different. People become delusional." He flipped a hand into the air and moved it in circles above his head. "They have hallucination. They see and hear things that aren't there."

His hand fluttered a moment then dropped to his knees with a thwack. "This rascal is quite a challenge to treat. I'll be honest with you, a lot of times people with schizophrenia can't hold down a job, or they go off their meds and end up homeless." He paused and looked hard at Maggie. "But you have to remember this isn't always the case. There are also many who stay on their meds and learn how to cope successfully with their disability."

"So..." Maggie began tentatively. "Max could have this a long time?" She stared past him at a birch tree fluttering in the wind outside the window. "His whole life?" she asked as her eyes swiveled back to his.

"It's possible, Mrs. Axline, but at least Max has you for support. You're doing what you can for him, and ...well, it's hard, but it isn't hopeless."

For a few moments Maggie watched his hands resting on his knees before he shifted his weight to stand.

She nodded, then followed his lead and stood.

Maggie was more confused than ever as she left Dr. Moon's office. She saw Max once more before she left, but the question-answer conversation was about the same.

She slipped into the car. Okay, she told herself, it could be worse. She had a little more time. Time while they weaned him off Thorazine and got him on Prolixin injections before she took him home. It sounded...promising, she decided.

Two weeks later, Maggie was once again headed to Olympia. She had talked to Dr. Moon on the phone. Max was doing well, appeared pretty stable, Braxton had his jaw set free, and she had made arrangements to make monthly payments on her $18,000 bill from St. Peter. She was ready to settle into some semblance of order in her world. Years later she would think back on this time and ask herself: if she had known then what lay ahead, would she have done anything differently?

CHAPTER 18

"Braxton! Time to get up!" It was another school day for Maggie and Braxton. Just one more of the 129 left before school was out. Braxton was finishing up football season and gearing up for basketball. Maggie was finishing up midterms and gearing up for Thanksgiving, Christmas, any day she could use as an excuse to sleep in. They couldn't come soon enough.

But Max? Well, he did seem better Maggie had to admit, but he still wouldn't go to school. He had tried a couple of times since coming him home from St. Peter, but both times he had become agitated and confrontational and had walked the three and a half miles home before school was dismissed. Now, he was back to his routine of sleeping most of the day and roaming the house most of the night.

The Prolixin was working pretty well, she presumed, but since she didn't have much to compare it to, she could only guess it was an improvement over Thorazine. After two more visits to Dr. Canseco, two injections, and two weeks of watching Max, she still wasn't sure. She tried to keep her mind on other things, but at school she would catch herself picking up the phone to call him to see how he was. At home she furtively scrutinized every move he made when he came out to the kitchen to get a bowl of ice cream, or listened for sounds that would tell her he was still in his room.

She simply couldn't shake the feeling of looming disaster. That there was something hidden around the corner getting ready to give her cage one more good rattle.

Now who's being paranoid?

When she got the call from her insurance company the next Saturday, she was almost relieved. Maybe this was the other shoe she had been waiting to hear drop. Now, at least she could face it head on, stare it down, and smack it around until it cowered in submission.

"Hi Maggie, this is Leslie Stalls."

Maggie turned down the stereo until Johnny Cash's lament about shooting a man in Reno just to watch him die was barely audible and out of habit picked up the pencil and note pad next to the phone. "Leslie, hi," she began. "I guess you've heard something about the insurance, huh?"

Face it head on.

"Well, I don't have all the information yet. I mean the bills are still coming in, but that may take a while. It looks like your policy will cover the medical portion of it and at least some of the additional damages. But, Maggie," Leslie paused. "Right now, at least, it looks like they will exceed your liability coverage. I thought you would want to know ahead of time."

"Right," Maggie said. She doodled *damages* on the tablet. "So, what you're suggesting is that I go ahead and hire an attorney? I mean, will it probably go to court? "

Stare it down.

"I can't really advise you," Leslie said, then dampered her voice. "It might be a good idea to get someone, Maggie."

Maggie scrawled *call Crandall.* "Okay, I'll call him today...but," her tone matched Leslie's conspiratorial air, "can they take everything I have? I mean, I feel terrible about what happened, but I really don't want to lose everything I have. Will I? I mean, you know, lose everything?"

"I can't say for sure." Leslie hesitated, lowered her volume another notch, and added, "Call your attorney, Maggie. He'll tell you what you need to do." Her voice perked up again,

"Gotta go Maggie, but I'll call you when I know anything new."

When Maggie hung up the phone she sucked in a big swig of air, held it for a second, and felt her lips motor-boat a long exhale.

Well, so much for smacking it into submission.

She picked up the receiver again to make an appointment

at Crandall, Biggs, and Sweetwater.

Bernard Elroy Crandall was out of town, according to Stella his receptionist, so she scheduled an appointment for two weeks out. Meanwhile, Stella said, she would do some "preliminary work" and send her a form for listing her assets.

Maggie could practically hear the "ca-chings" as they flipped over on the attorney hourly wage odometer. Nevertheless, even though she wasn't at all sure of what or how much "preliminary work" needed to be done, she gladly gave her Leslie Stalls' number so they could contact her insurance company. That was the least of her worries. Right now, keeping Max on an even keel was her focus. She was trying to maintain a normalcy in their lives; not exactly like there was nothing wrong, but more like the weirdness was just a part of the routine they called living. There was no point in ignoring it, or hiding it, or pretending it wasn't there. It was. Work with it, she told herself. You don't have to exactly embrace it, but don't shut it out, either.

Other than his appointments, Max hadn't been out of the house for over a week. Maggie knew he needed a more ordered routine and more interaction with the rest of the world. That weekend she would take him on a social outing, and she would start with the grandfathers.

CHAPTER 19

Max used to call Maggie's dad his "fancy grandpa." When he was in the fourth grade, he asked if he could take him to show and tell. James Braxton Parker, being the self-assured, perpetual PR man he was, gladly agreed, and walked into Elwood Elementary with as much panache as if he had been walking into the White House to discuss Reaganomics with the president. Whether presiding over meetings as head of the Portland Kiwanis or drinking a beer with his ninety-year-old neighbor, he was equally at home.

But since her mother died, Maggie had noticed his increasing fondness for alcohol, until eventually he crawled into that bottle of gin, became comfy with it, and decided to stay there. As much as she loved him, she doubted he was the best influence on Max right then. But her sons were still crazy about him. Besides, it would at least get Max out of the house for a while.

With Max in tow, Maggie pulled into the Wavy Lane parking lot. The aroma of dill infused the atmosphere under the Sellwood Bridge where a pickle factory had been ensconced for years. Maggie's weakness for Mrs. Nuesin's pickles had wedged itself into her taste-bud memory when her parents had moved into their houseboat fifteen years ago. Even today, as she got out of the car, she drew in the piquant bouquet and salivated.

The aluminum ramp clattered as they walked down to the string of houses gently bobbing on the Willamette. It was Sunday morning, and the current would be festooned with pink and blue condoms bragging of Saturday night conquests. Her father wasn't what she would call a "swinger," but the population of Wavy Lane was a quirky hodgepodge of eccentric lifestyles.

"Hi, Mrs. Popovich!" Maggie hollered when she spotted a tangle of bright orange curls.

A scrawny figure dressed in a pink and green plaid housecoat peeking out from a yellow mackintosh, stopped watering a mum on its last legs with a coffee can nailed to a broomstick, and turned. Her face was as shriveled as a windfall apple at the end of a hot summer. A bony hand flew to her head and she straightened the mop of wig that threatened to fall into the Willamette every time she bent over to dip the coffee can. A cigarette dangled from a shock-red, pencil-thin mouth, spidery veins of lipstick bleeding into the crevices that wreathed it. She squinted one eye to keep the smoke at bay and with claw-like fingers shaded the other from the crisp glare of the morning sun.

"Bagpipe, is that you?" she rasped.

Max glanced at Maggie and arched his brows. "Bagpipe?" he mouthed.

"She means Magpie," Maggie whispered and covertly tapped her head.

"Yeah, it's me, Mrs. Popovich. How've you been?"

"Happy as a box of monkeys," she said and wheezed a chuckle.

"And Mr. Popovich?"

"Aw hell, he's itchin' somethin' fierce. Probably got flea bit from that mangy dog down at the end of the dock. I told him if he doesn't stop playin' with that mutt, I'm gonna throw 'em both in the river." She lowered her voice, out of concern for Mr. Popovich's sensitive nature, Maggie assumed. "He's as dumb as a bag of hammers, ya know," she said behind her hand just as a scraggly cat the color of his owner's wig came strolling with great nonchalance around the corner of her house. It slinked past her, then turned tail up and sprayed the knee-highs that sagged around her ankles, before continuing its stroll down the dock. "Mr. Popovich, you mangy old flea bag, you get the hell back here!" She wielded her coffee can broomstick like it was a machete and doddered after him.

"Good to see you!" Maggie called after her, and she and

Max turned toward her dad's houseboat.

She knocked once and stuck her head in. "Dad?"

"Door's open!" he yelled from the living room.

Max trailed behind Maggie as they made their way down the long hall and took three steps up into the kitchen that overlooked the wide living room. Her father was enthroned in his recliner with—ah yes, there it was—a gin and tonic perched on the stretch of windowsill that framed an unparalleled view of the river.

He swiveled toward her. "Hey! How's my third favorite—" he began, as Max stepped out from behind Maggie. "Well, Max, you scoundrel! Get over here!"

"Hi, Grandpa," Max said as he stepped down into the living room.

"Grandpa? Who's this Grandpa fellow? My friends call me James, but you can call me Jimmy since you're my second favorite grandson." He rose to hug Max, then held him at arms-length. "Hey, who gave you permission to get so tall?"

It had been almost six months since her father had seen Max, but it felt as if an entire lifetime had passed. So much had happened. Neither she nor Max was the same person. Her father, unfortunately, was. Maggie glanced at the bottle of Tanqueray sitting on the kitchen counter and tried to gauge through the forest green glass how much was left. Not that it matters, she thought. There's always more where that came from.

"Hi, Dad," Maggie said and gave him a peck on the cheek. "Wow! Beautiful day for November, isn't it?" Her eyes scanned the river. "Chinook?" she asked.

"Huh?" He followed her gaze to a pontoon boat fifty yards out. "Oh. No, too late for that. Probably Steelhead." He backed into his chair, sat down, and picked up his highball. "Can I get you a drink, sweetheart?"

The look on Maggie's face must have answered his question. "Now, don't start with me, Magpie. The sun's over the yardarm somewhere." He glanced at Max. "Max, how about you? You old enough yet?"

Maggie rolled her eyes.

"Guess not," he said and jiggled his glass.

The tinkle of ice triggered a familiar disquiet in Maggie, and she wondered if coming had been a mistake.

Change the subject.

"Dad," she said with too much exuberance, "we ran into Mrs. Popovich on our way in. She was watering some mums."

James took another sip and growled, "That old witch!"

"What? You don't like her?"

"She's a nosy old biddy, that's what she is. She's always coming down here to borrow something." James frowned at his almost empty glass.

"Well, we all run out of stuff once in a while. You can afford an egg or two... or even a dozen, for that matter. Or does she come down to borrow a cup of flour on the pretense of seeing your 'etchings'," Maggie teased. "Is that what it is, Dad? A little Wavy Lane romance going on?"

"Hell, no! Hell, I'd give her five dozen eggs if she'd stay away. Oooh, no. No, she comes in here and wants to borrow a cup of gin, for Christ sakes! Gin!"

Max yawned, smirked, ambled to the kitchen and pulled two slices of stale bread out of a drawer and took them out on the deck that ran the length of the living room windows.

"Or vodka!" James went on. "Can you imagine that? Comes right in and says, 'Hey, Jimmy, mind if I borrow a cup of vodka?'" He twirled the ice in his glass again. "Where's she get off calling me 'Jimmy,' anyway. It's 'James' to her. No, it's '*Mr. Parker*' to her. Old hag," he groused and slurped his last few drops of gin.

They sat watching Max who was coaxing a Canada goose perched on the rail to take bread from his hand. He'd move two steps closer, the goose would move two steps back; he would step back, the goose would step closer. Finally, he threw the bread in the river, and the goose dove onto it, scooped it up, and sat bobbling on the water, keeping an eye on Max in case more good fortune should come its way. Max turned to his mom and grinned.

"His name's Cutty," James said to Maggie. "Named him that when he came up on the deck one day and tried to take a drink of my Cutty Sark whiskey sour. Knew there was a reason I didn't like those things." He tinkled the ice in his glass again.

She wasn't sure if he meant he didn't like whiskey sours or Canada geese. "Ah," she said and nodded.

"Hey, buddy," James said as Max came back in and plopped down in an oversized papasan chair between Maggie and him. "How's school going? Have a girlfriend yet?"

"Naw, school sucks," Max said as he thumbed through a *TV Guide.*

"Remember how I told you Max was in the hospital, Dad? He might go back to school later, but not yet."

James leaned forward and put his elbows on his knees. Maggie knew this posture. He was now the patriarch presiding over important family matters. He lowered his voice two octaves to his "more official" tone. "Max, if you're ever going to make something of yourself, you need an education."

"I know, Grandpa," Max said without looking up.

"Well doggone it, Max. Get back to school, buddy, or you'll never amount to anything."

"Okay, Grandpa," Max mumbled as he sprawled in the chair and closed his eyes.

James leaned back again, satisfied that he had done his grandfatherly duty. "That's okay, buddy. You take it easy for a few minutes." But Max was already asleep.

"It's one of the side effects of one of the medications he's on right now, Dad," Maggie said as they watched Max. "He's on antipsychotic drug injections, plus a bunch of side effects stuff. I don't remember the names, but the shots he gets make him lethargic."

Maggie turned to the window again and scrutinized another boat drifting under the bridge. "Looks cold out there...Thing is..." She paused. "Thing is, Dad, there are some other sideeffects, too, that I'm worried about."

"Like what?" James said. "Seems fine to me."

"Well, he's started kind of..." Maggie made a clicking sound with her mouth. "Kind of this clacky thing he does with his tongue. I don't think he even knows he's doing it, but it's getting worse." She looked down at Max. "Doctor says it could become permanent. They might change his medications. I just wish..." her voice trailed off.

"I'll bet he'll be fine in no time. Probably needs to outgrow

67

it." It was her father's way of being supportive. His words of wisdom were based on a world where nobody talked about mental illnesses, or if they did, it was always in hushed or derogatory terms. Schizophrenia was just for the movies, just for characters in *Sybil* or *The Three Faces of Eve*. It was for the forgotten faction that had nothing to do with "normal" people. In his eyes, Max couldn't have a serious mental illness. It didn't happen in the "real world."

"Yeah, maybe," she said, but she didn't really think so. Her future, their future, was all muddied up. For the first time in her life, she had no power over it. It was that complete lack of control that mucked up the tidy order of her world.

It was almost three when they got to the "plain" grandpa's house. As always, Coconut greeted them in a state of glee. Usually, Max dropped to the grass and went through the whole tummy rubbing, ear stroking, rump scratching routine, but today he took a seat in a frayed orange macraméd lawn chair on the patio and absentmindedly patted the dog's head. Coco lapped at his hand a few times, then, resigned to less than his fair share of attention, resolutely slumped down next to Max, huffed, and stared through the sliders at Clive who was sitting at the kitchen table drinking coffee.

Maggie let herself in, got her favorite faux carnival glass mug from the cupboard, poured herself half a cup, and sat down without saying a word.

"Any better?" Clive asked and tweaked his head in Max's direction.

"Mmmmmm, yeah," she said.

Clive didn't ask any more questions, and Maggie didn't volunteer any more information. She was emotionally sapped from the visit with her father and needed the unspoken solace of a friend for a while. In a cluttered kitchen full of dated furniture, worthless knick-knacks, and a jumble of old magazines, faded photographs, and half-done crossword puzzles, she found that solace. They talked about the weather, the *Farmer's Almanac*, *The Late Night Show*, and the unlikelihood of O.J.'s innocence.

Sometime during a discussion of the *Farmer's Almanac's*

68

report on the cost of a gallon of domestic beer versus a gallon of condensed clam chowder, Max came inside.

"Hey, twerp," Clive said.

"Hey, Gramps," Max said as he shuffled through to the living room and clicked on the TV.

Clive watched him a moment, then pushed his chair back. "Hey, turkey, come help me with somethin'," he said as he stood up. "I need to bring in that box of canning jars from the tack room."

The barn went mainly unused now, but at one time had housed Yum-yum and Sloppy Joe, a couple of Black Herefords, and Pickles, a Shetland pony the boys had attempted to ride before landing in the mud after a bucking fit that would have given a rodeo bronco a run for its money.

Max followed Clive out the door, and Coco tagged after them as they disappeared around the corner of the house. Maggie was sure Clive didn't really need help but figured it was an excuse to interact with Max for a while. She poured herself another half cup and tinkered around the kitchen, washing a kettle, putting glasses in the dishwasher, wiping the counter, then sat back down and picked up a week old *Oregonian* crossword puzzle. She was working on the lower left corner when Max came in carrying a box, followed by Clive and Coco.

"You're nuts," Clive was saying. "Ever heard of the Andrews Sisters? Give me "Boogie Woogie Bugle Boy" any day. Now there was a song. Or Glenn Miller. Ever heard of him?" He pointed to the laundry room. "Put it on the washing machine."

"Yeah, I heard of 'em," Max said as he took the jars into the next room." But I can't believe you never heard of Ozzy Ozbourne!" he hollered over his shoulder. "Black Sabbath? Not even Led Zeppelin? Mick Jagger?" He came back to the kitchen. "Ya gotta of heard of The Rolling Stones, at least."

"Jimmy Dorsey!" Clive fired at him.

"Kiss!" Max snapped back.

"Benny Goodman!"

Max was quiet for a moment. Maggie could almost hear the gears grinding.

"Ha!" Clive yelled.

"Ha, nothin', old man. Pearl Jam, Guns N' Roses, Pink

69

Floyd, AC/DC, Motley Crue, Metallica, VanHalen, Motorhead. Want me to go on?" Max sat down at the table and beamed.

"Yeah, well...more doesn't mean better," Clive said with a feeble smirk and jabbed Max in the shoulder.

They had been locked in a battle of generational superiority that neither had any hope of winning, but Maggie was thrilled. She hadn't seen Max this animated for over a month. Maybe everything was going to be okay.

CHAPTER 20

Two weeks later, Maggie was doing her best to stay calm as she waited. Bernard Elroy Crandall was twenty minutes late. Three and a half blocks from the Clark County Court House, Crandall, Biggs, and Sweetwater was in a refurbished vintage Victorian with a musty smell and floorboards that creaked when she walked across the lobby. She picked up a *National Geographic* and put it back down, then picked up a *Sports Illustrated* and flipped though to an article on the World Cup that had only slightly more appeal than the article on MLB salaries for outfielders.

"I'm sure he'll be here any minute." Stella glanced up from her computer, then looked at her wrist as if there was a watch there. "He must have been held up in court."

Maggie recognized the universal alibi for attorneys. Right out of high school she had worked for a firm in downtown Portland long enough to know when someone called the office every lawyer in the building was either "in court," "with another client," or "on a conference call," even if they were at a two-hour lunch or out on the back nine. That's why it had surprised her that first day she called when Crandall had actually talked to her. She was mulling over her options of staying or consulting another attorney, when a man blustered in the front door, strode to the front desk, and began rifling through his messages.

"Oh, good morning, Mr. Crandall, how was your court case this morning?" Stella's fib was smooth and obvious. "This is Mrs. Axline," she said opening her eyes a little wider and directing her gaze toward Maggie.

Crandall turned abruptly. He was a bristly sort of man with a thick barrel-chested torso and brows like two singed Ponderosa Pines. He was seventy if he was a day, and he was sporting a...fisherman's vest and baseball cap?

"Huh? Oh! Oh, of course it is," he gruffed. Then, like on the phone, his voice suddenly turned softer. "Mrs. Axline," he said as he came over, took her hand in two beefy paws, and gently pumped it. There was something about this man that made her feel sheltered.

He made no excuses for being late, but during their conference Maggie learned besides being a passionate fisherman, he was semi-retired, did pretty much what he "damned well pleased," and only took the cases he wanted to. She also got the impression that when he did take a case, he put his heart into it. It became like a special-needs child that required particular care and attention until he solved its predicament.

She sat in front of Crandall's massive mahogany desk in a muted green tartan-plaid armchair. It was worn, sagging, and very comfortable.

Crandall was scanning the assets form Stella had Maggie fill out when she made the appointment two weeks ago. His face went through a series of perplexing expressions ranging from pursed lips and one eyebrow quirked, to a faint smile and slight head bobbing. Meanwhile, Maggie picked at imaginary lint and tried to keep her knee from jiggling up and down.

After several minutes, he looked up.

"Whadda ya think?" she said leaning forward, anxious and tense.

"I think you're going to be okay, Mrs. Axline," he said as he quickly scanned the form one more time and put it down. "Right now, it doesn't look like you have much in the way of assets," he said. "Now, in some cases we might consider that a negative thing, but in this case, it's good."

"But what about my home? What about my equity in that."

"Well, it does look like the damages for this accident are going to exceed your coverage, all right, but unless there is criminal neglect, I doubt you have enough for them to bother

72

with. However, it could still go to civil court, but the chance of your home being compromised is... slight." Crandall hesitated but kept his eyes on Maggie. His chair squeaked as he leaned back. "Usually," he said. "Usually," he repeated a little louder, "liability beyond a person's coverage only stretches as far as their income." He paused again and tilted his head. "Look," he said, "it doesn't make a whole lot of sense to sue someone who can't even pay for the damages they've caused you. In this case, you could have several people trying to get more money."

Maggie nodded.

"As far as your home goes, it would be considered 'exempt property.' Same with one car. I assume the other one was totaled in the accident?"

"Yes, but....well....there is something else you need to know."

Crandall righted his chair and leaned forward, hands folded in front of him, waiting.

"Since the accident, Max has been diagnosed as having a disability. A mental disability."

Crandall lifted his porcupine brows and waited for more.

"The doctors say he has chronic schizophrenia. He was in the hospital for a month. Oh, I forgot to write that down. I have an outstanding medical bill of $18,000, too."

During a rush of scribbling on a legal pad, Crandall fired questions: When did you find out about this? Was it before or after the accident? Was his behavior suspicious before the accent? Had you given him permission to drive that night?

Maggie answered them truthfully and succinctly. Yes, they had suspected his illness but weren't sure before the accident, and yes, she did think he was acting pretty strange before that but had chalked it up to drug use or being a stupid teenager. That was why, no, she had not given him permission to drive that night. She had even hidden the keys, but he had found them anyway.

Crandall uh-huhed and nodded his way through her answers, all the while scratching out notes. When Maggie was through, he leaned back again and flicked his pencil up and down on the arm of his chair while he was thinking. "Good," he finally said. "Good," he said again with more head joggling. He sat up straight. "I know this is a terrible worry to you, Mrs. Axline, but I believe we're going to be fine."

Maggie like the way he included himself in this mess. She fought back tears. "You think so?"

"Yep, I do," Crandall said and smiled warmly. "Now, I need you to know there are no guarantees...but no one wants to bankrupt a single mother of two."

"But I keep thinking about all those people. They go out one night, you know, nice dinner, minding their own business, and then..." her voice withered as she tried to find words that would do their misfortune justice. "It's so....heartbreaking," she managed.

"Yes, it is." Crandall looked into Maggie's eyes. "It is heartbreaking, and I understand your sense of responsibility. But..." he said, "you are not Max. You did everything you could to keep him from driving, but in the end, he is the one who made the mistake...not you."

One corner of Maggie's mouth drew up, but she lowered her eyes and slowly shook her head. "I keep thinking I shoulda..."

"Now you can shoulda, and coulda, and if I'da only, 'til the cows come home, but none of that's going to change things, Maggie. Truth is, you did exactly what you were suppose to do. Exactly. No point second guessing yourself."

"I suppose..." Maggie said.

"Mind if I call you Maggie?" Crandall asked. "You just seem like a Maggie."

Maggie nodded.

"And I hope I just seem like a 'Bernie'."

"Well," Maggie said, "more than an Elroy."

"That's the ticket," Crandall said and laughed a great nourishing laugh.

No, she wouldn't change attorneys.

CHAPTER 21

There were no guarantees. That's what Bernie Crandall had said. That's what Dr. Moon had said. Maggie had always tried to be positive, but she had to admit it was taking more effort and more self-talk to stay that way. The half-full line on her life was getting blurry, and she knew if she wasn't careful, it wouldn't take much for it to morph into half-empty. Bernie had told her it could still be months, even a year or longer before the entire matter of the insurance and lawsuits was sorted out. After all, he reminded her, there were a total of seven people, some more deserving than others, who each wanted a piece of the pie. For the next few months she would need to gather her strength, put one foot in front of another, and remember her "one thing at a time" mantra.

They got through Thanksgiving and were approaching Christmas when Maggie got a letter from the Clark County Juvenile Justice System. They had set a date for Maxim's hearing. Of course! How could she have forgotten! About a month after the accident, she had been notified that Max would have to appear in court to determine his "retribution to society." His court date was set for January eighth.

Both Christmas and New Year's came and went without much hoopla. The morning of the eighth the temperature dropped and the clouds anchored themselves to the ground and threatened snow. On the drive to town for Max's hearing, the flakes started, and as they parked outside the courthouse, they swirled in front of the tires and dusted the sidewalk.

"Okay, kiddo, we can do this," Maggie said, and staunchly

got out of the car and marched to the huge limestone building. Well, Maggie marched, Max more or less slumped, despite Maggie's give-'em-hell-you-can-do this-the- game's-not-lost-yet pep talk all the way down the sidewalk, up the stairs, and through the massive brass and glass doors.

Inside, their heels clicked on the marble and granite tiles as they left a trail of melted snow to Juvenile Courtroom II. Max followed her to the front of the room, passing half a dozen other wayward teens sitting with their fretful parents. She patted him on the knee when they took a seat next to the aisle for easy access to the judge when their time came.

And that time came right after a teenager who had graffitied his neighbor's Lexus because he wouldn't give him a ride to a friend's house in the next block. When the judge asked him why he did it, his perfectly logical explanation was that, "the stupid old bastard was going that way anyway," just before his mother whapped his ear. The boy was told he had to make restitution by doing one hundred service hours, forty of which would be fulfilled by washing his neighbor's car twice a week for the next twenty weeks. They heard his grumbling and his mother's rebuking all the way down the aisle and out into the hall.

"Maxim Axline?"

Maggie stood up and yanked Max by the hood of his khaki sweatshirt.

Morosely, eyes still on the floor, Max rose.

"Go forward," Maggie whispered, then followed Max to the front. She had no idea what the parental protocol was. Encouraging but not too pushy? Reason told her to keep her mouth shut, it was not her sentencing; instinct told her to be supportive. She stood two feet behind Max and willed her feet not to shuffle.

As the judge scanned the papers, Maggie heard a scuffing behind her. She turned her head slightly, and caught a glimpse of a woman with a cane limping to the front. She sat behind them, so Maggie could not see her without making an obvious about-face.

One of the victims from the accident? It had to be.

She felt like slithering back down the aisle and under the

door, but instead, straightened her back a little and stared straight ahead. The judge laid a paper in front of him, meticulously smoothed it with his hands, took off his glasses, and peered at Max.

"Maxim," he began, "do you understand the seriousness of your actions?"

Max nodded.

"Look at me, son," the judge said and waited until Max lifted his eyes.

"You realize that seven people besides you were injured as a result of your carelessness? That's seven people whose lives have been changed because you were negligent."

Maggie was nodding, but Max was just staring. At least he wasn't smart-mouthing the judge, Maggie thought in a desperate attempt to save what was left of her motherly rationalization of his defense.

"Do you have representation today?" the judge asked Max, but his eyes slid over to Maggie.

"Only me, I guess, Your—"

"I can represent Maxim, Your Honor," a voice boomed from behind.

Maggie jerked her head to the back of the courtroom, and there he was like the Lone Ranger, Hopalong Cassidy, or Mighty Mouse himself. A flood of relief swept over her as "Here I come to save the day" flitted through her brain.

"Bernard Crandall," he said as he came forward. "Of Crandall, Biggs, and Swee..."

"Yes, Mr. Crandall," the judge said. "Do you have anything to say on behalf of Maxim?"

"Yes, Judge. First of all, although he's a little shy, Maxim is fully aware that his disregard for the lives of others caused this mess and takes responsibility for his actions. However," Crandall paused and put one hand on Max's shoulder. "I think we need to keep in mind that this is the boy's first offense. You'll notice he has had no other misdemeanors, no other delinquencies on his record, Your Honor."

"Yes, I see that," is what the judge said, but with the slight lift of his shoulders, it sounded more like, "So what?"

"Maxim can learn from this, Judge. He realizes he needs to

make restitution for his actions, but if the punishment is too severe, he might—"

"Fine!" The judge banged his gavel, perhaps a bit too hard, Maggie thought. "Thirty days in juvenile detention and fifty hours of community service," he bellowed. "See the court clerk on your way out."

Maggie was neither startled nor surprised at the sentence. In truth, she was rather relieved. It could have been much worse. She tugged at the tail of Max's sweatshirt and he swiveled to her.

"What?" he mumbled. The expression on his face reminded Maggie of the rabbits their cat used to bring into the house. It was the look of the dazed. The look of what's-happening-to-me.

"C'mon, honey," Maggie said, and she caught the crook of his arm. As they turned, the woman who had come in after them stood abruptly, clutched her cane with both hands, and leaned on it. Her eyes were defiant and full of anger, and they tracked Max as he passed. When they got to the door, Maggie glanced back. She was still standing, still glaring.

Bernie followed Maggie and Max out.

"Bernie," Maggie rested her hand on the sleeve of his camel-hair overcoat as they stepped into the hall. "Thank you," was all she could say.

"Well, I looked his court date up. I figured you could use a little help. Not really sure I did anything you couldn't have done, but I don't think I made it worse, anyway."

"Oh," Maggie turned to Max. "Max, this is Mr. Crandall. He's the one handling the lawsuits."

"Max," Bernie said and stuck his hand out.

"Thanks," Max murmured as they shook.

"You bet." Bernie turned back to Maggie. "I'll be in touch with you when I know more, Maggie. Meanwhile, try not to worry." He turned up his collar and snugged the opening a little tighter. "Well, snow or no snow, there are fish waiting to be caught," he said with a slight wave and turned to go.

Maggie watched him walk down the steps and out the door. "That man," she said to Max, "deserves to go to heaven with his slippers on."

They stopped at the clerk's office and got information on

when Max would do detention and where and how he would do community service hours. She also made arrangements to take Max out of JDH to go to his appointments with Dr. Canseco and to get his Prolixin shots. She had the clerk write a note on Max's intake plan that he had a mental illness and left three numbers to contact if they had any problems.

Outside, the snow had picked up momentum and accumulated at least an inch. On the way home they stopped at Les Schwab and walked to a nearby Elmer's for a long lunch. Five hours later, they were headed home again, and by the time they hit the higher elevation of their driveway, at least four inches had piled up.

"No school tomorrow!" Braxton yelled from his room when they came in.

"You sure?" Maggie hollered back. "Or is that wishful thinking?"

"Sure! I heard it on the news."

That was fine with Maggie. She would gladly make up a day at the end of the school year for a reprieve now. In a week, she would need to get Max in for his appointment and shot, and in two weeks she would take him to begin his detention. But for now, right this minute, her life was on a fairly even keel. And that life seemed almost...normal. Maggie sank into an amicable over-stuffed chair, sighed deeply, and mentally crossed her fingers.

The next two months went fairly smoothly. They got through winter without too much snow, much to Braxton's discontent. Max did his thirty days in detention, and Maggie signed him out once a week for sessions with Dr. Canseco and to get his injections. But the strain of the court hearing and his stay in JDH had clearly taken its toll. He was even more sullen than usual, and when she tried to carry on a conversation with him, he clipped it short.

But that wasn't all. Maggie had also noticed Max's movements were becoming even more stilted. His gait reminded her of the zombies in an old sci-fi movie. He carried his arms slightly out from his sides, and his fingers were stiff and splayed as he walked. The tongue clicking had also gotten

79

worse so Doctor Canseco had increased his side effects medication to see if it would help. So far, it hadn't.

CHAPTER 22

Max writhed and clawed at his stomach. Oh my God! Oh my God! They did it! They finally did it! Oh God! I can feel them. Razor blades! If I can hold on a few more minutes. If I can just... He inched to the curb and clutched the pole of a parking meter, then lugged himself upright. Phone. I need to get to a... The rain fell like acid on his bare shoulders. Fuck! He slumped to the sidewalk and lay there in a heap, then hoisted himself to his knees and crawled toward the light.

Maggie fumbled for the alarm clock. Two-fifteen.

Who could be calling at this... Max is downstairs in bed... isn't he?

The familiar feeling of dread gripped her. Her hand groped blindly for the phone. "Yes?"

Within two minutes she was in the car, ripping around the sharp curves that fed the arterial roads into town.

Where did he say he was? Main and Drake? There was no Drake Street in Vancouver, was there? Main and...

Max had said he was at an Arco station. There was only one on Main she knew of.

She pulled into the gas station and scanned the property. Not in front, not on the sidewalk. She drove around to the back. No one there. When she came around to the front again, the attendant was standing outside. She rolled down her window as he came toward her. "Over there," he said pointing toward a dumpster. "I was gonna call the police, but he said someone was coming for him. He okay?" He strained his neck forward as if he wanted to get a better look but didn't want to get any closer.

"I got it," Maggie said as she yanked on the parking brake and scrambled from the car. The streetlight glared, but the shadow of the dumpster obscured the huddled figure wedged between it and a chain-link fence. As she approached, she could hear the ping of rain against metal and a diffused whimper.

"Max?"

"Yeah." The voice was gravelly and muffled. "They got me real good this time," it said.

Maggie bundled Max into the back seat where he droned out a steady moan punctuated by expletives and mumblings about razor blades in his stomach. Vancouver Memorial wasn't very far, but it seemed like it took an hour to get there. The "Emergency Room" sign flickered bleakly and pointed to the back of the hospital. As she tore into the parking lot, she glanced back at Max. The same. She pulled on the brake. "Stay here," she said and trotted to the single door and tugged at it. Locked. A sign by the door read, "push for assistance," but before she could raise her hand, an orderly was there holding it open as she stepped inside.

"It's my son," she kept one foot in the door as she gasped out the words. "He's in the back of my car. I think he's having a psychotic break."

"Is he violent?" he asked, peering at the only car in the parking lot.

Maggie shook her head. "He thinks he swallowed razor blades," she said.

"Name?" he asked.

"Maxim. Maxim Axline."

The orderly yelled at another, and the two of them brought Max in. "It's okay, man," he kept saying to Max. "We're gonna take care of you." They strapped Max on to a gurney. "Someone will be out to talk to you," he said over his shoulder as they disappeared down the hall and slipped into another room.

There was one metal chair in the hallway, but Maggie had noticed a waiting room inside the main door. It felt small and dank, but the size suited the purpose. Maggie didn't think it functioned in a capacity other than mental-patient intake. Either way, it was a slow night at Vancouver Memorial.

It wasn't until she dropped onto the yellow plastic sofa that she allowed herself a slow exhale. Her fingers traced the splitting fissures in the arm as she gave her pounding heart a chance to slow in momentum and intensity. She knew even though this was another upheaval, at this moment at least, Max was safe.

Maggie thought back to another time she'd been to this hospital. A very different time almost eighteen years ago. She hadn't had a chance to linger in a waiting room then; she'd been rushed straight to the delivery room. When they had put that tiny marvel in her arms, she looked down at the mop of brown hair and two little eyes as dark and shiny as Halloween jellybeans and knew his whole future lay in front of him. But in her wildest imagination she couldn't have predicted this day. Seven pounds, eleven ounces. His grandfather had nicknamed him "Lucky" the minute he saw him. Maggie shook her head. "Huh! Lucky!" she scoffed and smoothed a wayward flap of yellow pleather. She puffed a small burst of air. *Ironic.*

She settled in for a long wait and wished she'd had time to bring a book with her, or a crossword puzzle, anything to keep her mind occupied. The ragtag collection of magazines and pamphlets on the steel and laminate coffee table didn't pique her interest, so she leaned back and stared at Van Gogh's sunflowers on the far wall. It wasn't a print. She wondered how long it had taken someone to reproduce it in oil.

Was it a work of love? Of pride? Or the upshot of an assembly line. Maybe there was a machine that spit out hundreds of them every hour.

She counted the flowers. *Thirteen.... No, there was part of one peeking out from behind than big one...fourteen.* She imagined Van Gogh painting the original one. His first of many. Had the paintings become wilder as he became more manic? Had the brushstrokes become more erratic? Why had he cut off part of his ear?

Maggie frowned. She couldn't remember...*lead poisoning?* She pinched her eyes shut and felt herself being pulled in to a sea of sunflowers.

"Mrs. Axline?"

Someone was jiggling her arm.

83

"Mrs. Axline?"

"Oh!" she blurted. "Oh, I'm sorry. Must have drifted off." She straightened herself and glanced at the clock over the door. Almost four.

The someone was sitting next to her. "That's okay." She patted Maggie's arm. "Hi, I'm Caroline. I'm an intake specialist here?" She smiled. "Mrs. Axline, we've done a preliminary evaluation on Max, and we'd like to keep him here a couple of days." She opened a manila folder in her hand and gave it a quick once-over. "I noticed he's been here before?"

Maggie nodded. "For a while before he went to St. Peter in Olympia."

"So, do we have your permission to admit him?"

"Oh, of course...except...I don't know how... I mean, I don't have insurance for it. I'm not sure what to do. But..."

Get hold of yourself, Maggie.

"But of course, you can keep him here." This wasn't a time to be wishy-washy, she told herself. She would have to work it out. She just had no idea how.

"I have some forms for you to fill out and sign," Caroline said, getting up. She paused in the doorway, turned around and leaned against the jamb. She sucked in a short breath and stood with her mouth open, as if she wanted to say something.

Maggie lifted her eyebrows. "Was there something else?" she asked.

"There might be a way to make it so you're not liable for his bills. Do you have time to come in tomorrow if I set up a meeting with a mental-health coordinator?"

Again Maggie called for a substitute, and again she found herself driving to the hospital, but this time for the meeting Caroline had set up. She hadn't been there that many times, but it was still odd and somewhat disturbing how familiar it seemed walking up to the psych ward on the second floor and ringing the buzzer. Dave let her in and took her to a conference room where two people from the mental health department awaited her. They both rose when she came in, shook hands, and introduced themselves. The three settled around a small oval table, Julia and Tom with papers, pamphlets, clipboards, and pens spread in front of them, and Maggie nervously clutching a red hobo handbag in her lap.

"Thank you for seeing us, Mrs. Axline," Julia began. "First of all, Tom and I want you to know we are here simply to offer some options for you to manage your life and expenses with Maxim."

Tom interrupted and blurted, "We do have suggestions, but we have no intention of forcing anything on you." He looked back at Julia. Nervous, Maggie thought. Nice, but tense.

"Tom's right, Mrs. Axline. We are advisors and facilitators, not decision-makers. All decisions will be made by you." Julia paused and scrutinized Maggie. "Do you understand what I'm saying?"

Maggie looked from Julia to Tom and back to Julia. "Well...yes," she finally said. This was not Einstein's theory of relativity they were trying to explain. Of course she understood, but she also understood they were probably used to dealing with people who were under duress and therefore had a harder time comprehending. They were also, Maggie assumed, covering their asses in case of complaints of coercion later.

"Good!" Julia said, and Tom concurred by nodding his head a few times. "First of all, do you think you could tell us a little about your background with Max? I mean about his illness? Maybe some of your concerns? Some of your experiences since all this started?"

Maggie sucked in air and whooshed it out. "Well... let me see." She stared at the table a moment. "Sure, I think I can." She took in another deep breath and sighed audibly when she released it. "I guess it was about ten or twelve months ago I started to notice some changes in Max. Nothing huge at first, but he was a little, oh, I don't know...off, I guess you could say." She looked up at Julia, who smiled warmly, and nodded her encouragement to go on.

"So, anyway, at first I figured it was just some typical teenage stuff going on. You know, drugs, hormones, well... testosterone, I suppose. I didn't really know what to do. I even started trying to think of what I might have done wrong. Was I too hard on him? Not hard enough? I'd smoked part of the time I was pregnant with him. I even thought it might be that. I was

85

kind of grasping at anything I could, but nothing really made sense to me. Anyway, enough of that." Maggie waved a hand in front of her face, dismissing her doubts for now.

"When he had his first 'psychotic episode,'" Maggie air quoted the term that was becoming familiar to her, "I took him to the county alcohol and drug treatment center, and they told me it was probably schizophrenia. Sooooo, I took him to a psychiatrist, Dr. Canseco. He's still seeing him. But since then, I've had to commit him twice. Once they sent him to a hospital in Olympia for a month. St. Peter?" Maggie looked at Julia and Tom, who nodded again. "And, of course, this time. He's here now. But I guess you knew that," she said as one corner of her mouth spiked slightly upwards.

"And have you talked to the doctor here yet?" Tom asked.

"No, have you?" Maggie's eyes shot to Tom. She was again in that want-to-but-don't-want-to know situation.

"No," Tom said. He drummed his fingers on the table a few times, patted the folder, and looked to Julia.

Yes, definitely nervous.

"We probably won't find out anything until you do, Mrs. Axline, but if they decide Maxim needs extended treatment again, we know it can get pretty costly," Julia said. "And that's where we might be able to help you."

"Well, I can sure use all the help I can get." Maggie crossed her arms and rested them on the table. She hesitated a moment, then shrugged her shoulders and said, "Okay, shoot!"

Julia and Tom tag-teamed the proposal.

"We understand Max has a birthday coming up?" Tom asked.

"That's right, the fourteenth of next month. Just a few weeks."

"And he'll be eighteen, right?"

Maggie nodded and waited for more. *Where is this going?*

"Good," Julia continued. "Sometimes, Mrs. Axline, people are unable to care for themselves because of a disability, but the parents are also not able to care for them," Julia paused, maybe giving the information a chance to percolate down. "In a case like this, the person with the disability can be determined incompetent to take care of himself, and a government agency

86

can be appointed to see that he is taken care of."

"Does that make sense?" Tom tagged.

"You mean the government would...what?...be responsible for him? Well, I couldn't..." Maggie reined herself in. Wait, she told herself. Listen. "Okay," she finally said, "so what does that mean?"

"Well, yes," Tom went on. "It does mean the government would be responsible for Max. He would be a 'ward of the state,' or a 'ward of the courts,' it's sometimes called. But that doesn't mean you'd lose Max."

Julia picked up. "What it means, Mrs. Axline, is that the government would be responsible for Maxim's welfare. You would still see Max, be with him, you know, take him to the doctor or hospital, but some of the...well, the burden of caring for Max would be off your shoulders. For example, it would pay for Max's hospitalization, and it would pay for his medications and his counseling. And, eventually," Julia skipped a beat before going on. "It might even lead to a type of Social Security income so he could live on his own."

Julia glanced at Tom, who said, "Of course there are some hoops to go through for that. I mean, he'd have to demonstrate to the court's satisfaction that he couldn't hold down a job."

"Oh, Lord." Maggie drew in a breath, squeezed her eyes shut for a moment, then suddenly opened them. "So," she said, "basically, what you're saying is that I wouldn't have the financial burden." She watched both people, strangers really, across from her. She hadn't had time to think about the future, Max's future. She had barely had time to think about what was happening right now.

There was a family photo album in her head. She had flipped through the pages many times. There was a baby taking a bath in the sink, the camera catching the look of astonishment the exact moment he discovered if he slapped the water with his fist, he got a face full of suds; a little boy with an almost toothless grin, standing in a blue and white checkered shirt, clutching a *Star Wars* lunchbox on his first day of school; a twelve-year-old on his chrome Diamond Back BMX bike doing his version of a pro's tricks on a homemade half-pipe. And a more recent one of a teenager, head bent over his Epiphone

87

bass guitar, dark hair falling in soft, fluid folds, fingers poised, ready to hit the next metallic chord.

She had always imagined the album would later be filled with photos of Max in his graduation cap and gown, Max and his bride (she was pretty, too) on their wedding day, and eventually, maybe him and his own son sharing a moment caught in time.

Now, the last half of that album was empty. Maggie had no frame of reference to fill it with a different set of photographs.

"You don't have to decide right away, Mrs. Axline," Julia said, "but it might be helpful to decide before Max's eighteenth birthday."

Maggie crinkled her brows and Julia explained, "Sometimes we find it a less...complicated process before a child is an adult. Then when he turns eighteen, he is eligible for at least a review to see if he also qualifies for social services as an adult. Usually the person is referred to our local human services agencies, like the mental health agency, so he can get the care he needs. He would be assigned a caseworker who would help him. You know, keep tabs on him, help him manage his finances, and probably get to know him pretty well."

Tom leaned forward. "We know how hard this is for you, Mrs. Axline. This is never easy for any parent, but sometimes there are circumstances where parents are not able to care for their children." He tilted his head. "It's obvious how much you love your son, Mrs. Axline. And like we said, we don't want to coerce you. But we do want to put this option out there. We're hoping you will at least take some time to consider it."

Maggie stared at the conference table. Yet another twist to deal with. Another decision to make. There was a three-ring extravaganza going on in her stomach; the elephants, the tightrope walker, the jugglers, all vying for her attention. And then there was Braxton. She was aware of how Max's mental state had affected his life. She was also aware of the prognosis, and it didn't look good. But give him up? Was this how a mother feels when she has to give a child up for adoption? What mother could do that without an aftermath of regret and guilt? Maggie knew she was sometimes too headstrong, but right or wrong, she had always trusted her instincts and made critical choices decisively. But this one, this was too much to ask. Too much.

She lifted her head and closed her eyes. "No," she said. "No, I won't take time to consider this."

Chapter 23

Maggie opened her eyes. She shook her head. "I don't need time. I really don't see that I have a choice. If you'll get the papers ready, I'll sign them."

Julia and Tom gave her three pages of literature on laws pertaining to becoming a ward of the state and six more on what to expect, patient responsibilities, and social services' responsibilities. Before she left, they made arrangements to meet with her again in two days. During that time, she could talk to Dr. Friedman to get an idea of how long Max would be there or if they would be sending him away again. She found herself hoping for a last ditch effort to save him. One last chance for the doctors to change their minds.

"We're astounded, Mrs. Axline. It looks as though Max is getting better," they would say.

"I never would have believed it," Dr. Friedman would pipe up, "Max has actually recovered. Now that's one for the *Journal of Psychiatry*," he would say between pauses, and waggle his head in bewilderment.

Maybe she'd even call Dr. Moon. He'd get a chuckle out of it.

"Huh," Maggie huffed, "it certainly *would* be one for the psychiatrists to discuss."

She didn't see Max that morning, but came back in the afternoon to talk to Dr. Friedman who methodically went over his evaluation with her. Unfortunately, that evaluation came nowhere close to Maggie's wishful thinking.

"Max is still confused," he began and paused as he skimmed Max's file. "And you have been taking Max in regularly for his Prolixin shots?"

She answered with a curt, "yes," impatient for him to get to the bottom line.

"Well," he picked up the file, "I've talked to Max and done an assessment." He put the file down and paused. "I believe he is going to need to stay here for a while longer. The next twenty-four hours should give us a better idea, but if he doesn't improve before long... he may need to go to another facility again."

Dr. Friedman put his clipboard on the table between them and peered at Maggie over his silver-rimmed bifocals. "I understand you're considering signing the forms for Max to become a ward of the courts?"

Maggie nodded and bit her lip. There were those blasted tears again, ready to pop out at a moment's notice. "Damn it!" she blurted.

"Well," the doctor said without hurry, "if it's any help, I think you're doing the right thing. Chronic schizophrenia can be very hard to deal with. I believe it can even be harder than a physical illness because the prognosis is so...unpredictable, so... volatile. We never really know what to expect. What's going to work, what's not, or when it's going to crop up again. It can play havoc with your own health, too."

He paused once again, and in an uncharacteristic gesture, patted Maggie's sweaty hands that were clamped together in front of her. "Now, you wouldn't be any help to Max at all if you went off the deep end yourself, now would you?"

Maggie shook her head. "No," she murmured. "No, I guess not."

"You can see Max for a while if you want to, even though he's pretty out of it today. But," Dr. Friedman said as he stood, "it would also be okay if you didn't want to." He waited for Maggie to rise.

"Right, I think I'll wait a day or two." At that moment seeing Max in this state was more than she could handle.

She walked with Dr. Friedman to the nurses' station and headed down the hall to the exit. "You'll call me then?" she asked, turning.

"Of course. We should know something before you sign

those papers."

Maggie was sitting at her desk two days later when they put the call through to her classroom. The last bell of the day had rung, and students were scurrying from the room in a hurry to be anywhere but there. Max wasn't improving very fast, Dr. Friedman told her, and there was more than a fair chance they would be sending him to another long-term facility for the duration of his recovery.

Maggie hung up the phone and stared through the slats of the Venetian blinds, crooked and bent from years of careless use. She'd expected nothing different, she told herself. She'd just have to deal with it.

The meeting with Julia and Tom from Social Services was at four o'clock that day, so Maggie finished grading the last of a stack of tests on punctuation, locked up her room, and headed for the hospital. The flurries of February and March had passed, the sky had turned clear and cold, and the afternoon was as crisp as any she'd seen the last few months. The leaves that hadn't blown away in the fall crackled under her feet and whirred around them as she walked to the car.

Tom was waiting for her inside the psych-ward door and buzzed her in. As she approached, his fingers fluttered by his side, then he patted his khakis a few times, smiled, and shook her hand. She followed him to the conference room.

"Okay," Maggie said as she sat down. She slapped her hands on the table in front of her, straightened her back, and smiled politely. "Let's get this over with."

Julia's eyes widened and her eyebrows arched. "Do you have any questions first?"

But Maggie never was one to second-guess herself once she had made up her mind, and she couldn't see the point of prolonging it. "Nope." Her response sounded too brusque, even to her, but she'd read the literature, and this was what needed to be done.

Before she left the hospital, Maggie stopped at the nurses' station. She was thankful Dave was on duty. "Hi, sorry to bother you," she began. *Why am I apologizing?* "But do you think this is a good time so see Max?"

"Sure. Let me show you where his room is."

She followed Dave down a dimly lit corridor lined with doors, most of them closed. The tan linoleum, randomly flecked with black swooshes, had an inlaid strip of maroon tiles on the outer edges that made the hallway feel narrower than it really was. Yet it gave her a solid feeling, like she couldn't lose her way here even if she tried. Maggie wondered if this had been on purpose or if it was someone's attempt at contemporary décor at the time it was installed. Dave stopped in front of a slightly ajar door. He glanced at Maggie, and a faint smile crossed his face as he opened the door.

"Max, ya got company, dude!"

Max lay on a narrow bed but sat up abruptly when they came in. "Hey, man, how's it goin'?"

Maggie couldn't tell if he was talking to Dave or to her, but it didn't really matter. She stepped forward and hugged him. He stood up, but his body was stiff and unyielding. He glowered at her. She slumped, then straightened her shoulders and drew in a deep breath.

This is going to be a long visit.

Maggie sat on the edge of the bed and motioned for Max to sit next to her. He hesitated briefly, then casually plunked himself down.

Dave had followed Maggie in and was slowly walking around the room, smoothing covers, picking up tissues, straightening magazines.

He's stalling, Maggie thought. He wants to make sure Max is going to behave himself before he leaves.

After a few minutes, Dave walked out but peeked back in. "I'll be right out here in the hall if you need anything," he said and subtly left the door slightly open.

Now that they were alone, Maggie was at a loss for words. It was clear that Max wasn't going to do much talking. To break the tension, Maggie bounced on the bed a few times. "Feels pretty comfy," she said.

Suddenly, Max rose and strode to the window where he stood to one side and covertly peered out.

Maggie watched him. "Max?"

93

"They're out there," he said and flicked his head toward the parking lot below.

Maggie went to the window, "Where? Who?"

"Get back!" Max half whispered, half yelled as he ducked back. "They'll see you."

"What is it Max? Who's out there?"

"Behind that dumpster. If they see you, I'm dead." With his back to the wall, Max edged over to the window again, carefully pulled the flimsy curtain aside, and peered out.

"Okay then," Maggie said. "I'm going to go sit down. Come on, Max. Come sit and talk to me a while."

Max followed her back to the bed and eased himself down beside her with a guarded watch still on the window.

"Hey!" Maggie said, trying to get his mind off the imagined threat outside, "Braxton's team won their last track meet. I think he placed first in the high—"

Max bolted up and ran to the window again.

"...jump." Maggie finished. "Please, Max, no one's going to hurt you as long as I'm here."

Max sat down again, but only for a moment. Every minute or two he was back at the window. There seemed to be nothing Maggie could do or say to deter him. After about twenty minutes, she was exhausted. "Well, sweetheart, I think it's time for me to get going."

Max didn't say goodbye, didn't walk her to the door, didn't acknowledge her departure.

As good as his word, Dave was right outside the door. He was talking to one of the clients but glanced at Maggie and nodded once when she came out of Max's room.

"Now, Frank, how many times have I told you, you cannot smoke in your room? Hand 'em over." Frank shuffled his feet and stared down the hall past Dave before he reached into his pocket and brought out a pack of Marlboros.

"That's a start." Dave put out his hand palm up, snapped his fingers, and waited.

Frank glared at him, but took out a book of matches and handed them over.

Dave still stood there with his hand out and his eyebrows raised. Finally, Frank yanked his hat off and forked over two more books of matches.

"You come see me during the smoke break, and I'll give you one then, but ya gotta stop sneaking them into your room, ya hear me?" Dave patted Frank on the shoulder and turned to walk Maggie down the hall.

"How do you think Max is doing today?"

"Hard to say." Maggie shrugged. "At least he isn't violent."

"Well," Dave consoled as they walked back down the hall, "it's bound to get better."

There was nothing more she could do now except put one foot in front of another, live one day at a time until Max improved. How long that would be was the elusive question. Would it be longer this time than last? What about the next time? Was this just the beginning? The future was formless, and if there was a light at the end of this tunnel, it was too dim to see. Right then, nothing seemed right in the world. Right then, she needed Braxton. She needed to see him, to talk to him, to know there was still something normal in her life. Something solid.

Dave buzzed the door open, and Maggie slogged down the stairs and stepped out into an angry wind.

CHAPTER 24

Life is too ridiculous, Maggie thought as made the 130-mile trip north on I-5. If anyone had told her even a year ago she would be driving to the state mental hospital to see her son, she would have called them crazy. Now, that word had a whole new meaning.

This was not the first visit since Max had been made a ward of the state. They had been kind, understanding, sympathetic. All of them. Julia, Tom, Dr. Friedman, but none more than Dave. Maybe, Maggie thought, it was because he was right down there in the trenches with the patients, or the "clients" as they called them. She was quickly realizing it took a very special person to work in a psych ward.

Max was kept at Vancouver Memorial for another two weeks, long enough to hurry the custodial process through before they shipped him off to Western Washington State Hospital in Steilacoom. It was necessary, Dr. Friedman had said. And Maggie knew in her heart he was right. Just like she knew it was necessary she sign the papers. But each time she made this trip, she replayed the options over and over in her mind. Each time she came to the same conclusion. Right now, this was the best for Max, and if she was being honest with herself, it was better for her and for Braxton, too.

When she had come home from Vancouver Memorial after signing the state custody papers, she picked up a pizza, and she and Braxton sat and talked for a while before he was off again to a friend's house to study for a test the next day. She didn't get to see him for very long, but it was enough to ground her again, if only temporarily, before she started driving to the state hospital. Braxton was soft-spoken most of the time, but he was strong. She had to believe that. She had to believe he would survive, despite this absurd turn of events in their lives.

On her second visit to Steilacoom she had brought a cake for Max's birthday. It was.... memorable. She'd asked for permission to light the candles, and she and three staff members celebrated Max's eighteenth birthday. Not quite the party most mothers would envision for their sons.

"Blow out the candles, Max," she had said. But Max stood there, one hand in his pocket, and frowned down at the homemade chocolate cake with "Happy Birthday Max" scrawled on the top in red gel frosting. Maggie urged him again, "Blow out the candles, hon." Max skewed his head to the side and stared at her. His face darkened. She couldn't tell if he was confused or angry.

"Here, I'll help y—" Maggie began. Suddenly, Max turned back to the cake and frantically waved one hand back and forth over the candles until they went out. She cut a piece of cake for Max and one for herself before asking an orderly to take the rest to the break room for the staff, then she sat with Max as he opened the gifts she had brought. It had been hard to think of something to buy he could actually use in the hospital. She finally settled on a new pair of slippers, a soft blanket with a picture of a deer on it, and a carton of Camel Straights, which she had given to the person at the desk so they could be doled out to him at his smoke-breaks. Max has started smoking over a year ago, and she had long since given up on trying to stop him, or even discourage him. You have to prioritize what's important, she often reminded herself.

Now, here she was, making her fourth visit to Western State Hospital. Every two weeks she came bearing perfunctory tokens: a carton of cigarettes, sometimes brownies, socks and underwear, and an *Easy Rider* magazine if she could find one. The trip was becoming almost routine. The only variation was in the weather. Today, she passed cars slick with spring rain, she passed the billboard "Christ Died To Save Sinners," she passed the double-trailer rigs, mud flaps with naked women silhouetted in chrome, maniacally dancing in their wake.

Michael Jackson lamented that he was tired of injustice

97

and the whole system sucked. Maggie clicked the radio off and reached for her Starbucks mug filled with Folgers Colombian-roast coffee she had made that morning. Lukewarm. She fumbled in the brown lunch bag for something to munch on to distract her from the monotony. Ranch-flavored Doritos and a bruised banana would do.

She tried to keep her thoughts in check, in the present, but they leapt ahead of her. What would he be like this time? Would he talk to her? Would he make sense? Well, if nothing else, it can...entertaining, Maggie thought. Never in the history of the world had such a diversity of so many important people been sequestered in one place. She'd met rock stars and film stars. She'd seen secret service men who had protected presidents, assassins who had tried to kill them, undercover agents who had spied on them, and once during a full moon, JFK himself. Never again could anyone convince Maggie that the lunar cycle didn't affect people's mental or emotional state.

A little south of Tacoma, the exit sign loomed ahead, and Maggie's heart jumped to her throat. The steering wheel stuck to her hands then slipped under them as she veered off the freeway at Fort Lewis. She liked taking the back way to the hospital. It was a scenic drive and gave her a quiet time to collect her thoughts before she saw Max. When she got to the town of Steilacoom, she knew she was almost there. She liked this little town. Its charm helped calm her, and she could catch glimpses of Puget Sound on her way through. Sometime, maybe when she was more rested, she would take a ferry from Steilacoom to one of the smaller islands in the San Juans. She even thought she wouldn't mind settling there...sometime... under different circumstances.

Maggie's grasp tightened as she turned across traffic and through the open iron gate of Western State Hospital. She splashed through puddles until she found a parking space, then sat in the car a few minutes listening to the swish-swish-swish of the wipers.

Come on, Maggie Axline. Stop being a wimp. You can do this.

She sucked in a breath, put the car in park, turned off the ignition, and forced herself to open the door.

The hospital was formidable, not only in size but also in its unyielding façade. Brick after brick, it seemed to stretch for blocks. Maggie had read up on it. The first one was built in the late 1800s and was called an "insane asylum," or worse yet, a "lunatic asylum." Maggie had cringed when she read that. It seemed as though people were stuffed into it and never came out. Today, stories of screaming apparitions and haunting "orbs" sighted in the shell of what was left of that original building still persisted. Everyone loves a good ghost story, Maggie thought, but her attitude about the subject of those stories was changing. The patients today, like those one hundred years earlier, were simply people who had been dealt a rocky hand. It wasn't as if they chose to be that way.

As soon as she stepped out of the car, her eyes were pulled up to the second story. Even with the drizzle, she could see partially obscured faces staring at her through chicken-wire windows covered with bars. She had tried to break that habit of looking at them, but every time she came she felt almost compelled to see if they were still there. She had no idea why. Maybe it was sympathy. Maybe it was curiosity. Or maybe she thought one day she would look and no one would be looking back.

Get a grip, Maggie! One thing at a time. Put one foot in front of another.

Go through the columns.

Open the glass doors.

Now, take one step at a time up to Ward B2.

On the second floor, she stood for a moment outside the unit and composed herself, then rang the buzzer. A minute later, she heard what sounded like a hundred keys jangling on a chain, then saw an arm swing the door open and hold it for her. "Good morning, Joseph," Maggie said.

"I think Max is right inside," he said. "Must have known you were coming."

"Well, that's a good sign, don't you think?"

Joseph smiled, but Maggie knew by now not to read anything into it. Still...

As she signed in at the small, glass enclosed nurses' station, she could see Max through the window, rocking from side to

99

side, waiting for her. She straightened her shoulders, put on her smile, and engulfed him in her arms. He was still unresponsive but he did, at least, act like he knew who she was.

He was wearing a pair of fuzzy pink slippers. "Where are your shoes?" Maggie asked.

"I can't go outside."

Max didn't embellish. Apparently, not being able to go outside explained everything. Maggie would have to fill in the blanks. She knew there was a fenced-in courtyard where they took the client to get some fresh air a couple of times a day. Whether Max was restricted from that area, or whether the rain prevented them from using it for a while, Maggie didn't know. She was going to ask him where his new slippers were but decided against it. It didn't really matter.

She took Max's hand. He didn't pull away, but it hung limp and impassive at his side as they strolled toward the smoking room. There were also certain times of the day the patients had smoke-breaks, but when they had guests, they bent the rules a little. Using the smoking room to visit was one of them.

"That's my van out there," Max said as they sat down at a square pock-marked table next to a smoke-filmed window.

"No, I don't think it is, Max," Maggie ventured.

"It is too!" he fired back. "I had to repossess it from a guy last week. I had to beat him up to get it."

Maggie sighed. "Geeze Louise," she muttered.

"Louise?" Max said. "Hey, I know her. I used to go with her."

Maggie lowered her head and breathed out a barely audible, "Jesus Christ."

"Jesus Christ?" Max said brightly. "I know him. He's a punk! I'm gonna crucify him!"

Maggie's gaze shot up, at first startled, but then more amused than anything else, and she laughed.

Max laughed too, and even though she doubted he knew exactly why he was laughing, it was good to hear it. But the next second, their laughter bounced through the empty room and was gone. Maggie was glad he was talking and decided this might be a good time to use the nod and listen strategy. Max was a prolific talker when he was younger. He could talk a one-

100

legged man into trying out to be the LA Rams' kicker. Sometimes he would talk so fast and furious, it seemed like he was trying to keep up with all the ideas whirling around in his head until they spilled out through his mouth. She often thought he would be a good trial lawyer when he got older...or a politician, she thought wryly.

But since he had been diagnosed, Maggie knew there were times it was not productive to "discuss" topics with him. "Discussions" soon turned to arguments. Arguments she had no hope of winning. At times like this, listening and nodding was an altogether better approach.

They had a one-sided conversation—and this time it was Max doing all the talking—for about an hour before other patients started drifting in for their morning smoke-break. Maggie had brought an extra pack of cigarettes. She handed one to Max and lit it for him. A winsome-looking young man with a face that would melt a mother's heart came over to them. "Can I have a cigarette?" he asked.

Then another approached. "Can I have a cigarette?" One after another they came slowly, like birds to a bird feeder.

When Maggie ran out, she had to turn down the last one, a gangly man that was all angles and sharp edges. He stood over them a few moments, then reached across the table and flicked a scrawny finger through the ashtray for a butt with a little life left on it.

On the other side of the room, a young woman took her clothes off—every stitch—and launched into an exercise routine with the enthusiasm of a drill sergeant. Maggie fidgeted and tried not to look, but no one else seemed to notice. "One – two! One – two! One – two!" Finally, one of the orderlies went over to her. Maggie couldn't hear what he said, but she reluctantly put her clothes on and marched out.

When the break was over, Maggie and Max trailed out after the rest and sauntered back down the hall. The institutional green walls had the remnants of carved names and cryptic messages on them, but the floor was spotless. A man, bent with age, gripped the handle of a mop; his gnarled hands worked it back and forth over the already clean floor. The same man had been mopping the same section when they had gone in.

As they came into the spacious, brightly lit commons lounge, Maggie noticed Max's toes poking out through holes in the pink slippers. "Good Lord, Max! Doesn't anyone around here ever cut your toenails?"

Max had once again become sullen, but he stopped a moment and glanced at his feet. "You can," he said.

Maggie got some toenail clippers from the staff and sat in a chair across from Max. "Give me a foot, Max." He lifted one foot, and Maggie clipped his nails, being careful not to cut the quick. "Tell me if I hurt you," she said and glanced up.

His head was cocked to one side, and there it was again, that bewildered expression. Like he was trying to figure out who she was and what she was doing with his foot. Maggie preferred his full of bravado moods, the ones when he talked about imaginary old girlfriends or even about punching someone's lights out.

While she was concentrating on the amateur pedicure, a string of patients formed a queue behind Max. They were quiet and respectful, but Maggie had the distinct impression they also wanted their nails clipped. Or maybe they just wanted some individual attention from a visitor, even if it wasn't their own. When she finished Max's nails, he stood up, and sure enough, the first person in line sat down in his chair.

Maggie emitted a weedy, involuntary groan. "Oh, why not?" she shrugged. "Okay, give me a foot." She smiled at the middle-aged woman across from her. As the woman lifted her foot, Maggie chuckled softly. "Well... might work better if you take your shoe off first," she said to her.

The angel-faced boy, the exercising woman, the gangly man, all stood in line. They, and a half dozen more, waited patiently to have their nails clipped. Some of them needed it badly, some not at all, but Maggie made an attempt to snip off at least something so they would feel like they "got their money's worth." Other than her, Max, the staff, and the people in line, the lounge was empty. In fact, in all her times there, Maggie had never seen another visitor.

A young girl with jet-black hair sat down. The black liner that rimmed her eyes drooled onto alabaster cheeks. She smiled timidly and raised a delicate foot. Maggie smiled back. Her toenails were painted the same color as her hair dye, but they were neat and clean, so Maggie sat for a few minutes and massaged her feet, kneading bird-like bones under pale flesh.

Where was her mother, Maggie thought. Where were all their mothers? Where was someone to ask them about their pink slippers? To clip their toenails? Where were their mothers who had once held their cherished bundles in their arms, sat up with them all night when they were colicky, put bandages on their owies, clapped with delight over every new word, every wobbly step?

But deep down, Maggie knew. She knew how much it hurt to see your child morph into someone you hardly recognized. That feeling of helplessness. Perhaps some had been there years. Many were much older than Max. Did they still have families? Maybe some of their grandfathers thought they would outgrow it or could "get over it" if they tried hard enough.

Maggie huffed a little laugh when she thought of her father.

Hey, maybe I should bring him with me next time. Wonder what he'd say then?

For the next hour, she smiled, clipped nails and tried to carry on a conversation with people she didn't know. Maggie had Max pull up a chair next to her so she could talk to him, too. But for the most part, he sat and watched without saying a word.

When she finished the last one, she and Max sat in the lounge for another hour and made sparse, superficial talk. Maggie wished she knew what had sparked the chatter in Max, but once he became taciturn there was no turning it around again.

After another hour of stilted conversation and one more visit to the smoking room, Maggie hugged Max goodbye with the promise to be back in two weeks. When they walked through the commons, the exercising woman had taken her clothes off again and was doing jumping jacks. An orderly let Maggie out, and she trudged down the stairs and across the wet parking lot.

With her hand on the car door, Maggie looked up. Max was staring at her through a chicken-wire window.

She waved.

He stared.

As she merged into the slipstream headed south to Vancouver, Maggie picked up her travel mug for a last slurp of energy. Her coffee was cold. She reached for the radio on-knob, but drew her hand back.

She rode home in silence.

CHAPTER 25

The next time Maggie went to visit Max she made an appointment to see the psychiatrist in charge of his recovery. Even though Max was now a ward of the state, and even though they did not need her permission to treat him, Maggie found they were usually willing and considerate when it came to discussing treatment with her.

Before she saw Max that time, she knocked on Dr. Jeremy Jansen's door and heard a fragile voice say, "Come in!" When she stuck her head in, she saw a delicate face the same age, she could swear, as her sophomores. "Uh, uh," Maggie stammered, then recovered. "Hello, I'm Maggie Axline, Max's mother."

"Of course," the boy said. "I'm Dr. Jansen. Please come in, Mrs. Axline."

You've gotta be kidding me.

"Oh, uh, glad to meet you, Doctor. Please, call me Maggie."

"Good to meet you, too, Mrs. Axline."

Maggie noticed he did not say, "Call me Jeremy." Oh, this was going to be hard.

"I'm glad we have this chance to talk," he chirped. "I'll bet you're wondering how Maxim is doing."

"Right."

"Let's see..." Doctor Jansen flipped open a folder and nodded a couple of times. "I won't lie to you, I think Max is going to be with us a while. So far, he hasn't responded favorably to treatment. We're hoping a different medication..." he waffled his hand back and forth, "...a different combination of meds and treatment...will bring him around. But so far..." his sentence trailed off into that ambiguous area of uncertain outcomes.

"So what now? He'll stay here for as long as it takes?"

"Yes, that's a good way to put it."

Dr. Jansen seemed nervous, and Maggie wanted to pat his hand to reassure him, but instead she pushed a smile. "Any idea how long that might be?"

He flipped through the papers in his file again, as if he might have missed something that would suddenly appear and give him a more definitive answer. "Not really," he hedged. "Could take a couple of months more..." he skewed his head and raised one shoulder, "could be a year. We never know for sure." He shuffled the papers one more time and pushed his chair back. "We'll do everything we can, Mrs. Axline."

"Of course." Maggie crinkled her brows and nodded in what she hoped was an expression of affirmation. Yes, she was frustrated, but she also knew this doctor, no matter how young he appeared, was probably telling her the same thing a more experienced doctor would tell her. He was trying to reassure her, but it did little to relieve the tension in her back and shoulders.

She stood. Her hands were damp, and she swiped them on her jacket to shake the doctor's hand as she left. "Well then, if there is anything I can do, I mean, other than come visit him, you'll tell me, won't you?"

The rest of her trips were similar. On the days when Max was more coherent, Maggie could almost picture him as he used to be, but more often than not, his behavior was irrational and bizarre or surly and brooding. Every four months, they escorted him to court where a judge talked to him and to his doctors and reviewed his case. Each time he was ordered to remain at Western State for another four months.

It became habit, her visits to Max. After a while, Maggie became so accustomed to the drive, so accustomed to seeing Max in this environment, it felt kind of okay.

She also became accustomed to only her and Braxton at home. It wasn't easy at first. She had a hard time sleeping and woke up at odd hours to listen for a noise that would let her know Max was in his bed downstairs, or she was often startled by phantom phone calls in the middle of the night. Sometimes, she'd even reach for the receiver before she realized it was an involuntary reflex to the wail of coyotes that had seeped into her dreams.

But usually, between trips to the hospital, she felt a reprieve, and eventually was able to relax enough to occasionally sleep through the night.

For the first few months, Max phoned her collect several times a day. Sometimes after she accepted a call, he wouldn't say anything, but she knew he was there, waiting for her to talk.

Maybe, Maggie would rationalize, he just wants to hear my voice. So she would begin that familiar unbalanced chat, telling him about everything that had gone on that day and asking questions she knew he wouldn't answer. But sooner or later she would have to hang up. "I've got to go now, Max," she would say. "I love you, honey." She'd pause to see if he might say goodbye, but there was only dead air or occasionally, shallow breathing. "Goodbye, honey...I love you, Max. I love you, but I'm hanging up now. I'll talk to you soon. I love you..." Then she would force herself to put the receiver down.

When he first went to Western State, she accepted every call, but after the wild heart palpitations caused by a couple of phone bills, she knew she had to curtail them, and she began accepting just one a day and finally cut it back to two a week. It broke her heart, but after a while Max got used to it, and the calls came less frequently. And so, Maggie settled into a new pattern of life.

Braxton was now a junior in high school and had settled into his own pattern: football, basketball, track, homework, girls, friends. To anyone who didn't know him well, he seemed like a typical teenager with a typical home life. And, Maggie had to admit, he was quite spectacular. But she also knew there was a side to Braxton not everyone saw. A darker side that harbored his worries deep inside, surrounded by armor that was almost impossible to penetrate. He had a stubborn edge, too. Once he made up his mind about something, there was no changing it.

Yet, despite his sometimes somber, mulish side, Maggie knew she had it pretty good. Although they had a few rows she could have done without, for the most part, he was a good kid.

When she had to pick him up from practices, or at one of his games, he was openly affectionate. Maggie liked that best about him. While his teammates were making every possible effort to avoid being seen with their parents, Braxton would always put his arms around her right there in front of the hordes of parents, families, and friends funneling out of a football stadium or across a basketball court.

They seldom spoke of Max, but Maggie knew the last year Max was home must have been almost as trying for Braxton as it was for her. As soon as Braxton had gotten his driver's license, he had made the most of his newfound freedom, and stayed away from the house as much as he could.

She did see him more, now that Max was in the hospital, but he was still wrapped up in plethora of academic, social, and athletic experiences that far outweighed staying home with his mom and watching television. He was a busy guy, and Maggie was glad for it.

It wasn't until February of the following year that Maggie began to see a positive consistency in Max's behavior. When she came into the lobby on B2, Max was waiting for her as usual, and she hugged him as usual, but this time his arms bent at the elbows and he came close to hugging her back. They walked to the smoking room, and Maggie lit a cigarette for him, then settled in for a conversation of either all listening or all talking.

"So, hon, how has it been going the last two weeks?"

Maggie paused for his answer. In education, they called it "wait-time." When she asked the class a question, she had to force herself to wait for at least ten seconds to give it time to register and time for students to formulate their answers. It was the longest ten seconds in the history of man. But when she was talking to Max, as to her students, sometimes answers never came.

Most days, the wait-time seemed to drag into eternity, but this day Max stared at the ashtray a few seconds, then peered out the window, and before Maggie could ask him if he'd been outside lately, his eyes suddenly flipped back to her and he said, "How's Braxton?"

Maggie's mouth gaped. She uttered a confused, "uhhhh."

Before this, Max had asked her if he could go home, but Maggie couldn't remember him asking a single conversational question.

Every time he asked if he could go home, it almost did Maggie in. It was a gut-twisting question she had no answer for. When he first started asking, she'd tried lengthy explanations. "Well, honey, the doctors are trying to get your medications right, so you can feel safe at home. They have lots of good ideas; they've tried (blah-blah-blah)...," but she could always tell by his vacant stare, Max wasn't really listening. After a few months, Maggie started saying, "I don't know, Max," which seemed to get the same reaction as her expansive clarification.

This time, however, the question, "How's Braxton?" was different. After he asked, he actually held his gaze, as if he was expecting an answer. After Maggie had recovered from her initial shock, she said, "Well, he's fine, Max. He said to tell you hi."

It was just a little lie. Only a fib, really. But she could justify it by figuring if she had asked Braxton if he wanted her to tell Max anything for him, that's what it would have been.

But the connection was fleeting. Maggie started to tell him about how Braxton was gearing up for track season, hoped to go to state for the high-jump, but by then Max's eyes had glazed over again, and he sat sullenly and smoked cigarette after cigarette and stared out the crusted window.

Maggie didn't want to get her hopes up, but they were buoyed by one tiny, two word question: "How's Braxton?"

She was not able to see a doctor on that visit, but before she left the hospital, she made an appointment to talk to Doctor Jansen when she returned in two weeks.

Two weeks later, Maggie's step was a little lighter on the stairs that led to the ward on the second floor. She'd told herself to be prepared for anything. That the last visit could have been a fluke. Or her imagination. Still, she couldn't completely control the feeling that Max was improving. She told herself that maybe it was faulty "motherly instinct," but she couldn't shake it.

109

Her appointment to see Doctor Jansen was at ten o'clock. He had definitely gotten his sea legs since that first time she'd met with him, and Maggie could tell he'd gained more confidence and, she had noticed, a bit of a swagger. He'd earned it, she decided. Anyone who had the gumption and tenacity to work right in the thick of it had the right to swagger a little.

"Doctor Jansen, good to see you." Maggie offered her hand as she approached his desk. He never did extend the invitation to call him by his first name, nor did he attempt to call her by her first name. Maggie didn't know if he had a "small-man's syndrome" and was always in a mental scuffle to maintain respect, or if the difference in their ages was a deterrent, but after reminding him a couple of times, she'd dropped it.

He stood and motioned her to a chair facing his desk, then sank down low into his own chair. He intertwined his fingers in front of him, lifted his brows, and smiled at her eagerly, as if he was waiting for her to make the first move. Maggie tried to scrunch down a little so they had a more even line of eye contact. The thought crossed her mind that maybe he should use a telephone book for a booster seat.

"Yes, well...I guess I was hoping you could give me an update on Max," she said as she scooched her chair a little closer to his desk.

Doctor Jansen quickly bobbled his head up and down a few times and said, "We're pretty pleased with the changes we've seen in Max over the past month or so. Now, of course I can't make any promises..."

Ah, yes. There it is again. The disclaimer.

"Of course," she responded automatically.

"But I think I can say with some confidence that if Max continues to improve, we may be able to release him in a few weeks."

The choices of words the doctors used, "some," "if," "may be able," all hedged the issue a little. Maggie knew why.

"Will Max have somewhere to go if he *is* released?" Doctor Jansen sat with his pen poised over Maxim's file.

"Well, um, yes. I assumed he would come home with me." Maggie's eyes darted back and forth momentarily, then she

110

added, "That's his home." She had never thought of Max going anywhere else, so the question came as a surprise. To her, it seemed obvious, but apparently not to Doctor Jansen.

"And will you be able to take him to his appointments in..." he glanced at his file, "Vancouver, is it?"

"Uh-huh. Yes, I'll get him to his appointments."

She answered several more questions. All the while, Doctor Jansen's pen scratched away. Although some of the questions seemed pointless, they made her feel optimistic.

"So," the doctor continued, "will you be able to provide food for Max?"

Okay, now this is just silly.

The corners of Maggie's mouth drew up. "Yeah," she said nonchalantly. "Yeah, I thought I'd slip some food under his door once a day."

Doctor Jansen's pen stopped in mid-scratch. He paused, his head was still bent over his writing, but his eyes rolled up to meet Maggie's. "Now you're teasing me, aren't you? That's what this is, right?"

"Yes, Doctor," Maggie reassured him. "Tell you what. When Max goes home with me, I promise I'll treat him as if he were my very own son."

The doctor grinned.

Maggie answered a few more questions, shook hands with him, and went to find Max. He was sitting in the lounge, but stood as soon as he saw her. He didn't exactly smile but seemed lively and pleased to see her. He even had shoes on! They weren't the same ones he had come with, but they were a step above fuzzy pink slippers with his toes poking out.

As they walked toward the smoking room, Maggie didn't mention her conversation with Doctor Jansen, but apparently Max already knew about it.

"Am I going home?" were the first words out of his mouth.

But this time, Maggie had a more hopeful answer. "Well," she said, "not today, Max, but you're doing so well, I think it will be soon now."

They sat down at their usual table, the smoke lingering in opaque layers around them. Maggie pulled out a cigarette, lit it, and handed it to Max. His face had clouded over and her heart

111

sank.

God, he must hate it here.

"You know, Doctor Jansen is very pleased with your progress." She kept her tone positive, struggling to get Max's lighter mood back. "You know who Doctor Jansen is, don't you?"

"Yeah," Max said. He paused, and his eyes drifted to the window again. Then, after a few seconds, "He's short."

Maggie laughed. Max sometimes had a succinct way of putting things in perspective. No beating around the bush.

"Yes." Maggie said. "He certainly is that."

A corner of Max's mouth tugged upwards. Maggie loved it when he knew he had said something that tickled her. This hadn't happened much lately, and it was like a little gift. This gift would keep her going until she came the next time to take him home.

CHAPTER 26

The next few weeks were a jumble of emotions for Maggie. On one hand, she was excited about Max coming home soon. On the other, dreading it. The two sensations were further confused by several phone calls from her father in one of his three-sheets-to-the-wind states. He was not a pleasant drunk.

"Maggie!" he would begin. "Thi's your father calling. " And that was the end of any pleasantries.

"Hi, Dad!" Maggie would turn on a cheerful air, hoping it would derail what she'd heard a million times.

"Well?"

"Well what, Dad?"

Why haven't you called me lately?"

Here we go.

"Sorry, Dad, I know it's been a week, but I've been kind of busy."

"A week? Hell, S'been a month!"

"No, Dad, I called you last Wednes—"

"The hell you did! I sh'know when you called! S'been a month!"

"Okay, Dad. A month."

"Damn it! I cou'be dead over here, and you wunn't know the diff'rence. Hell, I cou'be floatin' down the Willam't, and you wunn't care."

And once he got started, there was no turning the conversation around. It always ended with something about how miserable he was and how ungrateful she was.

113

Maggie often tried to picture her father the way he used to be. His infectious teasing, his tin-ear whistling, his charming ineptness at anything mechanical. Her mother was the one who fixed the toaster, hammered up shelves, painted the house, while her father danced around the living room with Maggie on his toes.

"The first thing I'm going to do," he had said when they were getting ready to move into their houseboat, "the very first thing I'm going to do is push the lawnmower over the side into the river." Then he'd stared at the maple leaves accumulating outside their fifty-year-old home in the west hills of Portland and said, "Along with the rake."

Maggie remembered the conversation clearly because he'd looked back at her mom and said, "And the second thing I'm going to do is pour myself a beer." Why hadn't she seen it coming? But how could she have known then that one event, the passing of the love of his life, would tip the scales from one beer a day to a trip to the liquor store a couple of days a week to stock up on gin, and eventually to a taxi delivery every other day.

After the reprimanding calls from her father, Maggie needed something in her life to counterbalance them. There was only one place she knew of that could soothe that disquiet in the pit of her stomach.

Maggie wove her way past an amusing assortment of outdoor folding chairs, minced gingerly over the remains of last summer's marigolds oozing slime down the sides of mossy terracotta planters, squeezed around rakes and shovels leaning precariously on a rusted wheelbarrow, and peered into the warmth of a cluttered kitchen. Clive sat at the faux walnut-laminate table with Coconut sprawled next to him on the tatty orange, indoor/outdoor carpet. As Maggie slid the door open, Coco jumped up, snorted, and went into a drowsy rendition of his exuberant welcome. Clive got up slowly, ambled over to the bottomless coffeepot and moseyed back to the table. He pushed a few envelopes, rubber bands, and half empty Burpee seed packets aside, and set the iridescent mug down at Maggie's tacitly appointed spot.

114

How can a place of such chaos be so tranquil?

Maggie scratched Coco's velvet ears and slumped into the swivel chair. She heaved an overdue sigh and cradled her coffee in her hands.

Clive spooned sugar into his cup, stirred, and took a tentative slurp. He put the cup down, stirred it again, raised it, blew on it, put it back down, and said, "Know anything yet?"

"Yeah, I think he's coming home in two weeks. They'll let me know for sure before I go up there."

Clive took another sip, but his eyes stayed on Maggie. "Good," he said. "Heard anything about the insurance lately?"

"Only that they're still working on it." Maggie gazed idly at a squirrel on the patio that was in a snit trying to find a suitable hiding place for a black walnut. "Bernie called the other day. Said they're still trying to keep my personal assets out of it. So..." Her voice trailed off and she shrugged.

Clive nodded. "Need any help?"

Maggie shook her head. "At least I don't think so," she said. "Can I get back to you on that?"

"Anytime." Clive set his cup down, paused a moment, and said brightly. "Hey, I got this great pie down at Tarbutton's Bakery. You gotta try this." And without waiting for an answer he went to the refrigerator. Soon Maggie found herself nibbling on a generous slice of lemon meringue pie at nine o'clock in the morning and swapping opinions about the news of the week, the weather, and the upcoming planting season with a man that made the world feel normal.

Maggie didn't want to ask herself if that feeling would last.

CHAPTER 27

When Maggie left to get Max at Western State Hospital she felt sure things were going to be better, Max was going to be healthier, life was going to be smoother.

By the time she pulled back in to the porte-cochere, she was already having serious doubts. She knew Max was better than when he been committed almost a year ago, but he was not the same person he was before all this began. Of course, Maggie told herself, he is older, more mature. Maybe that's the difference. Or his medications? But there was something else that didn't seem quite right...Maggie couldn't put her finger on it. She wished she'd thought to ask the doctor about it earlier.

She had talked with Dr. Jansen before she and Max left the hospital that morning. He seemed pleased with Max's current state of mental health, like he was confident that it was time for Max to go home. But he dropped clues here and there, almost like little qualifiers couched in smiles and affable language.

"Well, Mrs. Axline, I'm sure you know how happy we all are that Max has made such great progress," he said as he leaned back in his chair and entwined his fingers behind his head. "Yes," he continued, "Max is quite the success story."

"I'm so glad," Maggie had said. "So, do you have any instruction for me before I take him home?"

"Not too many," he said, leaning forward again and swinging his laced fingers back over his head so they rested on the desk in front of him. "I'll give you his list of medication. We've contacted the county mental health group in Vancouver, and they can help you get the system started so you and Max can access it easily. You know, for appointments, meds, any questions you have."

"Oh, good." Maggie was grateful to have support from the agency she was already familiar with. "Shall I call them Monday?"

"Yes, I think that would be a good idea. And you know they can be a big help to you if Max disassociates again."

Clue number one.

"Oh...yes...of course," Maggie had stumbled over the words for a moment, but quickly recovered. How many times had they told her there were no guarantees?

"But I think Max is going to do fine, Mrs. Axline." Dr. Jansen paused, smiled, and said, "Now, here's the emergency number for them if you should need it." He slid a card across his desk.

Clue number two.

There it sat. Small. White. Unassuming. A little piece of paper that held in it the weight of the future. Maggie stared at it for two seconds, then reached out quickly, snatched it up, and stuck it in her purse without looking at it again.

"Well," Dr. Jansen said as he stood. "I'll bet you're ready to take that son of yours home."

Maggie smiled and followed his lead. "Yep," she said, "I sure am. It's been a long haul."

"Indeed it has." He stepped around his desk. "And let's hope we don't have to see you anytime soon."

Clue number three.

"Yeah," she said faintly. "Let's hope."

Max was waiting for her in the lobby cradling a grocery bag filled with a few pairs of socks and underwear, black t-shirts, an extra pair of jeans, and his birthday blanket...no slippers. He was rocking from foot to foot as had become his habit when he was nervous. He melted Maggie's heart. So tall and lanky and so...vulnerable. She would never have used that word to describe Max a year ago. Now his jeans and Black Sabbath t-shirt hung loosely on an angular frame, and his rounded cheeks had lost their fullness and were sprinkled with a substantial

117

two-day growth. He had matured physically, but two dark, velvety eyes peering through strands of long espresso-colored hair, made him look naïve, almost innocent.

The ride home was uneventful. Max talked some, answered a few questions, but generally kept to himself and watched the cars passing or commented on a few business signs he could see from the freeway. "There's a Harley store," or "I wonder if that outlet mall has a guitar store." When Maggie tried to engage him more than that, he became passive again.

"You know what we ought to do?" she said, trying to spark some interest.

Max continued looking out the window and after a five-second-delay, when Maggie thought he might not have heard her, he said, "Huh-uh. What?"

"Maybe we should stop on the way home and get a pizza. Smokey's?"

"Sure," Max said, but the old enthusiasm wasn't there. He had always loved Smokey's pizza, and used to hound her to get it.

"What kind?" She already knew what he would want, but she was trying to draw out the conversation. The "hot oven combo" was their specialty, and that was always Max's choice. He reveled in the layers of sausage, Canadian bacon, pepperoni, and cheeses. It was a veritable symphony of taste bud glee. For the last fifteen years Maggie had asked him what "special" dinner he wanted her to fix for his birthday. For fifteen years his answer was, "Smokey's Hot Oven Combo." That was fine with Maggie; she loved it too. She loved not cooking even more.

But this time, Max said nothing and seemed deep in thought as he watched cars whizzing by.

"Max?" she prompted. "What kind?"

"Oh." Max thought a moment. "I don't care." Then after a pause said, "Pepperoni?"

Maggie drove around the circular driveway, flipped the gear-shift into park, breathed deeply, and looked at Max. "I'm so happy you're home, Max. I've missed you, ya know."

She reached out and grasped Max's hand, brought it to her cheek, then kissed it. When she saw no response, she dipped her head slightly, still watching for his reaction, and said, "Love you."

Max glanced at her, nodded, and smiled weakly, then slid his hand away and opened the car door. "Braxton home?" he asked, and without waiting for an answer, went inside.

Maggie sat for a moment. Her gut tightened and she squeezed her eyes shut.

One thing at a time.

She took a frayed breath, grabbed the pizza, and follow Max.

By the time she got inside, Max was in his room. "Braxton?" she hollered down the hall.

She heard Max's muffled "not here!" through his closed door.

Maggie tossed the box on the counter, pinched a piece of sausage and Canadian bacon off the top, and stretched the mozzarella out a foot before it freed itself. She stuck it in her mouth as she walked back to Max's room and rapped on his door. No answer. She rapped again, said, "Coming in, Max," and opened the door.

Max lay with his back to her, looking out the window. She eased herself onto the foot of his bed. "Is this kind of hard for you, honey? You know, coming home after such a long time?"

"No, not really," he said, then turned over. "I'm glad I'm home, Mom...really."

Max's gentle voice touched the part of her heart that she stoically tucked away, out of sight to the world. There was so much she wanted to say. But for now, this was enough.

"Me too," she said.

Braxton tromped in at seven, slammed the door behind him, and eyed the pizza on the counter. He glanced at Maggie sitting on a bar stool paying bills.

Maggie looked up and answered the unspoken question. "Yes," she said. "He's in his room. Why don't you go say hi?"

"Only if I can have some pizza." Braxton grinned and turned to go down the hall.

"Hey," Maggie called after him, "why so late?"

"Track," he said over his shoulder. Braxton was never one

to embellish. It had always pleased Maggie that her two sons were so different from one another. Max used to talk a blue streak–and Braxton was as tight-lipped as they came. Max teased and taunted–Braxton was restrained and down to earth.

"Oh, right." In the flurry of getting Max home, the beginning of track season had completely slipped her mind.

Braxton was seldom forthcoming with any news from school, so if Maggie wasn't paying attention, or didn't call the school or ask Braxton, the beginning of a sports season could squeeze right by her before she realized he was out of football and into basketball or out of basketball and into track. Sometimes she didn't know until she saw which uniform was in the wash. But once she knew, she never missed a game or a meet. It was pure joy to watch Braxton catch a football, embrace it in the crook of his arm, and weave between tight ends, high-step it over fallen players, and prance with the gracefulness of a ballerina into the end zone. There was something for every season. The deftness and dexterity of the dribble in the winter, and the torque and thrust of the Fosbury Flop in the spring.

The electric bill Maggie was writing out, blurred and her thoughts drifted sideways.

What would Max be doing if he hadn't developed schizophrenia. Music?

Any heavy metal arrangement sent him into raptures of animated air-guitar antics. When he was fourteen, he saved his money and bought a red Jackson Rhodes Flying V and began his quest to become a rock star. And the flute. He loved the melodic piping of a solo flute. Maggie had always marveled that Max could get so much enjoyment from two such polarized tones. *Would he be graduated from high school now and into some musical career? Maybe a music major in college?*

Maggie huffed. He had the brains for it, there was no question of that. But would he have the drive and dedication?

Oh stop it, Maggie! This doesn't do anyone any good!

She stood abruptly and repeated her mantra, "one thing at

a time," as she slid the pizza into the oven to reheat.

CHAPTER 28

"Are you being left behind in the business world? Are you tired of always being the last of your friends to find a job? Does the entire world seem to be passing you by?"

Maggie flopped onto her weary camelback sofa and thumbed through a *Games* magazine looking for a moderately easy cryptic crossword puzzle. A TV commercial droned out questions about the miserable lot of the undereducated, and Maggie mechanically droned out her answers, "Yes...yes...hmmm...Does it seem like the entire world is passing me by?" She shrugged. "Eh. Sometimes." She flipped the magazine open to a solitare version of Battleship.

"Isn't it time you did something about it?"

"No..."

"Isn't it time you took control of your life?"

"Ha! I wish," she scoffed, as she scanned the grid for a place a ship might be hiding.

"Well, now you can. The Everlast Adult Education and Trade Academy offers flexibility and credibility so you can decide when and how to get your GED."

Maggie flicked the remote to off. "Ah ha! There you are! Thought because you're a little destroyer you could hide from... What did that guy say?" She clicked the "on" button and the TV crackled and lit up.

"...your future. Call us at 1-800-555-7994. Remember, an Everlast degree will last forever."

Maggie jotted down "555-7994" at the top of her puzzle page and clicked the TV off again.

Max had been home almost two months now. He didn't

seem curious about anything; he was listless and apathetic. Maggie was getting used to his unfocused conversations and lack of concentration, but getting used to it and liking it were two different things. She made a mental note to ask his counselor if she could sit in on his next meeting. She would ask her if she thought Max was ready to get his GED. She wasn't about to give up on him. Resign him to the life of a fifty-year-old still dependent on his mother. She had more confidence in him than that.

She knew Max was capable, but she wasn't sure how to get him to that degree of autonomy. She also knew it wouldn't happen overnight, and she couldn't push too hard. Certainly there would be baby steps. There would be trial and error. But she had to believe there was a future for Max.

It would be easy to let it all ride and hope for the best, to let her grief paralyze her into stagnation so she floundered in her own sorrow. Her mother had been an advocate of the bootstrap theory. Even as a child, when she felt down, she never had the pleasure of wallowing in self-pity. "Grab hold of those bootstraps, Maggie!" she could hear her mother say. "Grab hold and pull yourself up!"

Maybe Max couldn't pull himself up by his bootstraps, but on the other hand, maybe he could. At the very least, Maggie was pretty sure he could do more than sit and listen to heavy metal music or watch reruns of *Gilligan's Island* all day.

When Max had come home from the hospital, Maggie had called Columbia River Mental Health and got him back in the system. Since then he had seen a psychiatrist that was prescribing his medications, been assigned a counselor for weekly appointments, and was working with social services to learn what had to be done to get and keep benefits he was entitled to.

Maggie phoned CRMH and asked if she could sit in on one of Max's appointments with his counselor.

The next week when his name was called, Maggie followed Max down the hall to Patty Cravitz's office.

The ten-by-twelve room was straight out of a dated, generic Best Western motel. Everything was mauve and brass. And beige! Beige walls, beige floor, beige atmosphere. The camelback loveseat and the two chairs that flanked it were mauve with muted turquoise and white swooshes, the coffee table and end tables were oak, glass, and brass, and the mauve table lamps were dimmed for, Maggie assumed, a soothing effect. Boxes of tissue were strategically placed next to the sofa and one of the chairs.

Max sat on the loveseat, but Maggie waited to see which direction the counselor was headed. She inched toward one of the chairs, but before she sat down, she leaned over and extended her hand. "Mrs. Axline? I'm Patty Cravitz."

"Nice to meet you, and it's Maggie." Maggie backed into the chair opposite her.

"And I'm Patty. Well, Maggie," Patty began. "I'm probably going to be talking to Max most of the time, but I'm sure your insight will be helpful, so be sure to add anything you want to. Interrupt me anytime you need to. I don't mind a bit."

Maggie nodded.

"Okay! Well, tell me how your week went, Max," Patty said as her gaze shot briefly to the door, probably to make sure it was closed, then swept past Maggie and back to Max.

"Pretty good," Max said, and Maggie wondered if this was going to be another one of those times when pulling the words out of Max was like pulling teeth.

"And what have you been doing?" Patty's pen rested on the green steno notebook in her lap.

Max thought a minute. "Well, I've been watching a lot of TV...and...I went to a friend's house a couple of times...and I went to the store with my mom..."

Maggie nodded in agreement.

"So, have you had any odd feelings lately?"

When Max stared at her, Patty added, "Like someone is after you, or telling you things?"

"What kinds of things?" Max said.

"Oh, I don't know...like telling you to do things? Or sending you messages through the television?" Almost imperceptibly, Patty lifted her pen.

"The TV? Yeah, I guess so," Max said.

"What kind of messages?" Patty prompted. She lifted her pen a little higher and poised it over her notebook.

124

"Oh, I dunno." Max stared at the floor and thought about it. "They've been telling me to buy stuff."

"What kind of stuff?"

"Oh, stuff like toothpaste, and cars, and cereal, and stuff." The corner of Max's mouth rose slightly, and Maggie could see a bit of the old mischief in his eyes. He was playing with her.

Patty's pen fell back on her notebook. "Oh, I get it. Ha-ha," she said, then looked at Maggie. "Max likes to tease, doesn't he? Last week he told me he was hearing voices over the telephone. I think it was your grandfather, wasn't it Max?"

"Yeah, I heard him again a couple of days ago," he said, "when he called to see if I wanted to come over."

"What about you, Mrs. Ax...Maggie? How do you think Max is doing? Any changes in mood or behavior that you've noticed?"

Maggie hesitated. She wasn't sure how to answer. There weren't any changes since he had been home, but there were huge changes from what she considered his "normal" behavior. Was she wrong to expect more of Max? Would he ever get back to his "old self" again? He didn't really seem unhappy right now. Just unreceptive, as if he was merely tolerating life. Should she be content that he was at least in touch with reality? This was unknown terrain and it was playing havoc with her usual self-assurance.

"Maggie?"

"Oh, well, no, I guess I haven't really noticed changes in the last month or two. He seems to be doing pretty good, as far as I can tell, but..." Maggie hunched both shoulders up.

Max watched her, his eyes both sad and vacant.

"But?" Patty prompted.

"Well, Max doesn't seem to be doing much at all." Maggie slid her eyes away from Max's. "I guess it seems like he should be starting to do more. Or making some progress. I dunno, maybe I'm expecting too much." Maggie lowered her shoulders.

Patty jotted something down, then said, "That seems reasonable. He is definitely doing better." She cocked her head toward Max. "What about you, Max? Do you want to do more?"

"Like what?" Max said. He wasn't being rude, but sounded as if the thought had never crossed his mind.

125

"Well, I'm not sure. Maybe your mother has some suggestions." Patty shifted her gaze back to Maggie.

Maggie's shoulders rose again slightly and she crooked her elbows with her hands out in front of her. "Oh, I don't know. I was thinking maybe there was a regular activity that could keep him a little more occupied. Like..." Did she dare say it? "Well, like, I was thinking maybe he would want to get his GED."

Maggie paused for a response, but both Max and Patty stared at her as if she had suggested he join the French Foreign Legion and start a revolution in Algeria.

Finally, Patty broke the silence. "Well, that's a very interesting idea."

Safe. Noncommittal.

She looked at Max. "What do you think, Max?"

"Doesn't sound very interesting to me," he said.

"See, Max," Maggie leaned toward him, "you're at home all day, and all you do is sleep or watch television. I thought maybe it would be good for you to have something regular, something more...oh, I don't know...more...stimulating to do."

When neither Max nor Patty said anything, she went on. "They have these classes you can go to, where..."

Max groaned softly.

Maggie quickly back-peddled. "No-no, not those kind of classes. Not like school. This is a small place downtown where they let you do some things on your own. You know, things you would need to pass the GED. English exercises, some simple math, that kind of stuff."

When Max didn't groan again, she sat up a little straighter and went on. "Then you would take the test to see if you passed it. You don't get a grade on it or anything. It's just pass or...or take it again if you need to. There's no pressure." Maggie stopped, leaned back, and knotted her hands in her lap. Four eyes focused on her. She avoided them, lowered her own, and waited.

Patty broke the tension. "Max? Is that something you think you could do?"

Max studied Maggie as if he were sizing her up, trying to figure out how serious she really was. Trying to decide if it was worth the effort to object.

126

When his gaze swung back to Patty, Maggie unclenched her hands and splayed her damp fingers on her lap.

"'Spose so," he said indifferently, but when she saw his shoulders droop slightly, her heart sank and her confidence dipped again.

But Patty kept the thread alive. "Good," she said with at least a modicum of enthusiasm, and wrote something in her notebook. "Actually, Max," she went on, "you're doing so well, it wouldn't be long before we would be asking you to begin looking for a part-time job or planning some regular activity anyway, so this will certainly fill that bill. We feel a routine would be good for you. Help keep you on an even keel."

Bless her little analytical heart, Maggie thought. She felt her pulse slow and the tightness in her chest begin to subside.

The arrangement was for Maggie to run home from school three times a week, pick Max up, take him downtown, and drop him off at the abandoned JC Penney building that now housed the Everlast School. The only reason this worked was because this semester her prep period backed up to her lunchtime. That gave her almost an hour and twenty minutes to make the clandestine run. She couldn't risk asking for permission to leave school; Maggie was sure the administration would not give its blessing. Besides, even if she was able to pull Max out of his groggy, medicated sleep when she left for school at six, Everlast didn't open until nine. Nope, this was the only way.

So Maggie shoved her guilt to the back burner, began arriving at school at 5:30 instead of her usual 6:30 to make up lost time, and entered into a scheme she hoped would help Max. When Max was through at the school, he was to take a bus to his grandfather's and wait for her until she could pick him up in the late afternoon.

At least, that was the plan.

127

CHAPTER 29

And for the first couple of weeks it seemed to work. Maggie tried to pick Max up from Clive's by 4 p.m. But that cut into her correcting and planning time after school There was an easy fix—she took more work home to do in the evenings.

Most of the time when she got there, Max was spread out in Clive's overtly puffy recliner, drinking pop and watching MTV.

"Hey, knuckle-head!" Clive would holler from the kitchen table. "Your mother's here. Get your lazy arse outta my favorite chair!" Then he'd give Max a good-humored punch in the arm as he went by.

"Bye, Gramps!" was all Max ever said as he slid out the door and into the car.

How she knew Max wasn't really going to the Everlast classes, Maggie never quite figured out. It was really just a hunch, but one day, when she had asked him for the umpteenth time how his session was that day, and for the umpteenth time he said, "It was okay," she knew. Maybe it was something in the consistency and flatness of his answers, or maybe it was simply a mother's intuition.

Maggie called Everlast the next day.

"I've checked our sign-in sheets, and I see Max has come...hmmmm...once since he signed up." The Everlast secretary sounded tentative. Maggie could almost see her running her finger over the lists, searching in vane to find Max's name more than once. "Oh, nope! Here's another one, that's two. He's been here two times in...let's see...oh. Two and

128

a half weeks," she said as her voice faded to almost a whisper.

Maggie felt a little sorry for her. She wasn't trying to put the girl on the spot. No one at the school was to blame. Max was making that choice, and apparently he chose not to get his GED. She wasn't really mad at him, but she felt like she had been scammed. There was a slow leak in that balloon of expectations.

When she picked up Max from Clive's that day, she waited until they were in the car to ask him about it. "Now, I'm not angry, Max," she began when they pulled out. "I just wonder why you decided not to go to Everlast. Don't you want to get your GED?"

Max stared straight ahead in silence.

"I guess I can't understand why you didn't tell me." The pitch in her voice grew to a squeak.

Calm down, Maggie. Remember, you're not mad. Lower your voice.

"I know it's your decision, but it hasn't been all that easy coming home all the time to get you and take you down there, you know," she said coolly. As she talked, she felt the blood rise to her cheeks, and even though she had said she wasn't, the longer she talked, the more she sounded like, yes, in fact, she was angry. And the quieter Max was, the louder she got.

"I wish you had let me know. You could have done that, couldn't you? You could have at least let me know. It isn't like I've got nothing else to do. I have a full-time job, you know. I feel like I've been wasting my time and let's not forget the cost of gas besides the cost of getting you enrolled and besides what in the hell have you been doing all day, walking around down town twiddling your thumbs?"

Maggie came up for a breath and glanced at Max.

"Sorry I didn't tell you, but...I don't have to go anymore," was all he said.

"Well, no, of course you don't have to go, it's just that...it's just that..." Maggie faltered.

The words wouldn't come because, well, maybe Max was right. She never really told him he had to go. And he never did fully buy into it, so why had she expected him to follow through?

129

They passed a church and Maggie turned right, and then took another hard right into the empty parking lot. She pulled to a stop, rolled down her window, and gulped the soggy spring air. She let her anger ebb, took another deep breath, and exhaled audibly before she turned to Max again. "I'm sorry, Max. Of course you don't have to go."

"No," he said, looking at Maggie, puzzled, "you don't get it."

"It's okay, Max, I do get it." Maggie put her hand on his. "I shouldn't have made you go."

"No," he said again. "I mean, I already took the test."

Maggie's brows knit together then arched. "You..." she looked at Max, then out the window, then back at Max. "You...what?"

"I took the test." Max shrugged. "I passed."

"Wait. When..."

"The second time I went. I didn't like going there, so I..." Max shrugged again, "took it."

"And you passed." It was more a statement of disbelief than a question.

"They're going to send me my certificate in a couple of weeks. Well, I guess anytime now."

Maggie cocked her head and vaulted her eyebrows again. "But, what have you been doing all this time?"

"Sometimes I walked around downtown, went to the pawn shops or to that guitar store on Broadway. But mostly Jonathan picked me up and we just screwed around. Then he dropped me off at Grandpa's."

Maggie's hands flew up and came down on the steering wheel with a thwap. "Well, I don't know what to say to that." She shook her head. "I don't even know what to say," she repeated, then added a final, "Huh!" before starting the car and pulling out into traffic.

She needed time to think about what to say to Max. If he did get his GED, that was good. Not telling her, well, that was bad. And hanging out with Jonathan instead of going to class, was even more of a concern.

She decided to wait a couple of days. She had planned to call the school to verify his story, but she didn't have to.

Two days later when she picked up the mail, sure enough,

there it was. His certificate of completion.

"Huh!" she said again, and shook her head all the way down the driveway.

Things were looking up. She had finished grading the last of the finals that day and had to get grades recorded and her classroom ready for the summer, and then...sweet relief for several weeks! She pulled up to the house with a sense of forthcoming liberation.

Even before she was inside she could make out lyrics. "Make...joke..will sigh."

"Max!" Maggie yelled when she came in the door. She strained to be heard over the metallic vibrations of Black Sabbath quaking through Max's bedroom door.

"Max!" she yelled again.

Ozzy wailed back something about laughing and crying.

Maggie opened Max's door and was hit with the impact of a sonic jet breaking the sound barrier. She covered an ear with one hand and fumbled for the volume control with the other, then changed her mind and punched at the "off" button until the agony known to Max as "music," stopped.

"Max?" Maggie peered around the now silent room as if she half expected him to crawl out from under the piles of dirty socks, torn jeans, T-shirts, shoes, McDonald's Big Mac wrappers, and soggy cigarette butts floating in the dregs of pop bottles. "This kid is seriously out of control," she mumbled to herself looking around. She wrinkled her nose at the stench of stale French fries, sweat, and smoke.

Typically disgusting; nothing out of the ordinary. She nodded resignation and started to turn. Except...

"What the hell?"

CHAPTER 30

Her gaze swiveled back to Max's bed. The sheets were crumpled in a pile at the foot of the mattress. His burgundy comforter was gone.

Mincing through the chaos, Maggie peeked under his bed, then opened the closet door. She glanced in Braxton's room, walked swiftly back down the hall, and quickly checked the living room, the stairwell, the den, and her bedroom.

No blanket. No Max.

She stood in the middle of the kitchen looking around. "What the hell?" she muttered again. Nothing much surprised her anymore, but that feeling of apprehension about what Max would do next always hung in the air like a wayward swirl of dust that wouldn't quite settle. As much as she wanted to, she knew that nebulous cloud could not be controlled. The only thing she could do was wait it out. Maggie had to believe sooner or later she'd hear from him. She closed her eyes, exhaled a thready sigh, and turned to the dishes backlogged in the sink.

One restless night dragged by, then two, then three. Maggie phoned Jonathan's house several times, but no one answered. In the early evening of the fourth night, Max called. It was all Maggie could do to keep from lashing out. "Max,' she said with forced composure, "where have you been?"

"Me and Jonathan have been staying downtown with a friend," he said as if it was the most normal thing in the world. And Maggie supposed under some circumstances, it would be "normal." But Max was not "normal."

Or was she making too much of this? He was, after all, nineteen now. What nineteen-year-old wants his mother running his life? Keeping a tight rein on anyone that age was like keeping a tight rein on droplets of mercury. Even if you got them together in one tidy spot, the slightest jiggle would send them scattering in all directions again. Maybe, she decided, she would have to reconsider her role in Max's life. She'd given up so much of him already, but maybe she'd have to give up more.

She decided to give it a try. Instead of asking, "What friend?" she asked, "So, do you know when you'll be home?"

"Probably in a couple of days," Max said.

"Okay, Max, but can you remember to go to your counseling appointment? You need your injection tomorrow."

Leave it alone, Maggie. Just leave it alone.

"Yeah, sure. I'll have Jonathan take me."

Maggie cringed but pursued it no further. "Okay," she said, then quickly added, "But Max, if you need me, you'll call, won't you?"

"Sure," he said again.

He didn't sound very convincing, but to Maggie's amazement he did exactly what he said he would. And two days after that, he lugged his comforter back home and was there when Maggie got home from school. She still wanted to talk to Max. To at least set some boundaries of consideration if he was going to live at home. But it was tricky. How could she make him feel independent without giving him free-range? The opportunity came the next day.

"Want some scrambled eggs?" Maggie glanced over her shoulder as Max shambled into the kitchen late Saturday morning and hauled himself onto a stool. She poured a cup of coffee and shoved it in front of him, pushed the toast down, and turned back to the stove. She knew better than to get into a discussion when he first woke up, but there were so much she needed to say. She decided to chance it and gently dipped a toe in the water. "So, how did your appointment go?"

"Mmmmm," Max growled.

Maggie tousled his hair and slid a plate of toast and eggs toward him. When he didn't slide them back, she gambled

133

another question. "You make any new plans when you saw Patty?"

Max's fork hovered over his plate. He nodded and stabbed at his eggs. "Kind of," he said as he put his fork down. He sipped his coffee in silence before he added, "Wants me to start looking for a part-time job."

Maggie struggled to be nonchalant. She sensed a show of enthusiasm might shut him down. "Oh?" She cracked two more eggs into the skillet. "Any leads?"

Max shrugged his shoulders. "Eh, maybe," he said as he examined a forkful of eggs, sniffed them, and took a tentative nibble. "Suppose to go to Bradley Boys next week."

Maggie stopped mid-scramble and turned around, whisk in hand. "Bradley's? You mean that one down on Andresen?"

Careful Maggie. Don't get eager.

Bradley's was a locally owned hardware store with a decent reputation, a good starting place for Max. She turned back to the frying pan. "Yeah, I know where that is."

"Gotta go there next Tuesday." He put his fork down and pushed his plate back across the counter. "You can take me if you want to. `Bout four."

"Sure," Maggie said casually. "Will you be home then?"

Max frowned at her over his coffee.

"It's just that if you're going to live here, Max, I really need for you to at least let me know when you're going to be gone."

When Max didn't say anything, she pulled up a stool across from him. "I'm not saying you have to tell me everywhere you go, Max. I'm not saying that. I know you're almost an adult. But..." Maggie paused and calmed her voice. "Well, I'm still your mom. I still need to know you're safe."

Max held his cup out, and Maggie reached for the coffeepot, poured a refill, and waited. "I guess," he finally said.

She hadn't intended to give him an ultimatum. It had probably grazed the edges of her thoughts, but she had never allowed it any deeper. It wasn't until that moment Maggie knew she couldn't continue to live in a state of constant anxiety for much longer. She composed herself, and jumped in. "If you can't do that, Max, we'll need to find somewhere else for you to live," she said gently.

"Okay," he said. "I'll try."

CHAPTER 31

Tuesday afternoon Maggie sat doing a crossword puzzle in her car as she waited for Max to finish his appointment at Bradley Boys. He'd been in a good mood for the last two days...almost too good. She knew she should be pleased to see him in high spirits, but his swings in temperament kept her on edge. Always guessing.

She had run home to pick him up after finishing some inventory work at school and barely tapped the horn before he dashed out to the car and slid in. Most of the drive to town Max chattered about bikes, cars, and the superiority of heavy metal music and the inferiority of all other music. "But Steve Miller he's okay and maybe the Eagles I like them but they might be all hard rock I don't think they're soft rock they're really better than that but I hate the rest of them I hate all of them so much I can't even think about them without throwing up heavy metal is so much better anyone like Pink Floyd and Ozzy or Led Zeppelin."

Maggie interrupted. "I like the Village People. You know, Y-M-C-A," she sang as she drove with one hand and tried to form the letters with the other arm.

Max's eyes edged over to her. "Mom. Stop. Really."

When they pulled up to Bradley's, Max jumped out of the car and strode confidently up to the door without saying goodbye.

Ten minutes later he came out with as much swagger as when he went in.

Maggie waited. "Well?" she finally said.

He shrugged his shoulders. "Went okay, I guess. Talked to this guy. Manager I think. Name's Steve. Drives a Triumph 880 Bonneville. Red."

"Oh, good, Max." Maggie started the car and pulled out. "But does that mean you're going to start working here? How much you going to be paid? When do you start?"

But Max was quiet. Maggie glanced at him. A cloud had come over him. He scowled out the window. "I'm not wearing one of those," he said.

"What? One of what?" Maggie followed Max's gaze to a gray-haired man watering flowers in front of the store. He had on a green apron with "Bradley Brothers" scripted in white on the front of it. "You mean one of those aprons?"

Max continued glaring at the man as they drove past him. Then as suddenly as he had turned sullen, he looked back at Maggie and cheerfully said, "Oh, I don't get paid."

"Oh?"

"It's part of a work program. You know, like they want to see what kinds of jobs you can do."

"Ah. Yes," Maggie said. One thing at a time, she thought as she turned toward home.

For a while, Max's job went smoothly, or at least that's what Maggie thought. Twice a week she would drop him off, then do errands or sit and read while she waited for him. At first, he seemed relatively content with the work he was doing, but the third week Maggie began to notice a subtle change.

"How'd the job go today?" she said on their way home.

"It was okay," Max said, but this time, instead of telling her what he did that day, he stared out the window.

"So, what did they have you doing today?" Maggie prompted.

"Oh, lotsa things," he said quietly.

"Like what?" Maggie said, trying to sound interested instead of nosy.

They drove half a mile before Max said, "Too many things."

Tread lightly, Maggie.

They drove for another half-mile before he continued. "There are too many people telling me what to do."

"Who?"

"Everyone," he grumbled. "Everyone is bossing me around." After another pause, he went on. "Someone tells me to put more plungers on the shelf, and before I can finish, someone else tells me to go to the back and help unload some stuff, and before I can finish that, I have to go up to the front to help carry some stuff out to a customer's car. Then that guy tells me I'm doin' it wrong."

Maggie felt the tension weighing her down. It was almost tangible.

"They said Steve would be telling me what to do. Now everyone does."

"Can you talk to Steve?" Maggie asked, but she knew the answer. Despite his sometimes façade of bravado, Max hated face-to-face confrontations. "Well, do you think it would help to at least talk to Patty at your next meeting? Let her know how hard that is for you?"

"I'm not going back."

Maggie's heart skipped a beat. "Where? You're not going back where?"

"Bradley's," Max said matter-of-factly.

Relief washed over her. She was glad it was only Bradley's he wasn't going back to, but his mood swings worried her. What was it? Bitterness? Aggravation? Maggie couldn't quite nail it, but something was askew. She'd keep an eye on it, and if it didn't get better, she'd go to another counseling session with him.

Reluctantly, Max began working as a busboy at Prindle's Pancake House two weeks later. He had talked to Patty about his problem with Bradley's. She assured him there would be less pressure as a busboy. And for some there probably was, but not for Max. When she came to pick him up the fourth time, he was sitting on the curb waiting for her. He shuffled out to the car and fell into the back seat.

"Max?" Maggie twisted around. "What happened, honey?"

Max muffled his voice in the crook of his arm. "They won't..."

"What? Max, I can't hear you. What happened?"

138

Max sat up. "They won't tell me how to do it. They want me to do things, but no one will show me how to do it."

"Like what?"

"Okay. Someone tells me they need more silverware and to go get some from the kitchen. So I do, and I come out there with a handful of forks and a handful of spoons and try to give them to one of the waitresses. And she gets all snotty and tells me to put them where they belong, so I go back to the kitchen and try to hand 'em to someone, and they tell me to go out and give 'em to the waitress. So I do, and she grabs 'em out of my hands and tells me to go away... so I did." Max heaved a sigh and flopped down on the seat again.

"Okay, well..." Maggie searched for the right words of encouragement. "You know, I'm sure they'll find the right job for you, Max. It just takes time."

"I'm thinking about the FBI," Max said as he sat up again.

Maggie laughed over her shoulder and started to pull out, "Yeah, wouldn't that be the ticket for you? You could..." but as she glimpsed Max in her rearview mirror, she realized he was dead serious.

CHAPTER 32

"Yeah, the FBI would be perfect." Max was once again animated. "I'd have to be an independent agent, though. I mean, maybe only one person telling me what to do. Like I'd work on my own and then just check in with one person once a month. Or maybe twice a month. But most of the time I'd be on my own."

They stopped at a red light, and Maggie craned her neck around. "Well, I think you have to be at least twenty-one," she said. "And I'm sure there are tests and requirements for—"

"You don't know!" Max yelled.

The light changed. "You're right, Max. I don't know for sure. It's just that..." As the traffic inched forward, she glanced at him in the mirror. "No, I don't know," she said and made a mental note to call Patty as soon as she got home.

"I suppose that's something to think about, Max, but it's a big decision." Patty was scribbling in her green steno pad as she talked. "Mom, what do you think of Max's idea?" Her eyes slid up to Maggie.

"Well... I don't...I guess I don't think much of it."

What am I supposed to say? That it's a stellar idea? That I have great confidence in Max? That I'm sure he can pull it off? Or is Patty passing the buck and hoping I'll tell Max this is the stupidest idea since someone had said, "Hey, let's make the Edsel!"?

Patty turned back to Max. "Max?" she said and sat back, pencil poised.

140

What? Is she actually taking this seriously?

Max sat with his arms crossed and frowned first at Maggie, then at Patty, then back to Maggie. He had determination in his posture and defiance in his voice. He looked straight at her. "Well," he blustered, "it's what I want to do!"

Patty seemed unruffled. "What type of work would this entail, Max?"

"I don't know for sure." Max paused, looked up at the ceiling, then narrowed his eyes. "Probably espionage work. You know surveillance, spying, intelligence stuff."

You've got to be kidding me!

"And how do you suppose you would go about getting hired for that?"

Maggie opened her eyes wide and forced herself not to roll them.

Oh, this otta be good. First, get ahold of Miss Moneypenny.

Max tilted his head and thought a moment. "I dunno. I'd probably have to call someone in the federal government."

Well, okay. That wasn't completely off base. Still, the FBI?

But as she listened, Maggie began to realize what Patty was doing. She was trying to get Max to recognize for himself the improbability of becoming an FBI agent, and she was also trying to gauge how in touch, or in this case, how out of touch with reality Max was. She never did tell him he couldn't do it, but after half an hour of asking questions, Max finally decided that he should at least wait until he was twenty-one to pursue a career as James Bond.

But what about then? What if he still wants to do it? What if he isn't any better? Maggie caught herself. *Reel it in, Maggie. You have no idea what he'll be like then.*

"And Mom?" Patty was looking at her.

"Uh...yes?" Maggie raised her brows and gawked at Max then Patty. What could she possibly say to such a harebrained idea?

Patty turned back to Max. "Max, I'd like to talk to your mom for a while. Do you think you could wait in the lobby?"

"I guess. Mom, give me the keys and I'll wait in the car."

Maggie certainly did not want to give Max the keys, but Patty saved her by saying, "I'd really like you to wait in the lobby, Max. I may want to talk to you a little more. Would that be okay?"

Max shrugged but nodded vaguely and went out.

"Maggie?" Patty asked when the door closed.

"Hmm?"

"How would you describe Max's behavior the last week or so?"

Maggie was tired. She didn't want to think. She didn't want to answer. She didn't want to be there anymore. But Patty's pencil tap – tap – tapped on her pad, waiting to write down her answer. Maggie bought a little time by pretending to be thinking. But she was distracted by that infernal pencil. She seached the room as if an answer might be revealed in the tacky painting of the Eiffel Tower or the wisteria scratching against the high window.

"Unstable," she finally said averting her eyes away from that the pencil and looking directly at Patty.

Oh Lord! Now she's going to ask me what I mean by—

"And what do you mean by 'unstable'," Patty said right on cue.

Maggie sucked in a deep breath and exhaled with a woosh. She leaned forward a little. "Well, I suppose I mean he doesn't seem very sound mentally. He's moody, gets angry quickly. Or one minute he's happy and talkative and the next minute he's...oh, I don't know, kind of aloof and cold. And to me, his thinking isn't as clear lately. Well, you heard what he wants to do. Spy for the FBI? Do you think that's normal?"

Maggie sat back.

There! You and your pencil can just write that down why don't you?

Whether Patty did not pick up on the intended brusqueness, or whether she was just trained to show no emotion, Maggie did not know. In her usual unperturbed and composed manner, she responded with the old platitude, "I understand how you must feel, Maggie."

Maggie melted, the fire building inside her was temporarily quelled. "But it worries me, Patty. And I'm so damned tired of

142

worrying." She knew her eyes pleaded, but she seemed to have no control over them or the whimper in her voice. Ever since she was a little girl, she had an aversion to whining. She could almost hear her mother saying, "Don't whine, my darling Maggie. Tell me what you want right out, but no simpering please." Now, "simpering" seemed to be all she could do.

"And can you tell me exactly what it is you are worried about?"

She didn't want to. She didn't want to say she was afraid that Max would break again, that he would end up in the hospital for another year...or longer. That she felt angry and guilty and sad and tired deep down in the marrow of her bones. She felt an overwhelming avalanche of grief, but she couldn't bring herself to say those words out loud.

So she cried.

She cried bottomless, unrelenting sobs. Sobs for her loss, and sobs for Max's fall from innocence. Sobs for all the things she wanted for him and sobs for all the things she wanted for herself. Sobs for the time they could never get back and sobs for their lives that had been changed forever.

CHAPTER 33

"Can anyone tell me the difference between simile and metaphor?" Maggie had hoisted herself up on a tall, paint-splattered draftsman's stool and scanned her fifth period class as she thumbed her notes spread out on a pockmarked dais in front of her. The rest of the summer had dragged by, and now thirty-three hormonal teenagers, some with eyes wide and alert, some with eyes half-mast, some with eyes searching for other eyes searching for them, sat squirming, slouched, or sprawled in a variety of acceptable inner-circle freshmen postures. She had read "Ars Poetica" by Archibald MacLeish, one of her favorite poems. But her heart wasn't in it. Neither was her mind.

She remembered Patty's parting words, "We need to keep you healthy, too, you know." Other than that, there was little Patty could do at that moment. She would talk to the doctor to see if she could either get a med increase for Max, or a different med, or a combo of both.

"Yes," Patty agreed, "it is a bit unusual to want to join the FBI, but we need to remember Max is only nineteen. Most boys are a bit...off kilter at nineteen."

Maggie had helped herself to fistfuls of Kleenex and pared down her wanton weeping to a few leftover sniffles. "Off kilter?" she sputtered as she swiped at mascara running down her cheeks.

Patty's expression had the right tinge of sympathy: head tilted, brows peaking in the middle, mouth faintly pouty with just a suggestion of a downward turn. "The problem, Maggie, is

144

that unless Max is a threat to himself or to someone else, my hands are tied." She picked up the empty box of Kleenex in front of Maggie and slid a full one across the coffee table.

Maggie plucked out two more tissues and blew. "Yeah, I know. I guess I was hoping..." She wasn't even sure what she was hoping. That Patty could fix Max? That she would say, "just give it time, and maybe it'll go away"? Or maybe that it was Maggie's imagination, and he was not getting worse. Maggie shrugged in resignation.

"There's legal criteria," Patty said as she put her pencil behind her ear and scooted forward in her chair. "But," she added, "call me if you notice other behavior that doesn't seem normal to you."

That was six weeks ago. Now, as she sat in front of the class, a student was making a feeble attempt to explain the difference between a metaphor and a simile, but Maggie could barely focus on his answer. Thinking about what Patty had said still popped into the forefront of her mind at the strangest times.

She puffed out a weak "huh" and smiled wryly.

I hardly know what's "normal" anymore.

The student had stopped talking and was staring at her.

Oh, God! What did he say?

"Okay, then. Well now. Let's see." She faux studied her book again. "So what do you think MacLeish meant when he said a poem should be "silent as the sleeve-worn stone?""

This prompted a droopy-eyed, droopy-haired, droopy-pantsed boy in the back to mumble, "You shouldn't ever have to hear it."

Another equally droopy boy in front of him turned around and high-fived him, and the class chuckled its admiration.

Maggie was about to explain that on some level he might not be too far off, when she glanced at the clock and decided it was too much effort. "Okay then. Let's go ahead and summarize what we've learned today. Anyone?" One or two hands shot into the air. Everyone else busied themselves avoiding eye contact.

"Katie?"

"We learned that the difference..."

145

Maggie's mind drifted again, and she was in the realm of "what-ifs."

What if I tried spending more time with Max? What if I just started hugging him more and telling him how much I love him? What if I took Max and Braxton on vaca—?

The bell jerked her back to real time. Papers shuffled, books thwacked shut, backpacks zipped. "Hold it, hold it!" Maggie yelled as the students trundled towards the door. "Tonight I want you to..." She eyed the stacks of papers already spilling over the top of the turn-in baskets. Four hours of correcting on Saturday and four on Sunday. If she was lucky. "Oh, never mind," she said. "Fly away, little ones. You are free!"

A few whoops went up, and the kids clattered to freedom.

"And remember!" Maggie hollered after them. They were already so used to her standard Friday night pronouncement, no one even faltered in their scuffle to be first through the door, but by rote a few chanted her weekend slogan with her, "Don't drink this weekend...and don't drive with anyone who's been drinking...I don't want to read about you in Sunday's paper... Ruin my whole weekend!" they droned.

"We won't, Mrs. Axline," the last girl out giggled over her shoulder, elbowing her two friends as they disappeared into the flume funneling down the hallway.

"Yeah, sure," Maggie mumbled to herself, stuffing her notes between the open pages of *Literary Perspectives* and slamming it shut. She had intended to get in two hours of correcting and take the rest home for the weekend. Instead she sat motionless and let the fading clamor calm the palpitations that had been fluttering in her chest all day.

An hour later, when the custodian came in with his push-broom, Maggie was still perched on her stool, her hands cradling her chin, wishing she was home, but not wanting to actually drive there. She didn't want to bother to gather up the papers to work on over the weekend. Didn't want to make the effort to stop at the office on her way out to check her mail.

She didn't want to talk to anyone. Even Max. Especially Max.

Maggie dragged herself off the stool, shoved papers in her tote, and lugged her feet out to the car. The sun flickered and glinted sporadically between rain-saturated clouds. By the time she pulled into the carport the dominant gray had badgered its way across every inch of blue sky and anchored itself to the spires of cedar and hemlock that stippled her property. She sat in the car for five minutes before willing herself to get out.

Move, Maggie! Take one step at a time just until Thanksgiving break. It's going to be fine.

"Hey, guys, I'm home!" she hollered when she came in the door.

An unnatural quiet swallowed her voice. "Max?"

Maggie flopped her tote on the kitchen counter and listened. Her footsteps scuffed on the hall carpet. "Braxton?" she said, opening his door.

Probably at practice.

She opened Max's door. The usual disarray. She scanned the room. Seeing his comforter in a heap on the floor, her muscles relaxed a little. The stereo hummed softly as if waiting to be released from sentinel duty. She flipped it off and went back to the kitchen.

Okay, nothing to worry about.

Was she trying to convince herself?

"Not like he's always here," she muttered.

She reached in her tote and pulled out a sheaf of papers.

Might as well get some done while it's quiet.

As she tossed them on the table where she could spread out, a single sheet puffed sideways, fluttered to the floor, and landed under a chair. Maggie started to pick it up, then flipped her hand at it and went upstairs to change.

A few minutes later she was back in the kitchen clad in very old, very faded navy sweats, pouring herself a very large glass of Chablis. She chugged a third of it, refilled, and turned back to her correcting. She lined up two mechanical pencils, a red pen, a bottle of Wite-Out, and her wine before she pulled the chair out far enough to pick up the paper that had slipped under it. Her lips pursed when she noticed only a few words on it.

"Yet another clever 'world's shortest essay'," she smirked. Then, she read it.

In Max's scrawl, it simply said, "GONE TO CALIFORNIA."

CHAPTER 34

"What's that thing people say? The Lord never gives you more than you can handle? I don't know. It doesn't seem fair. Does that mean that if you can't handle it, you don't get as much shit in your life?" She thought a moment. "Or if you can handle it, you get more?"

Maggie was back in Patty's office, blathering about whatever came into her mind. She had called her as soon as she'd read Max's note. Patty thought it would be "in Max's best interest" for her to come in Monday right after school to talk about it.

Max's best interest.

Maggie found that sardonically amusing. But she knew that Max, not she, was Patty's patient. Maybe this was her way of helping both of them.

"Oh yeah, here's another one: When God closes a door he opens a window. Or something like that." She sagged into the mauve chair and puffed. "Spare me!"

Patty let her ramble.

"Where's my window? That's what I want to know. Where's my window? I want my damned window!" Maggie slouched further into the chair. An east wind had swept down the Gorge that afternoon, and her eyes were drawn again to the bare wisteria ticking lightly against the pane, then slid back to Patty. She crossed her arms defiantly and grumbled, "I've earned a fuckin' window."

Patty nodded. Her tablet lay untouched on her lap, her pencil unpoised. The expression on her face was...well, not

148

exactly indifferent; maybe just patient, Maggie decided. Waiting. Waiting for her to fizzle out so they could get down to business. She was, after all, Max's counselor, she reminded herself again.

"Yes, you have earned it," Patty agreed. "But right now, tell me about your weekend. I assume you did not hear from Max?"

Maggie shook her head. "I called his friend's house. He has this friend, Jonathan? He's not all there himself. His mother said that all he told her was that he was taking a road trip. Said he'd bought a beat-up, '78 Chevy with bad tires. Barely ran, she said."

Maggie rolled her eyes and groused under her breath, "Now there's a combination. Two nuts loose on the open road with nothing between them and disaster but four bald tires and a flimsy prayer."

Patty's chuckle was fleeting, but it was there. Maggie wondered if she was afraid a hearty laugh might be construed as politically incorrect. Since Max had become ill, Maggie had to admit she did sometimes wince when she heard words like "nuts," "crazy," and "loony," casually tossed around, but she knew people weren't intentionally being insulting or mean. Today it was a part of the common vernacular.

"Besides," she had told Max, "everyone is a little nutty. The only difference between you and the rest of us is that you've been diagnosed and we haven't."

She smiled when she remembered the grin on Max's face when he said, "Yeah, I guess so. Besides, you know what they say, just because I'm paranoid doesn't mean they're not really after me."

Max got that from her, that wry sense of humor. Maggie had always been able to laugh at herself, and now Max could do the same. It helped. Maybe, she thought, that was her "window."

She hitched one shoulder. "But, I suppose you could say the weekend was okay... considering."

Then came the question that had been gnawing at Maggie. "Did he take his meds with him?"

Because he had been doing better, his doctor had changed his medications back to all oral. As far as Maggie could

149

remember, he should have more than a month's-worth with him. She took air deep into her lungs and exhaled loudly. "I sure hope so. At least I can't find them anywhere at home." She held up both hands with her fingers crossed, then knocked on the cheap oak table beside her. "I hope he has enough sense to take them."

"Well, we need to remember that Max has shown at least a measure of responsibility with his illness. He's come to his appointments, he's usually pretty open in expressing himself, he hasn't been belligerent when he's here."

Maggie nodded while Patty ticked off Max's merits, but that wasn't what she was thinking.

He comes to his appointments because I make him come. Open in expressing himself? Well, here maybe. But at home he's mastered the art of communicating in one-word sentences: "Hi." "Bye." "Yes." "No." "Dinner?" Either that or he sounds like he's auditioning for the job of an auctioneer.

She had to admit, though, he hadn't been belligerent lately. She was glad for that. "Yeah, maybe," she said. "Maybe he'll take his meds." She sighed again, relieving some of the tension building behind her eyes. "But when those two are together, I swear neither of them have the brains God gave a dust mite."

She left the clinic feeling a little better than when she had gone in. She and Patty had decided on a plan. The plan was there was no plan. At least until Max got in touch with her or came home. If Max called and said he needed money wired to him for an emergency or to make it back home was, even Patty had to admit, a bit of a sticky wicket. There was always a chance he might actually need it to get home, but there was just as much chance he might want it to stay there longer, or to buy booze, or pot, or, she could only hope, food. They decided if he did call for money, Maggie would send him enough to get home, but make it clear that after that, no matter what, he was on his own. She knew it would be hard to resist sending him more if it meant he might not come back, but she was determined to stick to the plan.

When she came in the door that evening, the phone was ringing.

CHAPTER 35

Maggie lunged for the phone and swept it up with a breathless, "Hello?"

"Maggie?"

"Oh, hi, Bernie."

"Well, hello to you too." Bernie paused a moment. "Is this a bad time? 'Cause I can call back later."

"Oh, no, gosh no, Bernie. I was expecting...someone else. I'm so glad it's you. How are you?" Maggie rambled.

"You okay, Maggie?"

"I'm fine, Bernie. Really." She hesitated. It wasn't easy telling anyone about her problems with Max, but Bernie seemed to take everything in stride. "Well, to tell the truth, Bernie, Max is gone."

" 'Gone' as in to the hospital? 'Gone' as over the deep end? Or 'gone' as in from home?"

"The last one," Maggie said. "He left a note Friday saying he was going to California.

"Aw, damn!" was all Bernie said.

"But never mind that right now. Do you have any news about the lawsuits?"

"Well, that's why I called. I wanted to give you an update," Bernie said. "Things are looking pretty good, Maggie. I've talked to two of the attorneys and told them in no uncertain terms that you don't have a pot to piss in, so to speak. Pardon the language."

"That's good news, Bernie." Maggie tried to sound appreciative and she was, really, but it was a struggle to stay positive.

"But those people, Bernie. I wish I could..."

"Now don't start that again, Maggie. I've let them all know how you feel about it and about all your other...problems. And that's all we can do. Your insurance may not stretch as far as they would like it to, but it will have to do."

"Of course you're right Bernie. This is great news about the lawsuit. And hey," she added, "I owe you a lot... much more than monetarily. But be sure to send that bill, and I'll get it paid off as soon as I can." Bernie had been sending her monthly accounts of the charges, but she knew it was always weighted in her favor. There was no way an attorney could cover all his expenses on the amount he had billed her.

"Well, it won't hurt too bad," he said.

"Now, Bernie, you need to at least make it worth your while. You saved my hiney, and you know it."

"Oh, you better believe I'll make it worth my while," he quipped. "At least enough to cover the cost of tackle and live bait for the rest of the year. Worms don't come cheap, ya know."

"Thanks, Bernie. I don't know what I would have done without you, and that's not just a figure of speech."

"You, my dear, are perfectly welcome," Bernie said, "...and Maggie?"

"Yeah?"

"I'm sorry as hell about Max. Will you let me know if there's anything I can do that would help? I have the time. Besides, you know it wouldn't kill me to miss a day or two in search of the elusive cutthroat on the Toutle."

"You can count on it. Even if I have to drive up the North Fork and drag you kicking and screaming from your favorite fishing hole."

And with his deep, rumbling chuckle, Bernie hung up.

Maggie sat in the kitchen a few minutes wishing it was Friday, wishing Braxton would come home so she could put her arms around him. Wishing, but afraid, that Max would call.

Talking to Bernie usually had a calming affect on her. Like Clive, he made her feel that everything would somehow be okay. Like there might be a glimmer of light at the end of that long, dark tunnel, or at least that she would somehow learn to navigate through it. But right now, she felt more like she was falling into a black hole of insanity herself. She wanted to go have a cup of coffee with Clive. To lick her wounds and heal. The thought crossed her mind that she should also go see her dad, but she didn't think she could face him right now. Her skin felt as thin as the paper layer on an onion. She was too vulnerable. Maybe just a phone call would do. Soon. Right now she had to get through this week.

Maggie did get though that week and several weeks after that. Her sleep was patchy and dark, but with no phone calls in the middle of the night, she had started to become acclimated again to only Braxton and herself at home. Although he had remained his same stoic self, Maggie knew she had neglected Braxton.

It was almost Thanksgiving. She wasn't planning a big dinner, but it would be a good time to catch up with Braxton. She was determined to talk to him more, spend more time with him. Maybe on the weekend they would go out for Chinese or pizza. Or maybe he would go with her to visit Clive. He loved his grandpa and the feeling was mutual.

Yes, Maggie thought, that would be good for both of them. But there was something else weighing on her.

Oh yeah, Dad.

She had called her father a couple of times since Max had been gone, but she had to admit she always put it off as long as she could. First thing tomorrow morning she would call him and get that out of the way.

But she didn't have to.

CHAPTER 36

"Mrs. Popovich! Slow down!" Maggie had groped for the phone, and a voice on the other end was squealing something about someone tumbling or stumbling or fumbling into a liver. The only way Maggie knew it was her father's sadly-coifed redheaded neighbor was that in the middle of her rant she yelled, "Mr. Popovich, get the hell down from there!"

"Mrs. Popovich!" Maggie hollered into the spew of tirade coming from the receiver. "Slow down! I can't understand a word you're saying!"

When the cacophony stopped, she continued, "Okay now. Stay calm Mrs. Popovich, and tell me again what happened."

"It's your father," she began, then abruptly halted.

"Yes?" Maggie prompted. "Mrs. Popovich, what's happened to my dad?"

"They took him away."

Maggie's breath caught for a spit-second. "And?" she urged again.

"And what?" Mrs. Popovich asked.

Maggie rolled her eyes and reined in her own verbal rant. "And where did they take him, Mrs. Popovich?" She measured her words with the cadence of a slow waltz.

"Well, they took him to the hospital, of course!" Mrs. Popovich shot back as if she could hardly believe Maggie's inability to track a simple conversation.

"Can you tell me what happened?"

Maggie heard an audible sigh, and now it was Mrs. Popovich who was measuring her words. "Like I said, he fell—in—to—the—ri—ver."

Maggie glanced at the clock. Three-thirty a.m. Somehow it wasn't making sense. "When did this happen?"

"It just happened. Just a little while ago. I heard them stumbling down the dock, your dad and that...woman!" The emphasis on "woman" could only mean one thing: Delilah Bouquet, or as Mrs. Popovich called her, "Mrs. Bucket."

"Do you know if he's all right?" As the gravity of the information seeped into her now fully alert mind, the threat of losing her father seemed very real. Carrying the phone with her, Maggie was already up, searching for her shoes, wondering where she put her keys, and trying to remember how much gas she had in the tank. "Where did they take him, Mrs. Popovich?"

"I'm not sure, but I think someone said Good Sam."

Maggie slammed the receiver down, jotted a quick note to Braxton, slipped her trench coat on over her pajamas, and was out the door before her sheets had cooled.

Good Samaritan was across the river in Portland. Maggie gauged the route and the number of bridges to get there. Only two. One over the Columbia and one over the Willamette. Once she was on the freeways, it was almost a straight shot. Forty-five minutes tops. But the time of morning would be in her favor. If the state patrol had given up on seeing much action this late into their shifts, she might make it in forty.

She thought of the last time she had been to this hospital when her mother died. Then there had been no rush to get there. Cancer dawdles and lurks and sucks the life out of everyone in its sluggish march to the end. But accidents are different. The initial shock of losing someone you love is devastating. She didn't know which was worse. She wouldn't wish either on an archenemy.

Thirty-eight minutes after she left home, she squealed into an emergency room slot, flew across a parking lot puddled with rain, and through the automated doors, soggy pajama bottoms flapping around her ankles. A receptionist slid the window open. "James Parker," Maggie panted. "Daughter," she wheezed out before the girl had time to ask if she was a relative.

The receptionist scanned the list. "Bed number...nine. Go through the double..."

But Maggie was already halfway there.

One, two, three, four, okay Maggie, slow down— five— breathe deep—six—seven—concentrate on the present—eight— one thing at a time—nine.

She closed her eyes, inhaled deeply, held the smells of antiseptic, blood, and fear in her lungs, blew out a slow, quivery draft of air, then cautiously drew aside the turquoise and peach striped curtain.

A nurse in yellow scrubs dotted with red cherries looked up from her blood pressure monitor, smiled, and raised one finger telling Maggie to hold on just a minute. Maggie edged forward. They already had her dad out of his wet clothes and into a faded blue hospital gown. As she got closer, his dark eyes opened weakly and closed again. His signature shock of wavy, silver-white hair, now seemed sprinkled with dishwater yellow and stuck out in frenzied confusion on his pillow. The tape securing an IV puckered the paper-thin skin on his arm. Instead of a vibrant, teasing, devil-may-care personality, she saw a frail, wan, rather bony seventy-eight-year-old, still and fragile.

The nurse recorded his vital signs. "You his daughter?" she asked. The Velcro screeched as she ripped the cuff off, wound the tube around it, and replaced it in a wire basket.

Maggie nodded.

"Well, he's stable right now," the nurse said as she found the pulse on his wrist and looked at her watch. Fifteen seconds later she added, "But he was pretty out of it when they brought him in. Cantankerous." Head still bent, she peered up at Maggie. "Does he drink much?"

Maggie's scoff must have told her what she wanted to know, because the nurse smiled warmly and nodded. "Well, we gave him something to help him relax so he should be all right for a few more hours, but I imagine they'll want to keep him overnight."

"So, you don't think he broke anything?"

"No, nothing's broken as far as we can tell right now, but he must have hit his head on something...a dock did they say? There's a lump in the back." She put a hand to the back of her head. "But our craniums are pretty hard back there." She knocked on it a few times as if to prove her point. "The doctor isn't too concerned about it," she said, pulling the curtain open to leave.

"Will the doctor be by so I can talk to him?"

"Oh, yes," she said turning. "But it might be an hour or more. We're a little busy tonight." She snickered as if that was the understatement of the century.

"Thanks, ah..." Maggie glanced at her badge, "Tanya."

Tanya stepped into the chaos outside the curtain, but poked her head back in. "Can I get you anything?" she asked, smiling. "Coffee? Crackers? Jell-O?"

Maggie waved her hand, "No, I'm fine."

"Oh, there was a woman that came in with your dad. I think she's waiting in the lobby if you want to see her," Tanya said and pulled the privacy curtain closed.

Maggie turned to her father again. As soon as she had seen her dad, relief had washed over her. But now that she knew he was all right, her practical side kicked in. She picked up a wilted hand, cradled it in hers.

How long will he be able to take care of himself? How long before a nursing home?

He wasn't that old, but living at Wavy Lane wasn't exactly conducive to a healthy, live-to-a-ripe-old-age existence. Mrs. Popovich and Mrs. "Bucket" were barely the tip of the iceberg. The place was swarming with lifestyles of the drunk and clueless.

How long can he last in a place like that? How long before he "fumbles into the liver" and kills himself?

A knot was tightening in the pit of Maggie's stomach, and that knot felt suspiciously like anger. She squeezed his hand and shook her head. "Damn it, Dad!"

As if on cue, he turned his head toward her and his eyes flickered open. "Oh, hi, Magpie," he slurred. "Sorry, I must have drifted off. How long you been here? I could sure use a gin and..." He closed his eyes again.

"Unbelievable," Maggie muttered and made her way to the lobby in search of the visitor Tanya had told her about.

Delilah Bouquet stood out like a sleazy evangelist in a room full of born-again converts. You couldn't miss the deceptive halo of over-bleached and over-permed hair atop an almost pin-like head attached to a tall, gaunt frame that oddly sported breasts the size of Mount Rainier and Mount Hood. She oiled her way around the waiting room with the deftness of a slick blackjack dealer, doling out advice to the huddled masses yearning to be anywhere but there.

From a distance her piercing blue eyes and bright cupid's bow lips made her seem almost pretty. But as she came into focus, Maggie could see the cracks in her generously powdered face, the fluorescent glow of Maybelline's Pink Disco lipstick seeping into web-like creases around her mouth, and the caked mascara that had begun sliding down her profusely rouged cheeks.

"Oh, heavens no," she heard her telling a woman wearing a green paisley babushka. "I can assure you there is nothing to worry about. They'll give him something, and the stones will ...pass right through." Her hand made a ballerina-like sweep from her sternum to her pelvis, indicating the ease and gracefulness with which those gallstones would be excised from her husband's body.

Maggie wondered what her father saw in her, then remembered him saying she kept an ample supply of booze under her bed. Undoubtedly Mount Rainier and Mount Hood had something to do with it, too.

Maggie waited at a respectful distance for her to finish her ministering, then stepped up before she could get to another sufferer. "Mrs. Buck..." *Damn!* "Mrs. Bouquet?"

Two surprisingly alert eyes blinked a series of coquettish flutters, and a voice corroded by fifty years of smoking answered, "Yes?"

"Hi, I'm Maggie, James'—"

"Of course you are!" Mrs. Bouquet reached out her manicured talons and grasped Maggie's hands in hers to pull her closer. "Magpie! I'd know you anywhere, although we did meet before, do you remember?" She tilted her head and raised her penciled-on brows in anticipation of a favorable response.

"Well, I ah, I think I, ah..." Maggie fumbled for something that sounded credible.

"Oh, you remember. It was last year. At the Wavy Lane Cinco De Mayo Bar-B-Q and Beer Fest?"

"Oooooh yes." Maggie did have a faint recollection of it. It was hard to completely erase the image of a bunch of young "swingers," middle-aged "players," and old "wanna-be-hip"senior citizens acting like sixteen-year-olds that had used fake ID to buy their first beer. "Yeah, I think I remember. Wasn't someone wearing a pink flamingo—"

"Hat!" Mrs. Bouquet finished. "That was me!" Her eyes lit up, and she splayed her fingers on top of her head to further explain the daring fashion statement.

Maggie responded with what she hoped was an unbiased nod, but apparently Mrs. Bouquet wanted more. She stood watching Maggie. Still grinning. Still blinking.

Maggie skirted the hat discussion. "I wanted to thank you for coming to the hospital with my dad," she hedged.

"Oh, it was nothing at all, dear. Nothing at all."

"No, really it wasn't nothing. You're a good friend to do that, Mrs. Bouquet."

"I didn't mind at all, Maggie. And please call me Dee. Everybody does. But how did you know I was here?'

"Oh, the nurse told me," Maggie said with a waft of her hand in the direction of the emergency room. "Well, and Mrs. Popovich called me, of course."

"Oh, I see. Mrs. Popovich," she said with an eye-roll that would have put Groucho Marx to shame.

Maggie deciphered Dee's body language. Apparently she and Mrs. Popovich belonged to a mutual abomination society. And, she had a little hunch tickling her intuition that both of them had designs on James Parker. If so, she was pretty sure the Cascade Range would win out.

She made sure Mrs. Bouquet had a ride home, wrote down her telephone number, and promised to call her as soon as she knew something. By that time it was almost 6:30 Saturday morning. Maggie wanted to curl up on one of the gurneys she passed in the hall on her way back to her father's room, but she figured she'd have plenty of time to sleep when she got home.

And after a nice long nap, she wanted to take Braxton to dinner and to visit Clive. But first she'd have to talk to the doctor to see what he had in store for her dad.

When she got back to her father's cubicle, his doctor was coming out. Maggie extended her hand. "Hi, I'm Maggie, James Parker's daughter," she said.

Two limp fingers and a thumb lightly touched Maggie's hand in what she took for a half-hearted attempt at a friendly bedside manner. Without making eye contact, and without introducing himself, he examined his clipboard. "It looks like your father slipped and fell into a river?" he asked without looking up.

"That's right," Maggie said. "The Willamette."

"What, does he live in a boathouse or something?"

"Yes," Maggie confirmed, "but it's actually a houseboat."

"Well, I think he'll be all right, but I'd like him to stay another twenty-four hours at least. He hit his head pretty hard. Huge knot in the back." He went back to James' bed and slid his hand under his head to feel the lump again. Then he bent close to his face and studied it more closely through bifocals that slipped to the tip of his nose. He straightened and took her dad's wrist and studied his watch as he counted the beats per second. "He drink much?" he asked quietly.

At first Maggie wasn't sure he was talking to her. She felt an odd mix of guilt and embarrassment even though, rationally, she knew she had nothing to feel guilty or embarrassed about. It was a simple, logical question that called for nothing more than a straightforward answer. "What? Oh, yeah. Yeah, he does drink much."

"Weeell..." The doctor drew out the word as if he might still be contemplating the best thing to do with James Braxton Parker. That was a feeling Maggie knew very well.

Finally, he said, "Yes, I think it would be better for him to stay here until he comes to. He might have to go through withdrawal before we can release him. Hard to say right now."

Maggie nodded in agreement. "I think that sounds reasonable," she said. "May I call tomorrow to see how he's doing and if I need to come pick him up?"

160

CHAPTER 37

As she left the hospital the Saturday morning traffic was already in full swing. She drove home, checked Max's room to see if he had returned, checked Braxton's room to make sure he was still sleeping, then fell into her bed. When she woke up, it was almost noon.

As she came down stairs, Braxton emerged from his room. "Going to take a shower," he mumbled and disappeared into the bathroom.

"Good!" she hollered after him. "I want you to go with me to see your Gramps when you get out."

This would give Maggie a little more time. While Max was known to shower faster than a pit-crew could change a tire, Braxton's marathon showers could take longer than the entire Indy 500. Maggie decided to make some calls as she waited for him to run the hot water tank dry.

At Good Samaritan, although she wasn't able to talk to a doctor, the day-shift nurse told Maggie her father was "doing fairly well," but as the ER doctor had predicted, he did have the DTs. She could visit if she wanted to, but right now he was so belligerent they had him strapped down. The nurse said he kept clawing at his IV to pull it out and had fallen down twice trying to get out of bed to "leave this lousy joint."

Maggie was not altogether unhappy they had decided to keep him a while. "Is there anything I could do for him if I come over there today?" She crossed her fingers.

The nurse paused and Maggie knew she was trying to come up with an appropriate answer. Finally, she said, "Well, you might be able to calm him down a little." She paused again.

161

Maggie held her breath and waited. "But," she went on, "right now, I'm not even sure he'd recognize you. So, I guess it's up to you."

Maggie exhaled. That's what she had been waiting for, an out. A little out that assuaged her guilt. She jumped on it. "Okay then, I'll call back later today to see how he's doing."

Then she bit the bullet and called Mrs. Bucket. Dee, Maggie reminded herself.

"Good Morning! It's a beautiful day at Wavy Lane," a raspy voice answered.

"Dee?"

"Yes, this is Dee. Is that you, Magpie?"

Maggie cringed when strangers used her father's private nickname for her. Not even her mother had called her Magpie, but when her father started to court and woo other women after her mom passed away, all of them seemed to take the liberty of using it, even if they had never met her.

"Yes, this is Magp..I mean Maggie. How are you doing today, Dee? Get any sleep last night?"

"Slept like a baby!" she croaked. "How's your dear father?"

Maggie filled Mrs. Bouquet in on the details and promised to let her know if there was any change and when she was going to bring him home. "But," Maggie added before she hung up, "I know the doctor is going to advise him to lay off the booze. It sure would be great if you could help him do that, Dee."

Without so much as a hiccup's hesitation, Mrs. Bouquet answered, "Well, of course, dear!"

Maggie wasn't convinced; she had a feeling Mrs. Bouquet's idea of "help" in that department was adding an extra teaspoon of vermouth to his dry-as-dust martinis. But she knew until her father made up his own mind to get sober, there was little anyone could do. She thanked her again for taking her dad to the hospital, hung up, and dialed again.

"Yeah?" Mrs. Popovich crackled on the other end of the receiver.

"Hi, Mrs. Popovich. This is Maggie."

"Yeah?"

"I wanted to thank you for calling me last night."

"Yeah?"

162

"About my father?" Maggie waited for a sign that Mrs. Popovich knew who was calling. When she heard none, she said, "Remember? You called me last night? He fell into the river? 'Member?"

"Well, of course I remember! I called you, didn't I?"

"Yes. Yes, you did, Mrs. Popovich, and I thought you might like to know how he's doing."

"Yeah? Well? How's he doing?"

"Oh, well, he's doing okay, I think, but he's still in the hospital for another day or two."

"Yeah?"

"Yeah. Apparently he was pretty intoxicated when they brought him in. The doctor wants him to dry out before they release him."

"Of course he does! They're not going to send him home still wet! He fell into the damned river. Do they know that? "

"Oh, yes, yes they certainly do." Maggie gave a little "huh" and gave up. She promised she would let Mrs. Popovich know if there was anything else she could do and hung up.

As Maggie had hoped, the rest of the day was uneventful. Just the way she liked it. She and Braxton stopped to have coffee with Clive where they talked about nothing in particular. Maxim's name came up only once when Clive asked if she'd heard from him, then dropped it.

Maggie did tell both of them about last night's incident with her father. Braxton rolled his eyes, and Clive shook his head and harrumphed once. Those simple acknowledgements were all Maggie wanted or needed. Discussing them to death wouldn't make Max come home earlier or her dad get sober faster.

After mountains of moo goo gai pan, Kung Pao chicken, lo mein, and enough egg rolls to stretch the entire length of the Great Wall of China, Maggie settled into a routine that renewed her determination to make the most of her time with Braxton.

Two days later, she picked up her father from Good Sam, took him home, and tried to have a heartfelt talk with him about not drinking. She knew she was preaching to the wind when he said, "Oh for crying-out-loud, Magpie! Stop harping. I can stop anytime I want to. I just don't want to. Besides, without it, my life isn't worth a plug nickel. At least let me enjoy it. What else do I have?"

"Well, if you'd stop drinking, maybe you'd find out." Maggie knew it was a weak retort. She knew that her father's gin-soaked existence had the numbing effect he needed to get through his days without the person who made his life worth a whole lot more than the plug nickel he was always referring to.

Booze blurred the edges of reality and made things almost bearable. Temporarily. There were times she had a few too many drinks herself. Maggie knew she could have easily fallen into than bottomless pit. Lord knows she was pushed to its brink during Max's psychotic episodes. But her father's phone calls when he was drunk, his slurred speech, his falls, were enough to remind her she didn't want to follow that same path of least resistance. In the long run it never paid off.

On her way home, Maggie once again renewed her self-promise to not worry about what she had no control over. She still had five glorious days of Thanksgiving break coming up, and come hell or high water, she was going to enjoy them.

CHAPTER 38

Despite days saturated with autumn's typically bitter rain and nights saturated with dreams of helpless children falling into rushing water, those five days were also dappled with splinters of sun, deep naps, and gentle talks with Braxton, all of which restored Maggie's resolve to take it one day at a time.

One day at a time turned in to one week at a time. By the beginning of December Maggie was once again immersed in the routine of school. Winter break was approaching, and then it was a long stretch to June twentieth, the end of the school year. Maggie had already decided to take the summer off from enrolling in classes, teaching summer school, going to conferences and workshops, and anything else that might cause stress.

But she knew that a stress-free life for anyone with teenagers was not possible. And for her, it was like waiting for a bomb to drop. The hard part was not knowing when it would happen or how big the explosion would be. Maggie wished she could build a shelter to protect herself and Braxton from the fallout. But she couldn't, so she did the next best thing—she tried to insulate herself by keeping her thoughts on the surface. Shallow thoughts were easier to deal with.

Yet, during quiet days and still nights, when she was alone, it was hard to wrench those thoughts away from Max. What was he doing? Was he safe? Was he taking his meds? Was he homeless?

The cold truth was that if he was not medicated, he could have another psychotic break. Then anything was possible. He could be lost, in a strange hospital, in jail...or worse.

There was always worse. It took every ounce of her strength not to dwell on what would happen when his medications ran out if, in fact, he was taking them at all.

She didn't have to wait long to find out.

Maggie was still in limbo as December rolled into January, even though she had kept a steadfast rein on her out-of-sight-out-of-mind philosophy as much as she was able to under the circumstances. So when she drove into the carport the first Thursday of the month, she was somewhat taken aback when she saw the front door wide open. For a fleeting moment she thought Braxton might be home, then she remembered he would still be at the basketball game. She had planned to grab a sandwich and head over to the school to catch the last half.

She stepped lightly across the front porch and stopped at the door to listen. Just the rat-a-tat-tat of a pileated woodpecker in the broken top of an alder. Cautiously, Maggie edged over the threshold and into the entry.

"Max?" Nothing.

She walked softly down the hall. Max's door was closed. She knew it had been open when she left for work.

She grasped the knob, hesitated, then inched it open. "Max?"

She peered into the darkened room, her pupils dilating, searching, her mind swirling, trying to comprehend.

She fumbled for the switch and flicked it up.

CHAPTER 39

Maggie flinched, then an involuntary spasm gripped her body.

The room she had cleaned and straightened more than three months ago was in shambles. The sheets and comforter had been ripped from the bed, the mattress was propped against the window shutting out the daylight. A half-eaten pizza lay limp across a greasy cardboard box tossed upside down on a mound of clothes flung from Max's closet and drawers. Cigarette butts had been ground into the carpet to extinguish them. An almost-empty bottle of Jim Beam lay next to the Army surplus duffel bag he had taken with him when he left.

But there was no Max.

That night Maggie lay on the couch, afraid to close her eyes, afraid she would fall asleep and not hear Max come in or call. After seeing his room, she had waited for an hour in case he showed up, then drove to the school just in time to see Braxton throw the last basket of the game. She waited an hour and caught him as he came out the exterior door of the locker room.

"Max is back."

"How's he doing?" he asked as they walked to their cars.

"Well, I haven't really seen him yet, but from the look of his room, I'd say he's not doing very well." Maggie stopped Braxton, gripped his shoulders, and turned him to her. "If you want to stay somewhere else tonight, it's okay, hon. I'm sure Greg's mom wouldn't mind. Or Jeff's? Or you could always stay at Grandpa's."

Braxton looked over her head at the field beyond. "Maybe I should come home tonight," he said.

At nearly six feet, Braxton was developing into a tall, responsible young man. Sometimes it still caught Maggie off guard, and she marveled at the curious nature of life, at the quirks and hitches that could dictate its outcome. How an incident, an event, a mishap, or yes, even an illness, could either elevate a life or send it on a frenzied path to devastation.

"You could..." Maggie started. Of all things, she didn't want Braxton to feel obligated to help her handle Max. There was no doubt he was affected by having a brother with schizophrenia, but he didn't need to take care of her, too. Maggie started again, "You could, but I don't think it's necessary. I really think I'll be fine by myself."

She searched Braxton's face. "Besides, who knows if he'll even come home tonight."

"Yeah." Braxton nodded and put his arms around her. "You sure?"

"Absolutely."

Maggie wasn't absolutely sure of anything right then, but she did know that whatever happened, Braxton wouldn't be able to prevent it. She left him with the understanding that he would come home and pick up his clothes for the next day and let her know where he would be that night.

So into the evening, as Maggie lay on the couch, cradling the phone and listening for footsteps on the front porch, she concentrated on the forlorn hoo-hooing of an old barn owl that had taken up residence in the rafters of the porte-cochere, and eventually drifted into a light sleep.

CHAPTER 40

Max plunged his hand deep into the muddy bank and scooped out a handful of muck. He smeared it on his forehead and across his cheeks, then swiped his hands on his jeans. I don't care what they do to me. They're not taking me alive. A car approached and he jumped into the sopping weeds. He crouched, waiting for the next threat. For more than a mile he had crawled on his belly through reedgrass, thistle, and blackberry vines growing alongside the road. If I can just get to home base I can get that Lugar, pick up some ammo. If I can just... He raised himself to his knees and looked up and down the road, then for the next five miles, he walked, ran, and crept his way home.

The front door flew open and banged against the wall, bounded back, and crashed shut with a resounding thwack that sent tremors through Maggie's chest and every window in the house. She shot upright, but before she could get to the entry, Max was standing in the living room, his arms crossed, defiant, daring. His hair was tangled with twigs and leaves. His face was covered in mud, his Levis and Black Sabbath T-shirt torn and stained with dirt and food, his arms and elbows scratched and bloody. It was three in the morning.

"Hi, Max." Maggie tried to control the quiver in her voice. "I'm glad you're home."

Max postured dominance but said nothing.

Maggie tried again. "Want something to eat?"

Without a word, Max spun around and stormed down the hall, slamming his bedroom door.

Should she go after him? Try to talk to him?

Maggie's heart told her yes, but her common sense told her no. There would be no point. If she let him be, maybe he'd sleep it off...she didn't even know what it was he would "sleep off" or even if he could, she just knew something was wrong again. If she waited, maybe she could get him into the center with no incident when they opened that morning.

For more than two hours she listened to the sounds of restlessness coming from Max's room. The closet door opened and banged shut, something thudded against the wall, what sounded like Jacob Marley's chains clanked and clattered to the floor. Then she heard Pink Floyd bellowing about skating on the thin ice of life. Then silence.

Maggie lay awake until eight o'clock before she dialed the center. The recording said if it was an emergency, to call the crisis hot line. She did.

"So, do you need us to call the police?" a volunteer asked after Maggie had blubbered for five minutes.

Did she? She'd heard nothing since Max had turned off his stereo. "Well, no, not really," she finally said. "At least I don't think so. But I need to bring him in to the center for an evaluation. Can you let them know I'm on my way? Or, I think I am anyway. I'm not sure he'll come with me, but I think he will. Can you tell them he may be having a psychotic break? Can you let them know? His counselor's name is Patty Cravitz."

Maggie hung up. She crept down the hall and listened at Max's door. She put her hand on the knob, then removed it. "Not yet," she whispered to herself and went back to the kitchen to do last night's dishes and put the coffee on, delaying the inevitable. She knew sooner or later she'd have to face it. "I'll give it until nine," she told herself and sat down to wait. But half an hour later, she heard his door open, then she heard the toilet flush and the shower being turned on.

Maggie forced herself to go back down the hall and tap on the bathroom door. "Max?"

"I'm taking a shower," he hollered over the gush of water.

"Want something to eat when you get out?"

170

"Yeah."

"Okay, this is just plain weird," she mumbled as she went back to the kitchen and plugged in the toaster. "Weird," she said again as she got a frying pan. "Just weird," she said as she cracked eggs into it.

Ten minutes later Max strolled into the kitchen as if he had never been gone. As if everything in his life was as it should be. Just another typical day in the Axline household. He pulled up a barstool and sat at the counter. "I'm hungry," he said as he watched Maggie at the stove. "Those for me? Could eat a horse."

But something about the way he was talking wasn't quite normal. She'd seen it before. He was almost too matter-of-fact. Too loud. Too...something.

"So, honey," Maggie probed, "how was your trip? Everything go okay?"

"Yeah, it was fine," Max blustered. "Got a lot of things done."

"Like what?"

"Oh, you know, people I needed to see. Contracts settled." Max took a sip of the coffee Maggie had put in front of him.

"What kind of contracts?" she said.

"Contracts," he repeated. "Documents."

There it was, that voice of bravado, of over-confidence. Like he was playing a role.

Maggie put a plate of fried eggs and toast in front of him.

Max pushed it away. "Not hungry. Got a lotta shit to do today."

"But," Maggie started to protest, then caught herself. There was no point. Instead, she said, "I'm going into town. Can I give you a ride?"

"Sure, let's get the hell outta here." And within ten seconds, Max was out the door and into the car. Maggie turned the stove off, yanked the plug to the coffeepot, grabbed her purse, and scrambled after him.

On their way to town, Max didn't say a word. After another attempt to find out where he was for the last four months, Maggie gave up and they drove in silence. She had no idea if she would ever know where he had been or what he had done, and

171

she wasn't entirely sure she wanted to. She also did not know if her plan to drive him to the center for an evaluation would work, but she had to try.

As they entered the parking lot, Maggie watched for Max's reaction. "I think this is the place, Max," she ventured.

Max scanned the lot and seemed to be taking in any activity, imagined or real. His eyes swept from the building, to the benches along the walkway leading up to it, to the path on the other side of the parking lot, and back to the building. "Yeah, this'll do," he said. As Maggie pulled into a spot, Max bolted and rushed inside.

And again, Maggie dashed after him, hoping he would go to the right place. Fortunately, he did. She found him telling a girl at the counter something about a meeting and that they were expecting him. Maggie came up behind him, nodded to the girl, and said, "Yes, this is Maxim Axline. I think they are expecting him."

"Oh yes, of course," she said. "Will you take a seat? The doc...they will be with you right away."

Maggie and Max sat on the long bench that ran the length of the wall opposite the receptionist. Other than chairs, a few built-in planters filled with fake philodendron, and a variety of outdated magazines, the room was empty.

At first, Max sat quietly, then he rested his elbows on his knees. Gone was his bravado. He looked forlorn, desolate, dejected. Not at all like he did less than five minutes ago.

Maggie's heart tightened in her chest. "It'll be okay, Max," she said. "It'll be okay," she said again and caressed his shoulder. His eyes flicked over to her hand. He seemed to be studying it or, Maggie thought, perhaps the one-carat diamond ring her mother had left her.

With his elbows still on his knees, Max twisted his face up to hers, his eyes saturated with a sadness that was lucid, yet at the same time, unreadable. Then they shifted back to the floor. Out of the blue, his hands came up and covered his eyes and he wept. Then, just as quickly, he sat up and scowled at Maggie through his tears. He grabbed her hand and wrenched the diamond ring from her finger and threw it across the room where it landed in a potted philodendron next to the door.

Maggie stayed cool, unemotional. Yelling or jumping up to get the ring would cause more confusion for Max. She glanced at the receptionist who had been watching the entire scenario. The girl tacitly nodded at Maggie. She knew then this dear person would retrieve the ring for her once Max had gone in for an evaluation.

Patty Cravitz was not there that day, but a moment later Doctor Perrin, the psychiatrist on duty, opened the door to the hall of counseling rooms. "Max?" he called, and Max stood up and again, as if in complete control, walked confidently across the room.

Maggie wasn't about to be left out of this conference and followed without being asked.

Doctor Perrin seemed puzzled, but said nothing and led Maggie and Max to his office. However, after introducing himself, the first thing he asked Max was, "Is this your mother, Max?" And then, "Is it all right with you if she stays and listens to us?"

His emphasis on "listens" did not go unnoticed by Maggie. She took that to mean an overbearing mother's input was not needed here, nor was it welcome.

Max didn't seem to notice, or at least didn't care. He shrugged his shoulders as if it was the least important thing in the world, settled into a chair and looked indifferently at a picture of a monarch butterfly on the wall.

Doctor Perrin took a few minutes to glance at a two-inch-thick file that would have taken him days to thoroughly understand, then turned to Max. "Well," he began. "How are you feeling today, Max?"

Max shrugged again. "Fine."

Then came the series of Psychiatry 101 questions. "Are you feeling anxious?'

Max slowly closed his eyes and opened them again. "Not really."

He's heard it all before.

"Are you hearing voices?"

"No."

"Is anyone trying to communicate with you through the walls or the wiring?"

173

Max looked at him as if he was the crazy one. "No."

Do you know what day it is today, Max?"

"Yeah."

"Can you tell me?"

Max appeared perturbed, but said, "Saturday."

"And what's the date?"

"February 2nd."

"The year?"

"1997."

Maggie sat silently and listened to Max's answers. To someone who didn't know him, he would have sounded perfectly normal. About this time Doctor Perrin must have been wondering why she had brought him in. But Maggie knew he simply wasn't asking the right questions. If he could ask Max a question he wasn't used to. He knew all the answers he should give to these.

"Well, you seem to be doing fine to me," the doctor finally said. He was talking to Max but looking at Maggie.

There had to be some way of revealing his real state of mind. There was some reason he had cried in the lobby and thrown her ring. What was it? What was he thinking at that moment?

Doctor Perrin started to get up. She knew her input wasn't appreciated, but she didn't have a choice. "Ask him who I am," she said quickly.

The doctor glowered but sat back down. "Who is this person, Max?" he asked motioning to Maggie.

"That's my mom," he said frankly.

Doctor Perrin tilted his head at Maggie, as if to say, "satisfied now?"

No, she wasn't. Okay, that wasn't the right question, but there has to be something... In desperation, Maggie said, "Ask him who you are."

She knew he was losing patience, but he turned to Max again, sighed condescendingly, and asked, "Who am I, Max?"

Max hesitated. He glanced first at Maggie, then back at the doctor. His mouth opened and he stared as if he could hardly believe anyone would ask him such an obvious question. "Why, you're my brother, of course," he said. "I love you, man."

174

Ha! I've got him!

Maggie smiled at the smug bastard sitting across from her, now with his mouth hanging open.

Doctor Perrin recovered quickly and began a series of Psychiatry 102 questions: What makes you think I'm your brother? How long have we known each other? Do you have any other brothers?

But for Max, it was all downhill from there.

Poor darling.

Maggie did feel a little guilty, but she also knew it had to come to this. She knew she couldn't take him home.

Finally, Doctor Perrin stopped asking questions. "I'd like to change your medications, Max. I think it will help you feel better," he said as he wrote in the overstuffed file.

Surely that isn't all. Surely they will need to admit him to the hospital for a while.

"And," he went on, "I think you should go to the recovery center for a while, Max." He looked up from the folder. "You know, so they can monitor your new meds for a week or two."

He glanced at Maggie who let out a pent-up breath and nodded.

"Do you think you could let your mom take you there now?" he asked Max.

Max shrugged, once again the casual, devil-may-care attitude.

On the way out, the receptionist put Maggie's ring on the counter. As she walked by Maggie mouthed "thank you," and swiftly swept it up.

CHAPTER 41

Max was on a seventy-two-hour involuntary hold while the doctor and staff worked on getting him straightened out. Maggie saw him once during that time. He was still confused and had fabricated a world that was as real to him as Maggie's world was to her. He kept his shades drawn against outside threats and, according to Dave, lurked around the entrance during the day and skulked down the halls at night. Finally, Dave said, they gave him something to help him sleep, and as they tried new medications, he began to come around.

After four days, Maggie was able to carry on a somewhat coherent conversation with him. But he was still off-kilter. She was relieved when they made the decision to keep him another two weeks. There was still something about the way he acted that made her uneasy. Again, it was hard to pinpoint or to explain, but she had the feeling he would be right back in there if they released him early.

On Wednesday, she drove to Vancouver Memorial after school to see him again. She took brownies, cigarettes, and the soft, fleece blanket she threw over herself in the evenings as she watched television. She called them "comfort-stuff." They were three things she thought might soothe Max during his stay.

As she came into the locked ward that day, Maggie left the cigarettes at the nurses' station. On her way to Max's room, Dave caught up with her. Until a couple of days ago, she hadn't talked to him for more than a year. She was glad to see he was still as she remembered: large, genial, and gentle.

"How do you think he's doing?" Maggie slowed her pace to give Dave time to answer before they got to room 207.

"I'm not sure," he said and stopped suddenly in the middle of the hall. "He's better than when he came in, I do know that, but..." Dave looked down the hall in the direction of Max's room. He scratched his jaw, and Maggie waited for him to find the words. "You know, I don't really know Max other than when he's been here. And then he's always kind of..."

"Loopy?" Maggie finished his thought for him.

Dave grinned. "Yeah, well, I guess you could say that. But what's he like when he's not..." he lowered his voice, "'loopy'?"

Maggie wasn't sure any more how to answer that. Was Max's loopy self becoming the norm? She had a clear image of him when he was a happy baby giggling at a butterfly, a stubborn toddler clamping his mouth shut when she tried to feed him strained peas, an adventurous little boy getting on the school bus with his Spiderman lunchbox. When had he changed?

Again, she worked her memory to pull up signs of psychotic onset. Was the erratic behavior of his early teenage years normal? Didn't they all have mood-swings? Take stupid chances? Neglect their homework? Max was her first child. She'd had nothing to compare to until Braxton.

"Well," she said to Dave, "I guess you could say he was kind of a free-spirit in a way. He laughed a lot." Maggie lowered her eyes and thought. "And he teased a lot. Especially his brother." She smiled when she remembered four-year-old Braxton's frustration as he complained to her that Max was "a aminal!"

"But you know," she said to Dave, "he had such a tender side, too."

Yes, he could be almost relentless in taunting his brother, but Maggie also remembered Max with his arm around Braxton's shoulder. They had been playing at the neighbor's when Braxton had put his hand down on a nail. It was really little more than a scratch, and Braxton was whimpering, that's for sure, but Max, well, he was sobbing when he brought Braxton home. He couldn't be consoled until she had washed Braxton's wound and put a Band-Aid on it. Then, as if nothing had happened, he was back to playing, laughing, and teasing.

"He kind of changed when he got older, though." She scowled. "Did some drugs, alcohol, that kind of garbage."

"Yeah, well that's pretty common." Dave titled his head. "You know that don't you?" When she didn't say anything, he went on. "I guess it's not my place to say, but we see that a lot in here. A lot of people do drugs or drink before they get to this place. The 'experts' think they are probably self-medicating."

He paused a moment, as if he didn't know how much he should say. "It's like they know there is something going on with their chemistry, like an imbalance or something, so they unconsciously start taking stuff to make themselves feel better."

Maggie remembered hearing that before, but it made her feel better that Dave cared enough to tell her.

They found Max in his room, lying curled up on his bed, blinds drawn against the world. He sat up when they came into the room and although he didn't smile, he did seem somewhat pleased to see her. She gave Max the blanket and offered them both some brownies.

"Brownies?" Dave said with enthusiasm. "This definitely calls for a little celebration. You two care to join me in the lunchroom for a glass of milk? Or coffee?"

It wasn't in Maggie's nature to turn down a good cup of coffee. Unfortunately, she knew this would not be "a good cup of coffee," but she said she would brave it anyway, and she and Max followed Dave back down the hall to the cafeteria.

"Hey, Max!" Dave filled two mugs with coffee as murky as pond water on a cloudy day. "Tell your mom what you did last night."

Max frowned. He opened the box of brownies and scrutinized them.

Dave put mugs down in front of Max and Maggie and went to get milk for himself. He had an amused smirk on his face as he came back to the table. "Come on, Max, tell her what you did."

"I didn't do nothin'," Max said as he took out a brownie.

The English teacher in Maggie cringed, but she held her tongue.

"Yes, you did. Don't play dumb with me, pal." Dave grinned broadly as he sat down.

178

A corner of Max's mouth went up. "Maybe someone was hungry," he said and shrugged one shoulder.

"Hungry, he says." Dave tipped his chair back and locked his fingers behind his head. "Boy, that's an understatement." He chuckled, clearly enjoying the banter. "Okay, if you won't tell her, I will."

"You don't have to, ya know," Max said, but Maggie could tell he was enjoying it, too.

"Oh, but I do." Dave righted his chair, crossed his arms on the table, and leaned toward Maggie. "Well, last night, *someone* broke into the kitchen. Now, I'm not saying who, or accusing anyone, but *whoever* it was took a gallon of rocky road ice cream out of the freezer and sat in here and ate almost half of it." Without moving his head, his eyes slipped over to Max. "Half!" he said again in either disbelief or admiration.

"Coulda been anyone," Max said as he studied his second brownie.

"True, true. Coulda been anyone." Dave seemed to be thinking this over. He picked up his glass, held it up to the light, took a gulp of milk, set it back down, and wiped his mouth with a napkin. "`Course, the chocolate smudges on the door handles and all the way down the hall leading to Max's room were a pretty good clue," he said without looking at Max.

She had to admit, that did sound like Max. Even on a good day, he was a tornado. He had only to walk through a room to leave a wake of destruction in his path. Once, when he'd been playing with his Match-Box cars in a mud puddle, she had to hose him off before she'd let him come inside. And he did so love Rocky Road ice cream.

Maggie nodded and said, "Always was his favorite."

After fifteen minutes and a refill of murky pond-water, Maggie got up to leave. "I'll walk you back to your room," she told Max and picked up their cups to put on the stainless steel serving ledge.

She turned to Dave. "You going our way?"

"Naw," I've got to wait for the guy to come and replace the lock on the kitchen door," he smirked, his eyes still twinkling with amusement. "And this time it'll be a better one. Not that

Mickey Mouse job that any old midnight rambler can break into with a nail file."

He raised his eyebrows and directed his gaze toward Max. "Or a kitchen table knife?"

Max peaked one corner of his mouth, both defiant and teasing.

Dave turned to leave. "Oh well, see you later, Max."

On the way to his room, Max started talking more. He told Maggie about a nurse he thought was pretty and some of the patients he thought were idiots. Maggie considered that visit successful. That time, at least, he really did seem like he was getting better. But each visit over the next week and a half was different. More ups and downs than a fiddler's elbow, as Clive was fond of saying.

The next time she went to see him he was so sullen and dour she could barely pull two words out of him. But on the visit after that, he talked so fast and furious she could barely get two words in.

The two-week hold was almost up when she went again. This time she had called ahead to ask if she could see the doctor and timed it so she could visit with Max before she saw him.

She slipped into the closest parking place and once again trudged up the the flight of concrete stairs to the second floor.

What will he be like this time?

She tapped on his door. When there was no answer, she cracked it open a little. "Max, you there?" She stuck her head it.

Max was standing by the window. The blind was closed, and he was peering through two slats.

"What are you looking at, honey," Maggie said as she walked over.

"There are a couple of guys down there by the dumpster. Been there all day." Max's tone was low and conspiratorial.

Maggie studied Max's face. She'd seen this look before. "What are they doing?" Maggie moved the blind slightly to look out.

Not again!

"Careful!" Max blurted in a loud whisper.

"But it looks like they're loading the dumpster on their truck to empty it." Maggie dropped the shade and turned to

180

Max. "It looks like they're garbage men. I don't think it's anything to be worried about, hon."

When he didn't move, Maggie said, "Come on Max, let's go get a cup of coffee or something."

"Can't," Max said, but turned away from the window.

And there it was again. The tough guy, the thug, the victim being stalked.

Maggie plopped down on the bed, bouncing once or twice to get comfortable. She knew she'd run out of things to say. She didn't want to be condescending, and she didn't want to be understanding. It wouldn't make any difference.

She didn't want to play this game anymore.

She sat in silence for a few minutes while Max kept a vigil on the alley below. She had decided to leave when there was a soft rap on the door and Dr. Friedman poked his head in.

"Mind if I come in and talk to you and your mom, Max?"

Max immediately came to the bed and sat beside Maggie, the threat outside the window forgotten.

The doctor sat on the twin bed opposite them and rested his hands on his knees. "Well," he said after a lengthy pause, "how are you feeling today, Max?"

"Fine," Max said with a tone that implied it was an unnecessary question.

"I see...and how would you feel about going home soon?"

"Okay."

"Do you feel like you're better, Max?"

Max looked at him as if that was just another pointless question and nodded.

Dr. Friedman asked Max a few more questions, all of which Max answered logically and intelligently.

And Maggie watched the entire show. As they talked, she slumped lower both physically and emotionally. She felt utterly defeated. She knew there was little she could do, but she had to give it one last try. She sucked in air and pulled herself upright, shoulders back. "It's not that I don't want him home," she began.

Doctor Friedman's eyebrows rose slightly. She turned to Max and picked up his hand. "It's not that I don't want you home, Max, but, well, I'm not sure you're ready."

She turned back to the doctor. His eyebrows were still elevated. Was there nothing she could say to help him see what she saw? She sighed and deflated like a party balloon with a pinhole. Her eyes dropped to her lap, she let go of Max's hand, and almost in a whisper, said, "I just don't think he's ready."

Doctor Friedman studied Maggie for a few seconds, then Max. "What do you think, Max?" Pause. "Do you think you're ready?"

Maggie picked up Max Friday after school and carted him home along with armloads of essays to correct. Earlier that week she had assigned some of her students take-home exams, critical essays on a novel they had read in class that year. To make it easy on herself, they were to be one-page minimum and two-pages maximum. Still, if most were turned in, she knew she was facing forty hours of correcting before the end of that week. Between those and the in-class semester finals, Maggie knew she'd better figure out a way to dog paddle through a sink-or-swim situation. If Max continued to stabilize, she could use Saturdays and Sundays to catch up, then tread water until spring break.

She put the folders in four neat stacks on the kitchen table, tapping in the corners to even them. She stood back, then straightened them again, making sure they were arranged in exact alignment. Maybe she had no control over Max, but damn it all, she did over these papers!

Maggie pulled up a chair and reached for the first essay. If it went well with Max at home, she could do it. Maybe she had been wrong. Maybe he was better than she thought. Maybe he would continue to improve. There was always maybe.

CHAPTER 42

I feel like shit. I wish I could fuckin' die. I could kill myself, then they'd see. Don't they know? I don't feel right. I don't feel right. Max's hands flew to his head. He squeezed his eyes tight and tried to shut out the voices. He dropped his hands to the workshop bench stained with oil and scattered with screwdrivers, wrenches, and hammers. *Maybe I should just do it.* Max glared at his left hand, palm flat, fingers spread on the bench. *Fuckin' pinkie finger. I hate it when people stick those out when they drink tea or something. Like they're all fancy or something. Like they're better than everyone else. I fuckin' hate those people.* His eyes pivoted from his hand to an ax leaning against a stud, then back to his hand. He reached for the ax. It felt cool and heavy. It felt right. *Maybe I should just do it. It's either that or kill myself. What choice do I have? Maybe they'll notice then. Maybe they'll see I need help.*

All the way home from school Maggie's mind was spinning with things that needed to be done in the next three weeks.

Finish correcting essays, review literary devices, let's see, personification, oxymoron, symbolism, oh, and critical analysis. Okay, there's ethos, logos, and... What was the other one? Sounded like another one of the Three Musketeers? Oh yeah, pathos!

She turned onto the half-mile gravel road leading to her house.

Oh, and record grades, call parents, lesson plans.

183

She stopped at the row of mailboxes half way down the road and picked up an assortment of flyers and bills.

And then there's Max.

She got back in the car. He'd been home from Vancouver Memorial two weeks and so far was pretty mellow, but he still stayed in his room most of the time, laughed little and moped lots. There had been no violence, no outbreaks, but his mood was disturbing. She tried to get him out of the house, if only to run errands with her or grab a bite at Burgerville. But as soon as they returned, he went straight to his room where he lolled the rest of the day. Jonathan often came over while she was at work and was still there when she came home.

On some level she was glad Max had someone to keep him company, and she knew there were times Jonathan had helped Max. As she had come in the door a week ago, he was yelling, "Come on dumb-ass! You look like a fuckin' robot! Move your arms like this."

When she looked in Max's room, Jonathan was demonstrating how he needed to move his arms back and forth as if he was grasping parallel bars when he walked. "Pretend you're a gymnast, dumb-ass! Walk like that!"

And it had helped. The side effects of some of the meds Max took made him stiff and clumsy. More or less...well...robotic, just as Jonathan had said.

Most of the time, however, he took off as soon as he heard Maggie come in. She had to admit it made her nervous and on edge that he was there so often. Would Max take off again? Would he start doing drugs or drinking again? Maggie was never quite sure what might happen with Jonathan around.

But right now, things certainly could have been worse. Braxton was into track season and his coach was grooming him to go to state for the high jump again. Other than that, he did homework and spent most of his time at friends' houses.

And her father was behaving himself as far as she knew. She forced herself to call him once a week, and even though he was usually on his way to being well-oiled, there had been no more emergency midnight runs lately.

So, Maggie thought as she turned into the driveway, yes, it certainly could be—

"I didn't do it! I didn't do it!" Jonathan flew to the car as Maggie pulled up.

What the hell?

"Didn't do what, Jonathan?" Maggie yanked on the brake. Jonathan's eyes were wide with terror.

"I didn't tell him to do it! I didn't want him to! He just did it!"

"Jonathan!" Maggie yelled, "Just tell me what you're..."

Jonathan's mouth gaped and his eyes were riveted on something beyond her.

Maggie's head twisted and followed his gaze to the workshop.

Max stood in the doorway. His eyes were black holes, sucking in everything that came near. His sneer was menacing. Elbow bent, he held one hand, fingers splayed, in front of his face. He flaunted it like a trophy. Blood ran down his arm.

It took a moment for it to register, then Maggie saw a red stump where one finger used to be.

In two strides she was next to him, guiding him to the car. "Go get a towel!" she yelled at Jonathan who stood frozen. "Any towel! Now!"

She got Max in the car, wrapped the towel around his hand and placed the fingers of his good hand on his wrist. "Push there," she said and clamped down on it.

They left Jonathan in the carport, his pale face and saucer eyes diminishing in her rearview mirror, as they tore out of the driveway and back towards town.

Maggie knew the county roads well enough to drive them blindfolded, but at this speed the sharp curves were treacherous. She skidded around them and barely slowed for stop signs. They came to the main road into town. She gave a fleeting look to the left, slid around the corner into the closest lane and accelerated. The speed limit was 35. She looked at the speedometer. It read 55.

They approached the crossroads of Mill Plain Boulevard and SR 500. Maggie scanned the confusion of stoplights, turn-lane arrows, and walk signs. "Shit! Shit! Shit!" She slowed for the red light, then blasted her horn and bullied her way through the intersection. Cars screeched to a halt or swerved out of the

185

way. People stared, but no one honked or yelled. Probably too startled to react, she figured. Her mind was racing. She didn't know what she'd do if police stopped her. Maybe she could roll down her window and yell, "Hospital!" Then she'd have Max hold up his bloody hand. Would they shoot her tires out if she didn't stop? Would they just ticket her?

Stop it! Focus!

She glanced at Max. He had taken the towel off and had his fingers spread in front of his face again. "Max," she sputtered. Then she saw his eyes. She knew it would do no good to tell him what to do.

She swung into the Southwest Washington hospital entrance, pulled up to the emergency room doors, and rolled down her window. What do you say in a situation like this? "My son lost a finger," she hollered at an attendant leaning against a post. He sauntered over to the car, unrushed, cocky. As he approached, Max lowered his hand. "Put your hand back up, Max," Maggie ordered.

The man bent down and peered in the open window. "Oh!" he said, "Oh dear!" He snapped his fingers and motioned to another assistant and then pointed at a wheelchair in the entry.

"I'll be right in," Maggie yelled as they got Max into the wheelchair.

By the time she got inside, Max was already on a gurney in triage. A doctor bent over him. "Well, what happened here, son?" he was asking as she approached.

Max glared.

"What'd you do, have an accident or something?"

Max glared.

"Yes, I guess you could call it that," Maggie panted behind him.

The doctor turned and gave Maggie a brief smile. "You got the finger?" he asked.

Maggie slapped her forehead. "Oh no," she moaned, "I forgot all about it. I'll call my neighbor right now."

"Have them put it on ice and get it here as soon as they can. Not sure yet if we can use it."

In less than an hour, Maggie's neighbor Roger sheepishly peeked into the bay where she sat with Max. He carried a

Tupperware bowl with a "blue airtight seal that keeps food fresh," Maggie thought ironically. "Ah, perfect for all my storage needs," she quipped.

Roger looked at her askance, as if he thought she might have had a couple of drinks, but Maggie had never been so sober. She'd been trying to talk to Max, or at least sit with him to reassure him he would be all right, but she was wasting her time. He wouldn't listen to her. He kept trying to get up, and when she'd gently push him back down, he would ramble on and on about his hatred for police, doctors, nurses, teachers, equestrians, church people, store people, and all people who drive vans or ride unicycles.

Once she knew he was going to be okay physically, her fear ebbed and her frustration intensified. By the time Roger got there, she was ready to take that damned finger and throw it in the hazardous waste receptacle. Instead, she said, "Thank you, Roger. I'm so sorry I had to call you."

"Oh, that's okay, Maggie. Braxton was home when I got there. He helped me. In fact, he's the one that found...it." Roger started to hand her the bowl filled with ice and the offending digit, but Maggie held both hands in front of her. "Would you mind giving that to the nurse?" She pointed to the nurse's station.

Poor Braxton. Of all the people to search for a severed finger, he would hate it the most. This wasn't going to help his aversion to blood, that was for sure.

Roger delivered the bowl to the nurse and came back. She knew he wanted to ask her what had happened, but she sidestepped his questions. "I'll let you know how he's doing as soon as I'm able to, Roger. Thanks again."

When they had the missing finger, the medical team went to work. They wheeled Max away, and while most mothers would pray their sons would be all right, Maggie prayed only that he would stay on the gurney and stop talking.

An hour later, an orderly wheeled him back, hand bandaged. He straightened the sheets, adjusted the IV, and checked the monitor. And, Maggie noticed, avoided eye contact with her. "The doctor will be right in to talk to you," he stammered and left.

The doctor didn't seem much more comfortable talking to Maggie. "We patched him up, but we didn't reattach the finger." He picked up Max's hand and examined the bandage. "We don't think he's..." He paused, looked at Max, and frowned. "A very good candidate for it."

He didn't have to say more. Maggie could only guess what Max must seem like to them: angry, stubborn, unstable, and well, just plain unlikable. She wondered what had taken place in that operating room. Did they have to strap him down? Had he railed at them? Had he cursed the establishment? Maggie could have asked or explained, but by then she was too void of anything even resembling gumption to care. Whether they knew why he was like that, was not her concern. "Yes," she sighed. "I think you're right."

The doctor softened a little. He allowed a transitory smile, and for a moment, Maggie detected a hint of understanding. "There's no reason to keep him here," he said. "Physically, he'll do okay." He put Max's hand down gently. "Unless he's a concert pianist," he added.

"No, no concert anything in this family," Maggie said, hoping it would lighten the mood a little. She thought of Max's love of guitar, but even that shouldn't be impacted, she decided. His fingering hand was unaffected, but his strumming hand would have to do with three fingers and one thumb. It would be fine.

Maggie took Max home late into the night. She was torn. He needed looking after while his finger mended, but he also badly needed a mental health evaluation. Before she left the hospital, they gave her a list of dos and don'ts. *Do* monitor him closely that night. *Do* keep his arm in the sling. *Do* give him pain medication as needed. *Don't* engage in any heavy activity for a week. *Don't* remove the bandage. *Don't* get the wound or bandage wet.

When they got home, Max went quietly to his room and closed the door. Each time Maggie checked on him he seemed to be sleeping soundly, so she lugged a couple of blankets and her pillow to the living room, curled up on the couch, and kept a sleepy vigil as she watched Johnny Carson.

188

Far into the night, after *The Late Night Show* had ended, after the "Star Spangled Banner" had sung its last strain reminding the night owls about the "home of the brave," Maggie fell asleep. When she woke, she was disoriented. It was still dark; the TV sizzled and hummed in monotone as the station's identification lit the room with an eerie glow. Maggie opened one eye, saw nothing out of the ordinary, and started to get up to turn off the television.

But something didn't feel right. Her body did an involuntary shudder, and goosebumps traveled down her arms. "Hello?" she said meekly into the darkness that fringed the room. She shaded her eyes from the glare of the TV and tried to adjust them to the dark places. "Max?"

She reached above her and clicked on the lamp next to the couch. She shot to a standing position. She teetered a moment, then fell backwards onto the couch again. Max was standing in the doorway. His bandages had been ripped off, and he was flaunting his hand like a trophy in front of his face. He was silent but scowled through his fingers at Maggie, his eyes as black and toxic as she had ever seen them.

"Oh, Max. It's...good to see you."

Instinctively, she knew she had to tread lightly.

"I see you took off your bandages." She tried to sound casual, but she couldn't keep the quiver out of her voice. "You think we'd better go into town and get that taken care of?"

As quickly as before, Max turned and went out to the car. Maggie was thankful she had slept in her clothes. The keys were still in her pocket, her sandals next to her on the floor, so she was out the door and into the car almost before Max could get settled.

How odd, she thought, that once again he would go with her. Especially given his obvious delusional state. Was there some part of Max that was still rational? Had she given him enough support to still warrant trust despite his psychosis? She hoped this was true, but that's all it was...hope.

They drove straight to the psych ward at Vancouver Memorial, no point beating around the bush. This is where he belonged, she was sure of it. Maggie swerved into the parking

189

lot, slammed the car into park, and started to get out, but Max sat still, staring straight ahead.

Maggie sagged for a moment, but recovered quickly. "You know this place, Max," she said brightly. "These people have always been nice to you. Remember Dave?"

Max's eyes slid over to the small entry door, and Maggie went on. "He's funny, isn't he? He likes you, Max. He thinks you're funny too, you know."

Max made no indication he was going anywhere. Finally in desperation, Maggie said, "Come on, Max. You're killin' me here." She scowled at him. "You going to make me go in there all by myself?"

Max still stared at the door.

"Damn it, Max!"

And at that moment, Max got out of the car and walked directly to the door.

Maggie scrambled after him and caught up just as he was raising his hand to show a nurse in the hall who appeared to be doing some clerical work. The nurse gaped at Max's hand, then peered around to Maggie standing behind him and raised her brows in a tacit question. "Ah, this is Maxim Axline, and he needs an evaluation," Maggie said. "He's been here before." Maggie noticed the papers she was thumbing through. "You have a file on him."

The nurse seemed to be stymied at first, but like the professional she was, she simply said, "Well, that's good, Maxim. I think you came to the right place. Why don't you come with me and we'll get someone to talk to you right away."

She put one hand lightly on his elbow and led Max down the hall. "I'll come back in a while and talk to...is that your mom?" She glanced over her shoulder and smiled. As they went into a room, Maggie heard her say, "Hey, that's quite a hand you got there. How did that happen?"

Max answered, but Maggie couldn't make out what he said. It didn't matter. Her pulse slowed as she went back to the miniscule waiting room and collapsed onto the stiff yellow sofa. Then, with the sudden release of anxiety, came a steady flow of saltwater down her face, as if it had been stored in a reservoir behind her eyes. When the floodgate finally opened, it liberated

190

a long overdue basin of emotion. It was both distressing and cathartic. Maggie was aware of the odd blend of feelings. Huh, she though wryly, oxymoron. Good example.

Forty-five minutes later, the nurse came to the waiting room and sat down next to Maggie. By then Maggie had stopped crying, but her swollen, red eyes must have been a dead giveaway. "Pretty rough, huh?" she said and put a hand over Maggie's.

This sent Maggie into another bout of releasing-more-water-over-the-dam, which got in the way of her words, so she nodded.

The nurse patted Maggie's hand. "That's okay," she said. "You sit there. I'll do the talking for a while."

Maggie sniffed and nodded again.

"Now, I can't say for sure, but it looks like Maxim's having a psychotic break again." She scrutinized Maggie's face to make sure she understood. "But that's really not for me to say. The doctor is on an emergency call right now, but we expect him back any minute. My guess is we'll probably admit Maxim today, for a while at least."

Maggie managed to say "good," then wiped at her eyes and blew her nose with the shredded Kleenex she had balled up in her fist.

"The only thing is," the nurse went on, "he got a bit out of control so we had to strap him down. But, if you want to, you can go sit with him until the doctor comes in."

"'kay." Maggie snuffled again and followed the nurse down a cold corridor lined with pale yellow subway tiles capped with green bullnose half way up the walls. They turned into the sparse room where Max was held. His hands and feet were secured with thick leather straps. A pillow had been propped under his head. "Hi, Max," Maggie said. "How you doin', sweetheart?"

Max turned his face to hers. It no longer had the look of insolence. In its place was the face of the five-year-old boy she remembered getting lost in the supermarket many years ago. He had been frightened then and he was frightened now, but this time when he gazed up at Maggie and asked, "Can we go

191

home now?" Maggie had to say, "No, honey. No, we can't go home."

CHAPTER 43

The next morning, even before Maggie could get back to see him, he was transported by ambulance directly to the hospital in Steilacoom. It was probably best, she thought. Apparently he had raised quite a fuss during the night, fluctuating between yelling and lashing out at anyone who came close to him and spells of wailing and crying about the approach of... something; they weren't sure what.

When she talked to Doctor Friedman later in the day, he told her Max was at risk of hurting himself again and had deteriorated too far to have a successful translation back into society anytime soon. That's how he put it, "translation back into society." Maggie thought it an odd choice of words, but she was pretty sure he was right.

For the first few weeks of Max's absence, it was difficult to juggle visiting him and teaching and all that came with it before spring break. But as time passed and the atmosphere relaxed at home, her neck and shoulders unknotted, and she and Braxton reacquainted themselves with what Maggie thought of as a "normal" life. Sure, there were still the twice-monthly trips to Steilacoom, and it took a few months to completely adjust, but finally, Maggie once again established a schedule that would eventually become as familiar to her as the cycles of the moon were to the pull of the sea.

Yet, within that sameness, each visit was a little different and variegated with colorful, yet often disturbing, episodes. For Maggie it became almost like a play with unpredictable and vibrant characters that ran the emotional gamut: one week ecstatically joyful; the next, in the depths of despair. And as the weeks turned to months, Maggie realized that this was a drama without an end. The players changed from time to time, but the troupe carried on the comedy and tragedy of the illness.

But it wasn't until mid-July that Maggie truly felt a paradigm shift. At first it was awkward, then it became more familiar, then comfortable, then routine. Then it became a way of life.

Max, too, had begun to adjust to his environment, although Maggie often thought about how hard it would be to become stabilized in an environment that seemed far from stable. But other than private care, this was the best thing for him. As far as she could tell, the hospital personnel treated him, guided him, and cared for him humanely and intelligently. If he was ever going to be well enough to come home, this was the place to do it.

So, on her way to Steilacoom one balmy Saturday morning in the middle of July, the traffic was light, her coffee was strong and hot, and Maggie's life seemed relatively ordinary. Or at least as ordinary as it could be if one were going to visit a son in a mental institution.

She cranked the wheel to the left, thumped through a chain of connecting chuckholes spanning the entrance, and drove the length of Western State Hospital to the west end. This time, Max was in a different unit. From what she could pick up, the clients were assigned to wards according to the type and severity of the illness. C3, B2, E4. Each had a little different atmosphere and different rules and restrictions, but to a visitor, the variances were subtle. Maggie was glad E4 where Max was kept this time didn't face the main parking lot. At least she didn't have to look up and see his face in the window every time she left.

Her tennis shoes squeaked on the worn marble tiles as she walked briskly to the elevators. No point putting this off, she thought as she pushed the "up" button. "C'mon, c'mon, c'mon," she muttered and jabbed at it again.

"Out of order," someone said as he slipped behind her and turned to go down the stairs next to the entrance. Maggie scanned the elevator for a sign, punched the button one more time, then sighed and chugged up the stairs to E4. On the fourth floor, she leaned panting against the banister then rang the buzzer to be let into the ward.

"Hi, Jesus," she wheezed as the doors swung open.

"Elevator still not working?" He grinned as they walked down the hall.

Maggie was thankful she had found another ally. Like Dave, it was a familiar face she could count on to boost her spirits. His demeanor was playful and his accent was thick, but they had no trouble communicating. When she first met him, he told her his name was Jesus, then added, "You know, like the savior, but not so santo," and smiled broadly at a pun he had probably made a thousand times.

"So," Maggie said as they walked toward the nurses' station to sign in, "anything new and exciting happen in the last two weeks?"

When Jesus paused, Maggie glanced at him. His brows were furrowed and his usual sunny expression was subdued. He seemed to be taking the question seriously, then suddenly he brightened. "Oh, you know, the same old stuff, mas o menos."

"And Max?"

"Oh, he's okay," he said, then after a few seconds added, "he's been very tranquilo... uh...quiet," he clarified.

"Well, that's good, isn't it?"

"Yes, that is good," Jesus said simply and, Maggie thought, unconvincingly.

"I'll go get him," he added and veered off toward Max's room as Maggie went to sign in.

Usually, the nurses' station was a hubbub of chatter, laughter, and covert inside jokes followed by furtive winks or a twinkle in someone's eye. And Maggie couldn't blame them. She was sure one of the questions on their work applications had to be: Do you have a talent for seeing humor in even the most tragic aspects of the human condition? If it wasn't, it should be.

Melanie was manning the nurses' station that day. She was usually jovial and breezy with a willingness to be diverted from her duties if she had the opportunity to listen to or tell a good anecdote. But today, she seemed to be studying a chart intently and was anything but cheery.

"Hi, Melanie," Maggie said as she reached for the pencil perpetually attached in bondage to the sign-in clipboard. "Anything new in the trenches lately?"

Melanie glanced up, "What? Oh, hi, Maggie," she said and immediately bowed her head again.

"Here are Max's cigarettes." Maggie put two cartons on the counter. "Hopefully these'll last him two weeks. I think they would if he'd stop giving them to the entire ward like I'm made out of money."

But Melanie was still engrossed in the chart. "Uh huh," she mumbled, but didn't look up.

Curious.

"Okay, I'll leave them..." Maggie's voice trailed off as she put the cartons behind the rim of the counter.

Maggie strolled into the lounge and sank into an orange-and-brown-plaid, butt-sprung sofa. She didn't mind waiting for Max. Watching and listening to the hum of the hospital was always interesting and, she had to admit, sometimes amusing. That day it was relatively quiet, but there was a nervousness around the edges she couldn't account for. Maybe it was something in the anxious faces or the slippered shuffle of the feet that passed by on their way to the smoking room. A few spoke to her: "Are you new?" "Do you have a cigarette?" "I'm Sandra, but they call me Spider. What's your name?"

But exchanges were brief and impersonal until one young man, as thin and wispy as a reed, came up to her. "Are you Max's mom?" he asked.

"Yep, I'm Maggie," she said and held out her hand. "You know Max?"

He didn't take her hand or answer her question, but dropped down next to her. "Did you hear what happened?" he said with the air of a person who has a tasty tidbit to share.

"No," Maggie said, expecting yet another flight of someone's imagination. "What happened?"

"Do you know Andre?" he asked, prolonging the morsel.

Maggie shook her head and waited.

His eyes slipped back and forth and he leaned in. "He killed himself," he whispered and waited for her reaction.

Maggie wasn't sure what to say. Did it really happen? She stared at him, not sure of how to respond.

"You know," he said and tilted his head to the side, then pulled at an imaginary rope above it and made a gagging sound. "Aaugg!" he choked out and lolled his tongue out of his mouth.

Maggie pulled back. Was this fact or fantasy? Given the slightly skewed behavior of everyone today, including the staff, it might be fact. Her eyes widened and her eyebrows rose. "He did? When did..." she began but stopped when Max scuffed over. The reed stood quickly and Max took his place on the sofa.

"Hi, honey," Maggie said and started to hug him, but something in his expression stopped her. "Max?" She put her hand tentatively on his knee.

Max's mouth hung open and his vacant eyes shifted first to her hand, then slid up to the man standing next to them. "Go away," he said impassively, and the patient turned, strolled to the other side of the room, and flopped into a chair where he sat watching them suspiciously.

"Max?" Maggie said again. "Are you all right?"

Max nodded. She followed his line of vision back to the man across the room. "He said something happened to Andre? Do you know Andre?"

Max nodded again. The lobby had cleared except for the three of them, and after a few minutes, the reed also got up and left. An eerie quiet spread over the room. Max sat stiff and unresponsive, and Maggie didn't know how to span the silence that separated them. She sensed it was best not to pursue the conversation about Andre, so she said, "Well. So. Tell me about your week, Max."

When Max didn't answer, she tried, "Hey, I've been meaning to ask you, how's the food here, anyway?"

Nothing.

"You know, I think maybe you've gained a pound or—"

"He wanted to know how to loop a belt over a pipe." Max dropped his eyes to the floor. His expression was lifeless, his voice flat.

"What? Who—"

197

"He asked me. I didn't know he was going to hang himself."

"You mean Andre? Oh, Max, I'm so—"

"I was walking by and there he was. Just hanging there."

"Ah, geeze, Max. I'm so sorry." Maggie's heart rose to her throat. She wanted to put her arms around him and make the hurt go away. Instead, she said, "Is there anything I can do for you? Do you want to talk about it?"

Max glanced first at Maggie, then at the hall that led to the smoking lounge. "I want a cigarette." He stood and began walking in that direction.

"Man, so do I. And a stiff drink," she mumbled and caught up with him. She clasped his hand in hers, acutely aware of one missing finger. Together they walked hand in hand in silence.

CHAPTER 44

When the phone calls began again, Maggie accepted all of them. She had felt so helpless when Max told her about Andre, she was encouraged that he would want to call her to at least talk. They began as once a day, usually in the evening, but after a few weeks it was twice, three times, and soon four to five times a day she would pick up the receiver to the familiar, "I have a collect call from Maxim Axline, will you accept the charges?"

Just as his last time at Western State, her phone bill was growing like an overfed albatross. Still, she hated to turn him down. At first, when the operator connected them, the familiar routine began. Max would say hello and, with one or two words, answer her questions. "How are you doing today, Max?" "Have you been outside?" "What did you have for lunch?" Are you out of cigarettes yet?" His answers varied between, "Fine," "Yes," "No," and "I don't remember."

She knew better. In her gut, she knew she would have to eventually stop the calls. But Andre's suicide weighed on her mind. Would Max try something like that? At least if he was calling, she knew he was still alive. And Maggie figured that between her visits to him, the calls were at least a familiar connection to Max's "regular" life, a more ordinary existence she didn't want him to completely lose touch with.

For a while, she played the charade of normalcy. However, as the weeks clicked by, his calls got more abundant and his answers got more scant until eventually, when Maggie accepted one of his calls, there was only deafening silence on the other

199

end. Yet she would keep up a one-sided conversation for a while, then say, "Okay, Max, I'm going to hang up now. I love you. Bye, honey. I love you. Bye," and force herself to put the receiver down.

One day when she opened the albatross from Ma Bell, the millstone had become so heavy she realized she had to make a choice: continue accepting Max's calls or continue to feed Braxton and herself.

Still, she didn't stop right away. The first few times he called she talked to him about it, let him know why she couldn't continue talking to him long distance, then she set a definite time after which she was not going to accept his calls, then counted down. "Okay, Max, you can make three more calls, and then I'm not going to be able to accept any more." Then, "Now remember, the next call is your last one." Finally, when the operator said, "I have a collect call, will you accept the charges?" Maggie said, "No." She had to say "no" fifteen more times before the calls stopped.

Getting no more collect calls was a mixed blessing. True, Maggie no longer had to sell her soul to AT&T for an equitable payment plan, but she couldn't help thinking that although she hadn't had in-depth conversations with Max, when he had called she at least knew he was on the other end of the line listening to her. This gave her a feeling of closeness and a modicum of ease. Then again, when he no longer called, there was always the "out of sight, out of mind" theory, or in this case "out of contact, out of mind." Between visits, because she didn't "talk" to him, she could keep up the charade that maybe, just maybe, this time he was improving. Unfortunately, when she saw him face to face, the farce dissolved into reality, and she knew he was not.

Meanwhile, Braxton was making the most of his last summer at home before taking off for college. Maggie had saved enough to send him with some friends to Hawaii after graduation, where she hoped he could relax and mend before taking off for Washington State University. And, although she knew Wazzu was only 270 miles away in Pullman, she had mixed feelings about that, too. She was thankful Braxton had

200

the opportunity to experience life away from home, but she also knew she was going to miss him like crazy.

But she'd be okay. She often reminded herself she would be back to work before she knew it. Then, as Clive would say, she'd be busier than a one-legged man in an ass-kicking contest, so maybe she wouldn't have time to miss him. Besides, it wasn't like Braxton wouldn't be coming home for holidays.

Maggie didn't want to think about the school year starting again. Between tying up loose ends last year and getting ready for the new one, she had six weeks to rejuvenate, and while her sleep was deeper and her laughter more frequent, an undercurrent of stress was always there, just below the whir of life. And even though there was a routine to her life, every two weeks, two days before she drove to see Max, her angst ramped up and stayed that way until two days after she came home.

During that four days, her stomach did its own little version of dancing to Hava Nigila, undeterred by Tums, a bland diet, or her continuum of groans, tears, and swearing. But for a good nine or ten days between, it settled into a pattern of acceptable behavior.

This gave her more time to visit at least briefly with Braxton as he flitted between home, dates, friends, and summer sports. And even though it also gave her more time to spend with her dad, she only saw him twice that summer: once on Father's Day and once on his birthday. Both times, on her way down the ramp, she chatted briefly with Mrs. Popovich watering geraniums with her can-on-a-pole device, but neither time did she run into Dee.

There were, however, obvious clues Dee was still in the picture: florescent lipstick rimming a highball glass in the kitchen sink, white ostrich feather mules peeking out from under the bed, and the amalgamated stench of a cheap Eau de Parfum and cigarettes lingering in the closeness of James Parker's living room. This prompted Maggie to leave the entry door open and fan the door in the living room at the other end of the houseboat to let the crisp breeze off the river blow through.

"What in thee hell are you doing, Magpie?" was her father's reaction.

201

When Maggie hedged that she was hot, he grumbled about the injustice of him being old enough to have a daughter going through menopause and consoled himself by pouring another gin and tonic.

More often, however, she dropped in on Clive where she watched the progress of radishes and string beans in his garden and helped chase crows away from sprouting corn until the stalks grew tall and the silk turned the color of August. Each time she left, she took with her a sense of composure, along with bushels of fresh produce, including enough zucchini to feed her entire neighborhood and then some.

Her visits to Max were less satisfying. Several times she had tried to see his doctor, but he was elusive. Maggie was sure it wasn't intentional. The staff was spread pretty thin and Max was, after all, a ward of the state. As far as their records or obligations went, they were not required to communicate with his family. Still, the support staff was considerate about answering her questions and making her feel she was still a part of Max's life.

It was well into summer before she finally made contact with Doctor Silva, a natty dresser with a penchant for flamboyant ties. "Mrs. Axline," he said as he rose to meet her in his office. The cordial extension of his hand, the grin peeking out of a scruffy salt and pepper beard, and the good-natured tenor of his voice put Maggie at ease.

"Nice tie," she said as she took his hand.

"Ya think so?"

No she didn't think so. But it was just so blatantly peculiar, it was the first thing that came to her mind.

Doctor Silva sat down and picked up the end of his tie and studied the upside-down pink flamingo sipping a daiquiri under a metallic blue palm tree. "My wife gave it to me." He chuckled. "I wasn't sure about the drink part of it, but then I thought, 'Ah, what the hell!'" He spoke with the confidence of a man who had faced the world and no longer worried about what it thought of him.

"Well, you know..." Maggie studied the sunglasses on the flamingo and searched for a suitable response. "It certainly is...appropriate...for...the summer!" she finished brightly.

202

"That's what I thought!" he said, slapping the palm of his hand down on the desk, immediately securing a bond of tie-expertise between them.

"Well, I'm sure you want to know how Max is doing." He swung his chair around to a vintage 1950s metal cabinet and used both hands and considerable effort to pull out Max's file. "Sorry," he said as he flopped the meaty folder on his desk, "forgot to get this out."

He really didn't need it. Maggie noticed that even with it in front of him, he never referred to it, never even opened it. "I met with Max this morning," he began, "but I still don't see much improvement." He rested his hand on the file as if he could read it by osmosis.

Still?

She had never seen or talked to Dr. Silva before now, but it sounded like he was the one that had been keeping tabs on him since he'd been here. She wasn't surprised at his evaluation, but she was disappointed. She had hoped there would be something more than what she had seen herself, maybe something only an expert with a trained eye and experience saw that she didn't. "So," she said, "he hasn't stabilized at all?"

"Mmmmmm..." His chin crinkled as he pursed his lips. "No. Not much that we can see."

We?

And as if he could read her thoughts, he said, "We have been discussing Max's case in our department meetings. And, I guess I can't say we haven't seen any improvement at all. We are trying new medication—some new combinations—and he has responded to a small degree. I don't think he is as delusional as when he first came, so that's good. But he definitely has reduced motivation and flat emotional expressiveness."

"Yeah, I noticed that," Maggie said. "It seems like he's walking around like a zombie or something. He kind of looks at me, but he doesn't talk to me, or..." She thought a moment, and sagged. "He won't hug me," she almost whined. Then she heard herself, and she sounded pitiful. She gave herself a mental slap and fought back the tears that threatened to puddle. She straightened herself. "I hate that," she concluded decisively.

"Well, we're going to do all we can to bring him around," Silva said and with one finger casually inched the box of tissues closer to Maggie.

"But what if..." the unfinished question hung in the air. It felt like suspended shards of glass waiting to slice her last bit of hope into slivers.

"I won't lie to you," the doctor said. "We have clients who have been here for years. But," he peered into Maggie's eyes, "the field of antipsychotics is really taking off. They're testing all sorts of new stuff right now. If he's not better next week, we're going to try adding an antidepressant. That may help some."

"So, there is a chance he'll get better." Maggie said this like a statement rather than a question. Maybe it was wishful thinking on her part, but she wanted desperately to believe there was still hope.

"Yes," he answered point-blank. "With everything we're trying there's a good chance of that." Dr. Silva lost eye contact with her and patted the monstrosity of a file in front of him. "You know," he began, almost as if he was talking to himself. "I think this is one of the hardest illnesses families have to face. It's so...damned unpredictable." He shook his head. "People are always asking me for a prognosis." He looked back at Maggie. "The prognosis is that there is no prognosis. Anything can happen. We simply do not know enough about it yet."

Maggie wilted. This isn't exactly what she wanted to hear, but she appreciated Dr. Silva's no-sugar-coating approach. Still, she had to believe Max would recover. She had to, for her own sake, keep that spark of optimism alive, no matter how murky it sometimes got.

That afternoon, on the ride home, Maggie gave herself her mother's pull-yourself-up-by-the-bootstraps pep talk and ended with a reinforcement to face one thing at a time. Yet, being a realist, she knew if and when that time came, if there was no more hope, she would have to confront that, too, and get on with her life, however challenging that might be.

There was little change in Max's condition that summer. Mentally Maggie wasn't ready for school to start again, but she figured when you have no choice, you hold your nose and jump into icy water feet first. The middle of August she splashed back into her classroom. Who knows, she told herself, with Max's situation being so unpredictable, she might have to tread water later. With the September flood closing in fast, best to get more done while she could. No point in moping around the house waiting for a change in Max. No point dwelling on Braxton's departure. Life goes on.

And, as she knew he would, the first week in September Braxton packed his clothes, stereo, coffeepot, a roll of stamps attached to a vague promise to write—and, Maggie suspected, a fake ID—into his red, 1981 Toyota Starlet hatchback, all 64 horsepower of her, and embarked on a new phase of life.

And Maggie, too, entered a new phase of life. One without either son at home.

CHAPTER 45

Winter was wicked. The wind blew in hostile gales through the Columbia River Gorge, the ground froze solid, and Maggie turned her collar against the inclement weather and Steilacoom. She hadn't meant to stretch her trips into every three weeks, but when the snow fell, the Interstate became dicey, and it was harder to rally herself into driving there. She was never sure, however, if she was using the weather as an excuse. If she truly wanted to see Max wouldn't she follow the postman's creed to keep her "appointed rounds" no matter what?

Her guilt tugged at her conscience and made an uncomfortable bedfellow on nights she had trouble sleeping. On weekends and school "snow days," however, a crackle-and-spit fire of tamarack and a glass of cabernet sauvignon became her trusted companions, and she was able to ignore, at least temporarily, that little moral voice in her head.

Maggie had no idea if her visits to Max did him any good. He was so impassive, so leaden. Sometimes it seemed he didn't even realize she was there. But on other visits he would walk with her to the smoking lounge, stroll around the lobby with her while she talked to the nurses or other patients, and every so often, he would answer a question or make a comment.

"I know him," he said once as they passed a man playing an air guitar.

Maggie jumped on it, trying to prolong the exchange. "Oh, you do? Is he a nice guy?" But Max closed down again and the connection was broken for that visit.

She learned to focus her attempts at conversations on the topic of music. This seemed to spark more responses than anything else, even though they were disjointed. "So," Maggie said once, "I was listening to Black Sabbath on the way here." No response. "Is it true that Ozzy used to bite the heads off chickens?" No response. "Oh man! Can you imagine him on the stage and—"

"That guy over there was on Ozzy's road crew," Max interrupted.

Maggie craned her neck trying to see who he was talking about. Was it the guy standing at the nurses' station? The one curled up on the couch? It didn't matter. What mattered was that Max had talked.

"Oh really!?!" she asked as if it was a genuine statement of fact. "Now, when was that, Max?"

No response.

"Did he actually get to know Ozzy personally?"

No response.

And so it went.

Max had been in the hospital for over eight months and Christmas came without fanfare. The skies cleared long enough for the sun to dry the roads, and although it was still cold, at least Braxton would be able to come home for Christmas. Max, of course, would not.

Three days before Christmas, Maggie packed her car with Rice Krispy squares, Mrs. See's fudge, an assortment of lop-sided, but well-intentioned homemade cookies, small token gifts for the hospital staff, along with a carton of Camel Straights and wrapped presents for Max. Besides the usual fleece throw—this time one with Jimmy Hendrix on it—Maggie had bought him new moccasins, a Harley Davidson T-shirt, and another T-shirt with a circle of multi-colored guitars on the front and a caption on the back stating, "Whoever has the most guitars wins."

She knew the cookies and candy would be shared among patients, but she also wanted to acknowledge her appreciation of that unique bunch of people who had the heart and strength to work with them day in and day out. As she got the packages ready the night before, she tried to remember the names. "Let's see..." She went over the faces in her mind. "Melanie, Carol, Sharon, Micco...Jesus, of course. Who was the one with red hair? Was it Peggy? Lisa?" She wrote as many names as she could remember on tags, threw in a couple of blank ones for good measure, and wrapped individual cellophane bags of caramel apples, peppermint bark, and what might pass for a relatively good attempt at making Almond Roca.

For Doctor Silva's she tucked in a tie that had a snowman with a bright yellow Mohawk and a nose ring; he was playing a broom guitar to an audience of reindeer. On the tag she wrote "Rock On!" Oh yes, she knew it was pure corn, but it was either that or the green "Merry Fishmas" one with dophins in Santa hats.

Under the weight of gifts, Maggie breathed a sigh of relief as the elevator door swooshed open at the hospital. She leaned against the cool metal interior and whispered, "You can do this, Maggie Axline. One thing at a time." With an over-stuffed shopping bag in one hand and the other arm juggling several boxes that obscured her view, she fumbled for the buzzer outside Ward B4.

"Feliz Navidad, Jesus!" she said, peeking over the tops of packages.

Jesus reached for some of the boxes. "That must be Max's madre."

"Yes, it must be," she said handing them over. "Do I have a choice?"

"I am afraid not." He grinned and took the shopping bag. "It is your destino."

The nurse with the curly reddish hair sat behind the sign-in desk. "'Morning Maggie," she chirped.

"Hi...." *Name–name–name–auburn hair, the color of spice...* "Ginger!" Maggie almost shouted. *That was the other one.* Maggie made a mental note and set the packages on the end of the long counter.

Ginger turned to Jesus, "Would you go down to the cafeteria and see if they've found anyone to help do the dishes on Christmas? Tell 'em I might have a volunteer if they're shorthanded." She pushed her rolling chair back and stood up. "Oh, but could you go get Max first?" she hollered after him.

As they were talking, Maggie wrote her name in the ledger, and quickly scribbled "Ginger" on one of the blank gift tags.

Ooooooo! Lookie at all this stuff!" Ginger said, turning her attention back to Maggie. "Aren't you just the regular Santa Claus?"

"Yeah, there are some cookies and candy for everybody, and there are some Christmas presents for Max, and the others, well, just think of them as an offering to all you saints who work with him."

Ginger began transferring them behind the counter. "Ya want to give these ones to Max now?" she asked. "Or do you want us to give them to him on Christmas?"

"Why don't I take just one right now," Maggie picked out the blanket wrapped in red paper with green polka-dots. "Speaking of which...how's he doing?

Ginger pooched her lips and raised the inside corners of her brows. "About the same, I'm afraid. We make him come out of his room several times a day, otherwise..." she shrugged her shoulders, "we'd never see him...except when he goes to have a smoke, of course."

"Doctor Silva here today?" Maggie asked.

"No, he's in court today; won't be back until..." Ginger scanned her schedule. "Oh, I guess he won't be in 'til tomorrow. Sorry. Want him to call you?"

"That's okay." Maggie waved her hand. "Unless there's something new to tell me," she added.

Maggie knew the minute Max came out to the lobby, he wasn't any better. Once again she put her arms around him. Once again she forced a smile. Once again her heart broke. "How you doing, darling?" she asked as they sat down.

Max's gaze drifted to the package on her lap. Good sign, she thought, even though she knew she was probably grasping at straws. "Yeah, this is for you. Wanna open it?"

When he didn't reach for it, Maggie put the present gently on Max's knees, but he only stared at it. "Want me to help you?" she asked. When there was still no answer, she reached over and slowly pulled back the Scotch Tape, hoping he would catch on.

She began to babble. "Can you believe it's Christmas already, Max? I asked fancy Grandpa if he wanted to come for dinner, but he said he was going to someone's house over there. Big surprise, you know what I mean? Well, that's okay. But I guess I'll have to take him his gifts tomorrow." Her tone turned sarcastic. "Gosh," she said, "I wonder what he got us?" She grinned at Max because they both knew that since her mother died he hadn't gotten them so much as a potholder or a yoyo.

But Max didn't react, and Maggie finished unwrapping the gift. "Wow!" she said as if she was seeing the throw for the first time. "Looks like Jimmy Hendrix. Is that who that is, Max?"

She watched him for some kind of reaction but seeing none she said, "Maybe you could put that on your bed... Well, maybe later." Maggie gathered up the paper and the blanket. "Do you want to go have a cigarette now?"

Max started to get up. *Ah ha! So he was listening.* "Wait a minute," she said, "I'll go leave these at the desk and get some cigarettes."

In the smoking lounge, the conversation didn't get any better. Maggie brought up everything she could think of, every tidbit of news from home; every question about the hospital, the staff, his fellow clients; every recent weather update. Max smoked several cigarettes, and Maggie gave several more to people who asked for them. She and Max strolled around the lobby and stood for a while outside on the balcony enclosed with chain-link fencing. Max didn't say a word. Not a peep.

When she was ready to leave, Maggie faced Max and took both his hands in hers. He didn't pull away. She looked into his eyes. "I love you, Maxim," she said, "and I know you're going to be coming home before long. You'll spend next Christmas with Braxton and me...you understand?"

Max still didn't say anything, but was that something in his eyes? Something more than a blank stare? A sadness? A pleading? Maggie couldn't tell for sure, but she thought maybe...

Just then Max rocked back and forth from one foot to another. Yes, she thought. Yes, it was at least something.

210

Jesus walked with her to the door. "How was your visit with Max?" he asked. "Did he say anything to you?"

Maggie raised one shoulder. That, along with a slight eye-roll, gave Jesus his answer.

"Mi abuelita had a saying: El hombre propone, Dios dispone." Jesus opened the door to let Maggie out. "It is all in God's hands," he clarified.

Maggie nodded. She walked to the elevator and jabbed the down-button. The door slid open and as she stepped in, she turned and saw Jesus still standing in the doorway. "Thank you, mi amigo," she said as the elevator hissed closed.

CHAPTER 46

She wanted this Christmas to be...well, not glum, so Maggie invited Clive to dinner as well as Sheri, an old friend who was in town from Gig Harbor; and Teresa, a born-again cowgirl who worked in a leather and saddle shop in Portland. All three were amicable and unpretentious, and Maggie knew they would get along. Teresa and Clive had a lot in common. Both were of the no-nonsense variety and came from backgrounds of horses, cows, chickens, geese, dogs, cats, and various other livestock and pets. Sheri was a loquacious, child-of-the-earth pagan who came close to owning a dog once, but thought better of it when she read in a magazine she would have to train it where to pee and poop, what to chew, and when it was appropriate to bark. She settled for a black cat she named Lola Falana that proved to be aloof and independent and needed no training at all. That was her kind of pet.

"Hey, Brax!" Clive said as they sat down to dinner. "When did you roll in?"

"A couple of days ago, but I don't have to go back for two weeks."

"I'm surprised that bucket of bolts could make it this far," Clive teased.

Maggie set corn biscuits between them on the table. "Me, too," she said. "I thought he'd never get here."

"Ida been here a lot sooner if I could get that hunka junk to go any faster." He forked six slices of turkey onto his plate and reached for three biscuits.

Maggie and Clive made fleeting amused eye contact. "Ya think ya got enough there, sport?" Clive said.

"Huh? Oh, yeah, this is plenty. You know, Mom, I really need a better car."

"Better how?" Maggie passed the green bean casserole to Teresa.

"He probably means 'better' as in 'faster,'" Teresa said as she took the dish. "What is it about men and speed? Give me a good Appaloosa anytime."

Braxton didn't deny the macho insinuation. "Well, let me put it this way," he said, "the entire population of Benton and Whitman Counties passed me on the way here."

Clive nodded, the two of them in complete male simpatico.

"You know that 50-mile stretch north of Kennewick?" Braxton looked at Clive. "Even with my foot on the floor, she tops out at 68.5." He took a bite of the potatoes and gravy that covered half his plate and added, "72 downhill," another bite, "on a good day," another bite, "with a hurricane tailwind."

Clive shook his head as if being able to go only the speed limit was man's supreme embarrassment.

Braxton's head was bent over his plate, but his eyes rolled up to meet his conspirator's. "Believe me, I tried," he said, and they both chuckled.

"Well, why on earth would you want to go faster than that, anyway?" Sheri chimed in, helping herself to a generous plate of salad and pouring another glass of chardonnay.

Clive and Braxton stopped in mid-chew, looked at her as if she had asked a question either so profound or so stupid it didn't warrant an answer, then looked back at each other, shrugged their shoulders at the same time, and returned to eating.

When the phone rang, Maggie leapt to answer it. She had called the hospital earlier but wasn't able to talk to Max, so left a request that they help Max call her sometime during the day when they had time. She didn't know if he would actually say anything, but her plan was to talk to him for a while, then pass the phone to Clive and then Braxton so they could also wish him a merry Christmas.

All that changed as soon as Max started talking.

213

"Hi, honey!" Maggie began. "Merry Chris—"

"I'm coming home now," Max interrupted in a low monotone.

"Oh. Right now?" Maggie was startled. She hadn't heard him say more than three words at a time for weeks.

"Can you come get me?" he asked. "I have my stuff packed."

"Well, I don't think I can right this—"

"I have a guy here who will bring me, then. He's a cop."

"Max, did they say you could—"

"The main guy, the president, said I could if I could get a ride." Max's voice was becoming more agitated and broken as if he was on the verge of tears. "Come get me," he said. "I'll wait downstairs."

"Well, darling, I can't come get you today, but I could call the president and come visit you tomorrow if you want me—"

Max hung up. Maggie stood for a moment staring at the receiver in her hand, then put it down. She turned back to the table. Sheri was jabbering about someone who opened a fast-food chicken franchise in India. "They have the right idea," she said. "Before they slaughter those poor chickens a holy man says a prayer over each and every one."

But neither Clive nor Braxton was listening to her; they were watching Maggie. "It's okay," she mouthed. In a haze, she opened the refrigerator and stood there searching for something. *Oh. Pie...and... something else. What was it?* She took out a pumpkin pie, set it on the counter, and went back to the refrigerator. *Something else. Something else. Oh, yeah.* She reached behind the milk and pulled out a can of whipped cream.

"Who wants pie?" Maggie asked. All hands were raised, but she didn't notice them. Without looking she began putting slices on plates.

"Well, imagine that," Clive said, drawn back into the conversation but with his eyes still riveted on Maggie, "and we ate a great big turkey without so much as a howdy-do before we cooked it. Hey, Maggie, ya know any priests who could come sprinkle some holy water on this carcass?" His brows were furrowed, but he seemed to be enjoying ribbing Sheri about what he clearly thought was the ultimate in ridiculousness.

"Imam."

"Huh?"

"A Muslim holy man. He's called an Imam," Sheri said as though she clearly thought Clive was the ultimate in ignorance.

Maggie passed out pie, sat down, got up to get the whipped cream, sat down, got up to get the coffeepot, filled cups, sat down, got up to get clean forks, and sat down again before she noticed everyone was silently watching her.

"Mom?" Braxton said.

"Huh?" Maggie looked around the table. "Oh. Oh, no, I'm fine. Uh, that was Max on the phone."

"He okay?" Braxton asked.

"Oh...yes. Yes, he seems fine." Maggie squirted whipped cream onto her pie with one hand and picked up her fork in the other. "Really," she said, scanning the anxious faces.

"Sounded like he had something to say," Clive urged.

"Well, yes, as a matter of fact he did. He wanted me to come pick him up today." Maggie let out a ragged sigh, and everyone at the table held their breaths. Again she skimmed four pairs of apprehensive eyes. She shrugged one shoulder. "Not going to, though," she said with a timid smile. "No matter what the president says." And as she spoke, she heard the absurdity of it and giggled. "Anyone want some whipped cream?"

For a brief second there was a puzzled silence, but then the tension broke and mollified laughs rippled around the table. "Now. Clive, were you saying something about a priest?"

So, as Maggie had hoped, Christmas was not glum. In fact, somewhere among the aroma of roasting turkey, the soft tinkle of silverware, and the second bottle of chardonnay, Sheri started to sing "Silent Night," followed by "O, Tannenbaum," explaining that being Pagan didn't deter her from loving Christmas carols. Clive and Braxton got into a lively argument on which year Corvettes were first manufactured, Teresa wove some leather scraps she had in her pocket into a bracelet for Maggie, and then everyone, even the guys, helped clean up.

She would call the hospital tomorrow.

CHAPTER 47

Maggie slept fitfully that night, and "tomorrow" came early. She stacked kindling and logs in the fireplace, gathered up the remains of stray Christmas wrap and ribbons, scrubbed the turkey pan that had been soaking all night, and tidied up the kitchen as she waited for light to infuse itself into the morning and a reasonable time to call Steilacoom.

At 8:00 she steeled herself and dialed. Unconsciously, she counted the rings as she waited. "Four...five...six..." Maggie's heart did little flip-flops. "Seven...eight...oh, hi, this is Maggie Axline, is this Sharon?" The low, steady voice on the other end was reassuring. "Sounds like you're busy this morning." Maggie tried to sound upbeat.

"Sorry," Sharon said. "I was trying to find someone's teeth, believe it or not."

"Did you?"

"Yep! Found 'em in someone else's mouth." Sharon sounded pleased. "Made my day," she added. "Just don't ask me how they got there."

Maggie savored the droll moment but knew she had to ask. "Well, I wanted to find out how Max is doing this morning. He called me yesterday, and he seemed more agitated than usual. Said he was coming home."

"You know, I just came on. Let me check with Carol before she leaves."

As Maggie waited on hold, she thought about Christmas day and about how unpredictable life can be with all its curveballs, sliders, and strikes and how every once in a while

216

there might be a great high lob into center field that goes sailing over the chain-link fence and leaves you feeling exhilarated, like maybe life is more than a long series of errors and outs and disappointing pop flies. Yesterday, for the most part was a solid hit day. Today would be, at best, a day of sitting on the bench waiting. Sometimes it felt like that's all she ever did. Wait. Wait for Max to get better. Wait for her next visit to him. Wait for school to be out. Wait for Braxton to come home. It wasn't that she was bored, or lonely, or even unhappy; she just felt like she was somewhere in limbo, waiting to get a toehold in life. Waiting for a home run she knew might never happen.

"Hi, Maggie, this is Carol. I was just leaving, but Sharon said you asked about Max?"

It was like Carol to take the call before she went off duty. Maggie pictured her on the phone, and at the same time, tying up all the loose ends of her night shift, writing in her planner, and mapping out her stops for the quickest route home. A real multi-tasker, that one.

"Yeah, Carol. I got a call from him last night and he sounded...oh, I don't know..."

How did he sound? There were many times he sounded agitated, or out of touch, or down, or...

"Well, I guess he sounded kind of different," she finally decided. "I was wondering how he seems to you lately."

"Oh, yes," Carol began. "I think maybe he was a little restless last night. Actually, quite a few clients were having some difficulty. I guess it's probably because they realized it was Christmas. It can cause some agitation, all right."

"Of course. That makes sense."

"I gave him the presents you left for him," Carol went on. "He didn't open them, but in hindsight, I'm wondering if that was the best thing to do yesterday."

"Who knows," Maggie said. "I did ask you to give them to him. I never thought about it being upsetting. Anyway, he wanted me to come pick him up. Permission from the upper echelon, the president himself, he said."

Carol's laugh was wry. She must have heard this type of thing many times.

217

"Anyway, I was wondering if you thought I should come up there to see him today. Or tomorrow. He may have forgotten all about it, but I wasn't sure."

"I haven't seen Max today," Carol said. "I think he's still asleep. But Dr. Silva is going to be in later today. Why don't I have him call you?"

So, Maggie settled in for the day, once again, waiting.

When the phone rang, Maggie was somewhere between asleep and awake, stuck in a twilight dream of trying to get to someone. Max? Braxton? She didn't remember, but she did remember that it left her with the same frustration she had when she couldn't finish a task. There were loose ends that needed to be found, tucked in, and tidied up.

The blare of the ring tore her out of the unsettling reverie, and caused her arm to flail up, sending the phone flying to the floor. She rolled off the couch, bellied to it, and scrabbled for the receiver. "Hello? Hello?" She turned the receiver around. "Hello?"

There was a pause, then, "Hello? May I speak with Mrs. Axline. Dr. Silva calling."

"Oh, hi, Dr. Silva. This is Maggie Axline. Sorry, I, ah, dropped the phone. How are you? How was your yesterday? I mean, how's everything up there?" Maggie took a deep breath and started again. "Thanks for calling, Dr. Silva, how was your Christmas?"

"It was great. Oh, thanks for the tie, by the way. My son thinks I'm a 'righteous dude' now."

This amused Maggie, and she wondered if his son actually thought he was more of a "righteous nerd," but instead she said, "I'm so glad you both liked it." She took a deep breath. "Say, I got a call from Max yesterday. He said I could come pick him up."

When there was no response, Maggie went on. "I told him I couldn't, but he said he could get a ride home then. He said he had permission from the president, so I figured I was pretty safe not keeping the light on for him."

"I think you figured correctly," Silva said with a slight chuckle, "but I'm a little surprised he talked to you at all. He's

218

clammed up again today. I talked to him...well, I guess I should say I talked *at* him. He didn't say anything. I'm not even sure he heard me."

"I was wondering if I should come up there tomorrow. Maybe I could draw him out a little? You know, just sit and talk?"

"I don't really know, but it couldn't hurt." Dr. Silva let out a loud puff of air. "It would be good to see some positive change in him. If not..." he paused and Maggie held her breath. "Well, let's see what happens. We may have to try some different treatments on him."

Maggie didn't ask what kinds of treatments he was talking about. She'd seen *One Flew Over the Cuckoo's Nest*. Surely it wouldn't be like that. She wasn't usually the ostrich-with-its-head-in-the-sand type, but right now she just didn't think she was ready to hear what the doctor had to say.

The next morning, Maggie stopped at Starbucks and picked up a blueberry scone and a vente dark roast and pulled into the I-5 surge headed north. At the Longview exit, the traffic thinned and she let her mind drift lightly through memories of better times. Times of making newspaper and crepe-paper hats for birthday parties, of taking the boys to the Dollar Store and letting them pick out one toy each, of putting Shoe Goo on the bottoms of their tenny-runners to make them last one more month. They had never let her live that one down, but it didn't matter. That was the stuff of memories. Maggie wondered if her mind was being selective. Probably. But wasn't that the beauty of it? She chose to flip through her mental catalog and pull out the times she wanted to think about and, at least for now, let the others remain deep inside the murky pages. She'd pull those out when she felt stronger. But not now. Not on her way to see Max in the hospital.

Keeping her thoughts clear of all the what-ifs, the maybes, the I-hopes, made the drive go faster and kept her mind less muddled. When she drove into the parking lot, the hospital didn't seem quite as austere and ominous as usual. It wasn't until she stepped out of the car and approached the granite steps that her heart ricocheted from her chest, to her stomach,

219

to her throat. She paused for a moment, collected herself, and walked through the massive doors.

What would Max be like today? It was fear of the unknown that kept her off balance. *Didn't Shakespeare say something about that?*

She was still trying to remember which play it was when Melanie buzzed her in.

"Sorry you had to wait," she said. "Jesus is out today, and it's like the Florida Everglades in here."

"The Everglades?" Maggie asked.

"We're swamped." Melanie's grin was broad and infectious and Maggie felt better already.

Melanie walked with her over to Max who was already sitting in the lobby. His vacant-eyed stare told her this was not going to be an easy visit, but she plunged in. "Hey there, Toots! How're you doing?" She sat on the couch next to him and took his hand. He didn't pull it away. Her eyes met Melanie's.

"Been that way for a couple of days," Melanie said. "Haven't you, Max? Tell your mom about how I've been hounding you relentlessly to talk to me." She bent down and peered straight into his glassy eyes. "If you don't say something to me before long, I'm going to think you don't like me anymore. And then..." she edged closer, raised her hands, and wiggled her fingers. "And then...comes...the tickle!" Her eyes glistened and flickered to Maggie's and back. "And, if you dare to laugh, so much as a giggle, fair warning! I'm going to start calling you Elmo."

When Max didn't respond, Melanie straightened and sighed. "You are a man of few words, Max." She tousled his hair. "Always was a sucker for the strong, silent type. Well," she said to Maggie, "I'll leave you two alone and get back to the joy that is my job." She grinned again and returned to the desk.

So Maggie sat with Max for three hours, at first trying to cajole him into talking, then trying to tempt him to go the smoking room for a cigarette, then trying to appeal to his curiosity about what might be in the Christmas gifts left to unwrap. But after a while, she resorted to the drone of the one-sided conversation that had become so familiar to her, and then finally, she just sat next to him and held his hand as she

220

watched the coming and going of patients and staff. When she felt there was nothing more she could say or do that would help pull Max out of his static state, she kissed him goodbye and left.

Had it helped? Did her coming up here have any affect? Any at all? She fished in her purse for her car keys. Well, at least now she knew he was not better. How long before he—

Hamlet! That was the one!

"The undiscover'd country" he called it. Does it really make us "...bear the ills we have /Than to fly to others that we know not of?" But he was talking about death. That was the 'undiscover'd country.' Surely that couldn't be the answer. When he was contemplating whether to be or not to be, all he knew then was his mother had married his uncle. Big deal! He never had a kid in a mental institution. He never had Max.

No, death was never the answer. She prayed it wouldn't be for Max, either.

Maggie scoffed and meshed into the traffic. What did Shakespeare know anyway? Besides, she thought, I don't think I even own a bare bodkin.

On the way home, Maggie tugged on her boot straps, repeated her mantra about a hundred times, and pep-talked her way into believing that everything would be all right in the end. "Need to remember," she said to herself, "if this is as bad as it gets, we'll be okay. Yep, we'll survive as long as it doesn't get any worse."

And then it did.

CHAPTER 48

New Year's Eve was uneventful, school started again with no hoopla, and Braxton returned to school. It was still early January, a drab month at best. But at least occasional snippets of sun whispered the promise of an early spring. And while it was too early to predict, Maggie grasped at any straws that could keep her moving in a forward direction.

The weather was holding dry and steady, and Maggie was trying to decide the next best time to drive to Steilacoom. The weekend coming up would make it less than two weeks, but the following weekend would make it more than two weeks. She rationalized, with a little pang of guilt, that if she waited a little longer, it would give Max more time to improve to the point of perhaps actually talking to her. However, a few days later, when she got a message to call Dr. Silva, her thoughts detoured immediately to the worst possible scenario.

When she got home that Friday, as Maggie dropped her purse and homework folder on the counter, she noticed the red button on the telephone glaring at her. She punched the message button. "You have-one-new message," the machine told her. She punched it again. "This is Doctor Silva calling. Please have Mrs. Axline call me at Western State Hospital at her earliest convenience."

Now don't read anything into that, Maggie. He didn't say "immediately," he said "earliest convenience." Besides, if it was an emergency wouldn't they have called me at school? Unless they knew it would be too upsetting to tell me at work. Oh that's silly; they would have figured out a way.

222

But this message was left—she glanced at the recorder— *over three hours ago. I would have known by now if it really was an emergency. Wouldn't I?*

"Oh for heaven's sake, pick up the damned phone and call!" Maggie dialed the number.

"Silva here," a bright voice said.

Okay, this is a good sign.

"Hi, Doctor Silva. This is Maggie Axline. You left a message for me to call you?

"I sure did, Mrs. Axline, how are you doing today?"

"Fine. But how's Max?"

"Well, that is what I called you about. I know Max is a ward of the state, so I don't need to clear this with you, but I thought it was..." the doctor searched for the right word. "Oh, I don't know, more considerate, I guess, if I at least let you know what was going on."

"Oh, I see," Maggie said calmly. "I know you've been concerned about Max's progress lately. Of course. Me too. What's happening?" She forced a slow, steady, clear dialogue. To her ear it sounded flat and hollow and not at all like the tirade that was trying its best to sucker punch its way from her gut to her mouth. But she put the screws to it, bullied it back down and said, "I can't tell you how much I appreciate this, Doctor Silva."

Dr. Silva sucked in a deep breath, coughed, and cleared his throat. Then he got down to business. And as he talked, Maggie picked up a pen and began scribbling on the note pad next to the phone. She did this sometimes when she knew it was going to be a lot to take in: a scuffle with the telephone company; a squabble with the bank... life-altering information on her son's insanity.

She wrote as fast as she could, jotting down key words that would help her remember when she would go over it a hundred times in her mind after she had hung up. "Catatonic." "Mute." "Shutting down." "Wheelchair."

When he was through, it was crystal clear that Max's mental state was deteriorating. He was in a stupor. Dr. Silva called it "Catatonic Schizophrenia," a condition in which a person loses complete touch with reality. Max was not

223

responding to any external stimuli. His motor activity was almost non-existent so they had him in a wheelchair most of the time to see if they could prompt him to react to something. He made little or no eye contact with other people, would not, or could not talk, and remained rigid almost constantly.

By the time Dr. Silva wound down, Maggie had lost her calm exterior and felt lost in a sea of unfathomable data. "But...but..." she stammered. "But does he eat? I mean if he doesn't eat..." the unfinished sentence weighted the air between them. She couldn't say it out loud.

"Oh! No, we have that covered, Mrs. Axline." Doctor Silva said quickly. "No, Max is a young, physically healthy twenty-year-old, and we're going to keep it that way."

Until then, the information had been clinically astute, but now a touch of empathy found its way in. "Don't you worry about that. We have begun feeding Max." He hesitated as if he was trying to decide if he should say more. "Through a tube," he finally said. "Down his nose."

"His nose?" Maggie's stomach did another summersault. "But why, I mean how, why does this happen?" Maggie had stopped writing and was in a semi-dazed state herself.

"Now that's a question I would love to have an answer for." Dr. Silva paused again, and Maggie heard the audible tic-tic-tic of a pencil against a desk. "We do know that people with schizophrenia have too much of this chemical—dopamine they call it. We all have it.

And yet another pause, perhaps searching for the right words. "But some people have too much of it, like Max. So when his brain processes things, they get mixed up. So we try to block some of this chemical, this dopamine, so he can think straight. With catatonia...well, we just aren't sure exactly why some people develop it and some don't. Some researchers say that people in this state may be shutting down...preparing to die. But we don't really know."

Suddenly he sounded tired, spent. "But we're not going to let that happen," he added.

There were questions that needed to be asked, but they wouldn't come. Maggie felt like a sponge that badly needed wringing out. Saturated. Heavy with unwelcome knowledge.

Dr. Silva drew in another audible breath, let it out, and continued. "We discussed this...at length," he emphasized, "at our meeting this morning. Up 'til now we've been trying different medications on Max, but so far...well, you see the results...or maybe I should say 'lack of results.' Anyway, we are going to try a different approach for a while."

"Oh?" was all Maggie could muster.

"In cases like this, electroconvulsive therapy can be an effective treatment."

"Oh?" Maggie said again and knew, but this time didn't care, that she sounded pitiful. She released an involuntary moan. "Is that electroshock therapy?"

"Now, I know what you're thinking. Nurse Ratched, right? Believe me, Mrs. Axline, this isn't like that at all. That movie, I swear it's done more to take the public image of psychiatry back to The Dark Ages than anything else I know. No, I promise you, this is a cautious, humane treatment for Max's...uh...condition."

Maggie nodded dumbly. "I feel so...helpless," she finally said. "Is there something I could be doing? Like, coming up there more often?"

And just like that, her mind switched into the maternal instinct protection mode, fighting for the live of her cub. "I could get time off work. Maybe find someplace to stay by the hospital. Come sit with him during the days? Maybe I could read to him. Something about guitars...or motorcycles...or, I know! Rock stars! Ozzy...uh...Pink Floyd."

Dr. Silva waited for her to finish before he said, "All those things would be good, I'm sure. But I have a feeling they would help you more than they would help Max right now."

Maggie couldn't say she was altogether sorry to hear him say that. Not that she couldn't do it, not that she wouldn't do it, but if she gave it more thought, her spur-of-the-moment plan could be more than a little problematic. There was, after all, the small matter of mortgage payments, Braxton's schooling, buying groceries, having heat, putting gas in the car. "Well, do you think I should come up tomorrow at least?"

"Actually, no. That is," Dr. Silva added quickly, "you certainly may, if you would like to, but in all honesty, at this time, I doubt that Max would even know you're here. Besides, we're going to be giving him his treatments for a while, so we'll be monitoring him closely, and right now, I'm not even sure he will be in this unit. We may decide to move him to a different part of the hospital until he's..." There was a slight pause before the doctor said, "...better."

"For a while, why don't we keep in touch by phone a couple of times a week?" he suggested. "I gave you the number where you can reach me directly, didn't I?"

"Yes, you did. You don't mind if I call you every few days?"

"Nope, not at all. But," he paused, "try not to worry, Mrs. Axline. I...we, all of us, are going to do everything we can to get Max back on track. Worrying about it isn't going to do anyone any good. Especially you."

"Right," Maggie said, knowing full well that was much easier said than done. "And, Dr. Silva?"

"Yes?"

"Could you wear a lucky tie?"

CHAPTER 49

The answer was always the same: No change. No change. Sorry, Mrs. Axline, no change.

For two weeks she had done her best to detach her worry gene from Max's situation despite the seed of maternal intuition that was rooted firmly in her heart. Now, heading into the third week that seed had again germinated, spreading its tendrils into every nook and cranny of her being until she could stay away no longer. She called ahead to see if she could meet with Dr. Silva, and with trepidation, put the usual staples in her car—cigarettes, magazine, Snickers bars—and lit out for Steilacoom.

She had to see Max, if only for a while; if only to look at his face; if only to hold his hand. She knew it would be hard, maybe even devastating, but she couldn't ignore her natural instincts any longer. It was like a magnetic field pulling her north. Pulling her toward her child.

Jesus held the door open, and she stepped into E4. He had only to look at Maggie to know the question. "About the same." He splayed the fingers of one hand and waggled it back and forth. "Mas o menos," he added.

Maggie's eyes immediately swiveled to his. "More or less?" She felt a little spasm of hope in her gut.

"Not really." Jesus started to walk down the hall, then stopped. "Maybe I shouldn't say, but..." he turned to face her. "I thought he tried to say something this morning."

"What?"

227

"No," Jesus said.

"Why not?"

"No. I thought he said 'no'." He shrugged his shoulders. "I may be wrong, but..."

Maggie knew better than to feel optimistic, but she couldn't control the flutter in her chest.

"Anyway," Jesus continued. "Dr. Silva is waiting for you in his office. I'm supposed to go get Max and bring him in there while you talk to the doctor. Do you know where his office is?"

In the lobby they branched off, Jesus to get Max, and Maggie to Dr. Silva's office. His door was ajar. She tapped on it and peeked in.

"Come on in, Mrs. Axline." He waved her over.

Even under the unpleasant circumstances, Dr. Silva's voice was a comfort to Maggie. As she sat down, he rolled his chair around to the side of his desk, leaving enough room between them for Max. He put his elbows on his knees and clasped his hands together. "Well," he said, "are we ready for this?"

His casual tone forced a weak, putting-up-a-brave-front smile to Maggie's face. "To tell you the truth, I'm not sure," she said. "Anything I should know before Max gets here?"

Dr. Silva also smiled. "Well, the good news is that Max is physically healthy. He's probably lost some strength, especially in his legs due to his immobility. And...now I don't want to get your hopes up," he went on, "but I believe I've seen some small signs that he has a cognitive awareness of the people around him."

When Maggie sat up straighter in her chair, he continued. "Just small things. Like the other day he looked right at one of the nurses, and yesterday he frowned. I mean it was a real frown. Purposeful, like something was actually bothering him." Dr. Silva leaned back in his chair. "I know it's vague, but it's a good sign. And right now we'll take whatever we can get."

Maggie choked back the lump in her throat. She nodded. Then she noticed Dr. Silva's tie. "Hey!" she said, thankful for the distraction. She pointed at the most garish tie she'd ever seen: neon green, sprinkled with silver horseshoes and gold shamrocks. "Perfect!"

Dr. Silva looked down at his tie. "Oh yeah, I wore my lucky tie. See?" He looked back at Maggie, "I was listening."

There was a rap at the door, and Maggie's attention pivoted toward it. She held her breath.

Jesus wheeled Max in and parked him between her and the doctor, nodded to Maggie, doffed a finger to his forehead at Dr. Silva, and left.

This was the first time Maggie had seen Max in a wheelchair. She hadn't thought to prepare herself for this moment by visualizing it first, and words failed her.

Fortunately, they did not fail Dr. Silva. "Max!" he said, "Glad you're here." He talked to Max as he would anyone who had strolled into his office. "Hey, buddy! How're you doing today? Your mom's here to see you, Max. You want to tell her hello? I'll bet she'd like that. No? Maybe a hug? Okay, fella, then how about just a 'hi'?"

Between each sentence he paused a moment to wait for a reaction, but Max sat rigid in the wheelchair, his head inclined slightly, eyes void of life, staring at the floor.

Little Orphan Annie eyes.

Dr. Silva continued, "What, not even a smile? Okay, Axline," he turned the wheelchair to face him, pulled it closer, and with both hands clenching the arm rail bars he looked straight at Max and said, "This is your final chance to redeem yourself before you're back on my shit-list."

Maggie glanced at the doctor and saw he was clearly teasing Max. She was grateful for his candid sense of humor. Just what she could relate to and maybe just what Max needed.

He waited a moment, then laughed and patted Max's knee. "It's okay, buddy, I still love ya," he said and turned Max around so Maggie could see his face.

"Well," he said to Maggie, "I was hoping this might be a breakthrough, but I wasn't expecting it."

Maggie searched Max's face for a reaction, but it was stony and unyielding. She reached over and brushed a few rebellious strands of hair away from eyes as dark as Greek olives.

He could use a haircut. And a good scrubbing.

She noticed a smudge on his cheek and restrained herself from licking her thumb and rubbing it. Her eye caught an ashtray on the corner of the desk. "Do you think I could see if he...?"

"Oh, sure. Go ahead and try it."

She pulled a cigarette from the pack in her purse. "You want one, Max?" She held it out to him. "Here, I'll light it for you."

She lit the Camel and held it out again. He didn't look at her or take it. "Here you go," she tried again and put it between two fingers that lay stiff on the arm of his chair. It fell to the floor. "Okay," she said as she picked it up and put it out in the ashtray, "you can let me know when you're ready for one."

Dr. Silva bobbed his head a couple of times. "It's one hell of an illness." He was talking to Maggie, but watching Max. Then he turned his attention to her. "His electroconvulsive treatments have been going well. I think we should see some results soon."

Maggie finally pulled her gaze away from Max. "I guess I'm confused," she said. "It all seems so...surreal somehow. I still just don't get it. So you don't have any idea at all what happens to cause this?"

"Not really." Dr. Silva shook his head. "They believe that underlying problems with the brain are probably the cause. Like we talked about on the phone, it's like the brain chemicals called neurotransmitters get, well," he stopped and scratched the scruff of a beard on his jaw, "mixed up, you might say. They've done some image studies and they do show differences in the brain structure." He shrugged one shoulder. "But they don't know why."

"But you think Max will come out of this...whatever it is he's in?"

"No promises, but I believe he will. Catatonic schizophrenia is pretty rare," he said, "but not to eventually come out of it is even rarer." Dr. Silva smiled gently at Maggie. "But you should be aware that if he, I mean *when* he does, part of his memory may be compromised. Some of it may be short-term, but Max could also have some long-term loss."

Maggie sighed and studied her hands in her lap. *When did these hands get so old? Do I look as old as they do?*

230

She tucked her fingers in and curled her hands into balls. *How long? Dear God, how much longer?*

She dodged eye contact with Dr. Silva by scanning the room. Four degrees, two licenses, and a photograph of what she assumed to be his sons flanking a red Harley.

They look normal. A couple of regular guys. I wonder....

She let her gaze linger on a painting of ducks swimming in the reflection of stars on a pond, then forced herself to look at Dr. Silva again. "Any idea of how long..." but before she could get the question out, she heard a low, raspy voice.

"I'm here."

She gasped and her eyes flew to Max.

Dr. Silva grinned. "Well, good morning, Max. Good of you to join us."

CHAPTER 50

"I'm right here. Don't talk about me like I'm not here," Max grumbled and scowled at Dr. Silva.

"Well, I can see that." The doctor flicked his chin toward Maggie. "Hey, your mom's here. She came to see you."

When Maggie was able to speak, she said, "Hi, sweetheart, I'm so glad you...came back."

The words caught in her throat. Her fingernails dug into the palms of her hands. She forced them open and spread them on her knees but couldn't stop the trembling. "You were...gone...for a while. I missed you. How are you feeling?" The expression on Max's face kept her from leaping out of her chair and embracing him. "Are you okay?"

Max didn't look at her or answer. He sat silently brooding for a moment, then took one foot off the footrest of the wheelchair and put it on the floor. He grimaced with the effort and tried the other foot.

"Oh, I see," Dr. Silva teased, "now you're a big shot, huh? Gonna try to stand up on your own." Nonchalantly, he reached over and pushed a button on his phone, then put a hand on Max's shoulder. "You know, Max, you're going to fall right on your keister if you try to stand up too soon. Why don't you hang on a minute and someone will be here to help you."

"Please, Max." Maggie reached out and touched his arm.

Max glared and narrowed his eyes to slits, then his face went soft, and for a moment his eyes turned moist. He stared at her, angry, sad, confused.

He had to be disoriented, she thought. How could he not be? "Max?" Her shaky fingers trailed lightly along his cheek. "It's going to get better now, Max. I promise." Why had she promised? What she really meant was, "I hope."

Dr. Silva leaned in. "Your mom's right, Max, but for now why don't you relax another minute? We'll help you stand up pretty soon."

But Max wasn't about to relax another minute. The darkness swept over his face again, and now with bare feet on the floor, he scooted himself to the front of the chair and struggled to hoist himself up. His face contorted as he grimaced, moaned, and hefted himself into a standing position. He took his hands off the chair arms, freelanced for two seconds, teetered, and fell back with a thunk!

Dr. Silva jumped forward and helped Max ease himself into the chair. "Okay, you showed us you can do it. Now will you wait until we get some help?"

Max glowered at him. "Stupid tie," he said.

Dr. Silva tilted his head toward Maggie. "Your son thinks he's a connoisseur of ties. He has an opinion on every one I wear." Then he smiled at Max. "'Course, so far, the only one he's liked is the one that says, 'Live to ride, Ride to live,' on it."

There was a faint rap at the door and Jesus stuck his head in.

Dr. Silva waved him over. "Give us a hand, Jesus. Mr. Axline here is trying his best to prove he's super human."

"Hey, it's good to see you, amigo." Jesus strode over and hoisted a hip onto the corner of the desk right in front of Max. "Where you been, man? All the ladies been askin' about you."

As Jesus talked, Maggie watched Max. She could see he was trying to make sense out of something that must have been so nonsensical to him it was like falling down a rabbit hole and waking up in a world of Cheshire Cats and hookah-smoking caterpillars asking him "awhoooo...R...U?". There were so many things she wanted to say to him—so many questions to ask him. Questions he may or may not be able to answer. But she knew she had to take it slow. Like Alice, Max had to make discoveries on his own and in his own time. Whether those discoveries would clear his head or muddle it more remained to be seen.

233

The sound of Max's voice jerked her back to the real world.

"I'm hungry," he was saying.

Dr. Silva chuckled. "That's good, Max. That's real good. Jesus, you think you could wheel Max into the cafeteria and see if you can rustle up something fit for a superhero?"

"You bet I can," Jesus said turning Max's wheelchair.

"And Max?" Jesus stopped, and the doctor went on. "After you eat, Jesus will take you into the physical therapy room and they'll help you get those legs in shape again. We'll have you up and around before you can say 'The Incredible Hulk'."

Max nodded slightly, and his eyes slid over to Maggie.

Dr. Silva caught it. "Your mom's going to stay here a while and talk to me, but she'll come in and visit with you before she leaves, okay?"

"'kay," he murmured, and Jesus wheeled him out.

"Well now!" Dr. Silva slapped his hands on his knees. "That was something, wasn't it?" He shook his head and kick-pushed his chair back around his desk so he was again sitting across from Maggie. "This illness continues to amaze me."

"So, what do we do now?"

"Now..." Silva paused a moment as if he was trying to decide. "Now, we see how Max does on a different medication." He studied Max's file in front of him. "But it's tricky. We've tried so many...Lithium...let's see...no, we tried that one. Haldol? No... Melaril? No... Thorazine?" He made a little clicking sound with his tongue as he scanned the file. "tk-tk-tk-tk-tk. You know, we'll be discussing this at our next meeting. Now that he's out of his catatonia, we'll be watching him very closely to try to prevent a relapse."

"Try to prevent a relapse" rang in her ears like the wail of an air raid siren. Would the bomb be dropped again? How bad would the devastation be next time? A missile could hit the same place only so many times before complete annihilation. If it happened again, would Max be able to recover, rebuild his life?

Maggie didn't have the answers, but sadly, neither did Dr. Silva. He had always been upfront with her. "There are no guarantees, Mrs. Axline," echoed in her mind.

But now, right now, Max was better. And right now, she needed to embrace that little pearl of delight that was trying to manifest itself into something close to giddiness. And while she listened to the doctor, she realized she couldn't hang on to the worry of what might happen. All the "what-ifs" and the "might-nevers" in the world weren't going to do her a bit of good. That air raid siren would have to remain silent while she celebrated the moment. And that moment was joy.

Maggie leaned forward in her chair and beamed. "But this is wonderful!" The giggle that had been trying to surface finally did; then it morphed into an uninhibited laugh. That laugh provoked a laugh in Dr. Silva. And together the two of them basked in that brief flash of success.

CHAPTER 51

When Maggie came home from Steilacoom and flopped face first onto her rumpled bed, the last thing that went through her mind, other than Dr. Silva's well-intended but absurdly gaudy tie, was a quote from *Macbeth*. She let her eyelids drop softly and thought, "Sleep that knits up the ravel'd sleave of care." Sleep... the "balm of hurt minds." She took a deep breath and hoped Will was right. And that night, for the first time in many months, Maggie fell into a deep, cavernous sleep with no murky bottom, no dark corners, no sharp edges.

If someone had told her three years ago she would be relieved her son had only chronic paranoid schizophrenia instead of catatonic schizophrenia, she would have laughed herself silly. But now she had acclimated herself to a different way of thinking, and while it was still disturbing, Maggie was finding it harder each day to imagine her life if Max had not have gotten sick. Now, even the smallest improvement was cause for celebration. So, when she awoke from that vast, dreamless sleep, Maggie felt almost...good.

She floated on that tiny cloud of euphoria for the next two weeks and actually broke out in a chorus of "The Sun Will Come Out Tomorrow" on her next visit to Steilacoom.

Before she had left the hospital last time, she had sat with Max a couple of hours. Although he hadn't said much, he did at least respond to her questions and showed a modicum of interest in what she was saying. Since then, she had also called the nurses' station a couple of times and was told, without elaboration, that Max was "doing better."

That's why she was a little taken aback this time when Jesus hesitated. They were walking toward the lounge when Maggie asked, "How's Max today?"

When he didn't answer right away, she glanced at him. For a moment she thought he must not have heard her, but then he said, "Well..."

She waited for it.

"He's..." And she waited for it. "*Pretty* good," Jesus finished. But Maggie had become so attuned to voice inflections and innuendos, she heard the emphasis on "pretty," which left plenty of room for interpretation.

"'*Pretty* good?'" Maggie parroted.

"He's better," Jesus said simply. "I'll go tell him you're here." He clipped the conversation short and went off across the room to find Max.

Maggie signed in, said hi to Ginger, and then watched and listened to the rhythms of the hospital. Today, the room was full of hubbub. Nurses and orderlies talked to patients, carried trays, administered meds, coaxed, cajoled, comforted. In one corner several people watched President Clinton on TV declare no wrongdoing in his relationship with White House intern Monica Lewinsky. On the other side, two patients were in a heated discussion about which cartoon was better, *Beavis and Butthead* or *South Park,* when another patient walked over and threw his hat into the ring with, "Aw, you're both nuts; everyone knows it's *The Simpsons.*"

Then, Maggie saw Max across the room. He held an aluminum cane that he was tapping and swinging in front of him as he made his way toward her. The cane would tap, tap, tap on the linoleum floor and veer from side to side as he encountered a chair or a table.

Maggie shot to standing. "Max?"

Max ticked the cane along the edge of the sofa, then felt his way around it with his hands, patted the cushion, and sat down.

Maggie dropped next to him, her eyes wide, her jaw slack. "Max?" she said again.

Max stared straight ahead and with no emotion, said, "I'm blind."

237

Maggie wasn't sure she heard right. Her brows furrowed and her face pinched with disbelief. "What?" she blurted.

"I'm blind," Max said again.

No! This can't be happening again. No, no, no! I will not go through this again!

Then with the full force of a mother's ultimate frustration behind it, she yelled, "The hell you are! God damn it, Max, you are not blind!"

The room went silent. Every head swiveled towards her, including Max's. But while the others seemed startled, or amused, or embarrassed, Max seemed puzzled. He stared at Maggie for a few seconds, then said, "I'm not?"

"No!" Maggie yelled again, then caught herself and brought her volume down a few decibels. "I mean, no, Max."

Max looked around the room with the bewilderment of a lost puppy.

"Max. Max, look at me." Maggie took his face in her hands and turned it toward her. His eyes followed. "Max," she said again. "You are not blind. You can see me, right?"

Max's eyes slowly met hers and he nodded.

"Good," she said matter-of-factly. "I'm glad you can see again. So, you won't be needing this." And with that, Maggie gently pulled the cane from his hands and took it to the nurses' station where she and Ginger exchanged quirky grins and eye-rolls before she walked back to Max.

From then on, for many years, Maggie measured time by the day Max "went blind." She wasn't sure why; maybe because she thought it was so absurdly bizarre and, she couldn't deny, rather funny.

"Oh yeah," she would say. "I think *Titanic* won best picture the year Max went blind.

Or, "You remember that really weird late snow storm? Oh, you remember, it was right after Max went blind."

And, it was only a couple of months after Max "went blind" that things started to turn around long enough for Maggie to catch her breath, at least temporarily. In March, 1998, Max had been at Western State Hospital a year, and each time she went to see him, it seemed like he was doing a little better. By the time he turned twenty-one in May, Maggie knew if he kept improving, he would be coming home before too long.

Home. She had waited so long for it, but now that it was approaching, there was something in the pit of her stomach that didn't feel right.

At first, she couldn't identify the cause. It felt like what she imagined a fur-ball would feel like if she were a cat. Like if she coughed hard enough, up it would come, and she would say, "Oh yeah, there is it. That's what was bothering me." But no matter how hard she tried to bring it to the surface, no matter how hard she tried to figure it out, it was elusive. At the same time, she couldn't ignore it. It was a slight tickling feeling that became her constant, irritating, companion.

That's why, on her trip to Steilacoom the first of June, she was pleased when Jesus greeted her with, "Hey, the big guy wants to see you while you're here today."

"Dr. Silva?"

"Si, el gran jefe." Jesus ginned just as if Maggie knew what he was saying.

"What about?" she asked.

"No se`," Jesus shrugged, "but he asked me to send you to his office as soon as you got here."

Maggie was actually glad to talk to Dr. Silva that day. She'd been wondering what his take was on how Max was doing. Besides, she thought, maybe he could shed some light on this peculiar, anxious feeling she couldn't shake. She rapped lightly on his partially open door. "Dr. Silva?"

"Ah, Mrs. Axline." Dr. Silva walked around his desk to greet her. He motioned to a chair. "How are you doing today?"

Maggie smiled and nodded. "Good," she said and waited for the doctor to carry the conversation.

"Max will be in pretty soon, but I wanted to run a couple of ideas by you first," he said after a few moments of mutual grinning. "I guess you know how happy we are with Max's improvement over the last few months. Still, I'd like to keep him a while longer, but his court date is coming up in a week, and I think they might decide to release him."

The fur-ball spun around a few times.

239

"Soooooo," Dr. Silva dramatized, "I want to have a plan in place in case they do."

There it was again, that prickling in her stomach.

Could it be...? Naw. This is what I've hoped for ever since Max came here. I want him to come home...don't I?

"Mrs. Axline?"

"Oh, I'm sorry, I was just thinking. Yes, a plan. That's a good idea."

"There are several options," Dr. Silva went on. "Of course, we could always release him and he could go home like he did before."

Maggie rubbed her stomach.

"But there's another option that I think would be really good for Max."

"Oh?"

"There's a unit here called PALS. Stands for 'Program for Adapted Living Skills.' It's a transition unit, but they only take volunteer patients. Now, if we could get Max to go to that unit on a volunteer basis, he could be under our care a while longer, and we would help get him ready to translate back into society."

Maggie was starting to feel better. "That sounds like it would be good for him, don't you think?"

"I do." Dr. Silva leaned in toward Maggie. "The only thing is, Mrs. Axline, I don't think we can convince him to do this, unless—and here's where you come into it—unless you tell him he can't live at your home anymore."

And there it was! Without so much as another hiccup, the churning in her stomach subsided.

She knew now, as much as she loved Max, in her heart—and apparently in her stomach—she simply didn't want him to live at home anymore. Her home. If she...they...could just get him in a position where he could be self-sufficient. If he could learn how to manage his illness, his meds, his life. He was twenty-one. Wasn't it time? Surely this illness didn't mean the end of her own freedom? No. She knew there had to be a better way.

Maggie's stomach felt better, but her head was reeling with the possibilities.

What about after that? What about next year? What happens if he breaks again?

She took a deep breath.

One thing at a time, Maggie.

Dr. Silva's reassuring voice jerked her back to the present. "What do you think, Mrs. Axline? Do you think that's something you could do?"

Maggie grinned. "Yes," she said.

They went over the plan and were deep in a discussion of whether Sean Connery or Roger Moore was the best James Bond when Max knocked on the door. "Hey, Max, come on in. You can settle an argument for us. Who was the best James Bond ever?"

Max's eye flicked between his mom and the doctor. His forehead crinkled as if the future of all Bond movies depended on his answer. He sat down, thought a few moments, then looked up. "Pierce Brosnan," he said.

"Awwww! Jeeze! Just when I thought you were well enough to get out of this joint!" Dr. Silva feigned. "Pierce Brosnan? Jeeze, Axline, what am I supposed to do with an answer like that?"

Max scooted back in his seat, clearly satisfied with the doctor's reaction.

"Hi, honey," Maggie said and reached over and squeezed his hand.

"Hey, Mom." To Maggie's delight, he squeezed back.

Still shaking his head, Dr. Silva went around his desk and leaned back in his chair. "Well, you'd better watch it, Axline, you know you go to court next week to see if they'll release you."

"Yeah, I know," Max said. "I think they're going to let me go."

"They might, but to tell you the truth, I'd like to keep you around a while longer. I'm going to be there and I'll be wearing my lucky tie, so don't get your hopes up too much." Dr. Silva picked up the end of the green and yellow polka-dot tie he currently had on and flapped it a few times to get his point across. "If I get my way, you'll be mine for six more months, Axline."

241

"Aw, even you wouldn't be mean enough to do that," Max said, but the corners of his mouth drew up, and Maggie knew these two had gone through a lot together, and not all of it was bad.

The doctor bobbled his head up and down a few times, then folded his hands in front of him and, although he still had a pleasant look, Maggie could tell his demeanor had now shifted to a serious mode.

"Listen, Max," he began. "I'm not certain, but I do think there's a good chance they'll cut you loose. And I want you to know, both your mother and I...hell, the whole staff...are very proud of what you've accomplished here." He paused a moment to make sure Max understood. "You do know that, don't you, Max?"

Maggie felt a little like a third wheel. She figured if she was going to break some difficult news to Max, she'd better be a part of the conversation now. "He's right, Max. I tell ya, when I think of what you've been through and how far you've come in just the last few months, I couldn't be more proud. And, well," she struggled with the words. "Well, I guess I want to make sure you keep growing and making progress."

She didn't mean to look at Dr. Silva for approval, but her eyes flickered over to him, and she raised her eyebrows as if to say, "Did I do good?"

Dr. Silva picked up the thread. He leaned into the desk a little further. "You've come so far. Both your mom and I want to make sure you keep heading in that direction, but you're an adult now, Max, and the major part of that responsibility is up to you."

Max shifted in his seat and lowered his head, but kept his eyes glued on the doctor. One knee started a rhythmic bouncing.

Oh shit! Here it comes!

She'd seen this look before. He wasn't liking what he heard, and Maggie wasn't liking what she saw. She sat up straight, squared her shoulders toward Max, and kept her voice low, steady, and firm...very firm. "Max," she said, "I know you are a wonderful person, and we both know you're intelligent and have a lot of potential. But..." she paused, glanced at the doctor,

242

drew herself up, and said, "you can't reach that potential if you're living at home."

Max's eyes shot to hers. At first he frowned, then his expression softened, and for a split-second Maggie thought he was going to cry. But he didn't. Instead, very softly he murmured, "I know."

And all Maggie could say was, "You do?"

"Of course you do!" Dr. Silva snagged the ball and ran with it. "You're no one's fool, Max. Everyone knows that, and we also know you've been through too much to let you slip back into the same state you were in before. 'Course," he hunched his shoulders, and tilted back nonchalantly, "we could just boot you out the door, or, oh, I don't know, maybe drop you off at the bus stop with a one-way ticket to Relapseville."

He leaned forward again. "But we wouldn't do that, Max. You'd be right back in here before you could say Jack Robinson. So, we," he gestured toward Maggie, "your mom and I, have some ideas we'd like to go over with you."

And then, Dr. Silva laid out the plan. A beautiful plan. At least to Maggie's ears. But would Max see it that way?

If Max was released, he would voluntarily go to the PALS unit where he would have more therapy, more freedom, more say-so in his day to day routine. He could go off-unit whenever he wanted during daylight hours, have free-run of the unit, and access to the vending machines. Max listened with little enthusiasm. But when Dr. Silva said, "Hey, Max, you can even smoke and drink coffee whenever you feel like it," Max's raised his eyebrows, and he smiled briefly.

"Still," Dr. Silva said as he wound down, "I don't want to mislead you, Max. I'm still going to wear my lucky tie next week, and I still want to keep you right here on E4 a while longer. But..." he cocked his head, "if you agree to go to PALS voluntarily, there is a much better chance they'll kick you out of here."

Max looked at Maggie and then back to Dr. Silva. "Who's Jack Robinson?"

The doctor stared at him a moment. "Huh?"

"Who's Jack Rob—"

Dr. Silva waved his hand as if to dismiss the question. "Oh, I don't know. Some guy. Some legendary guy."

"Was he fast?"

"Well, I guess so. He was some guy who would come to visit you and then leave before you could say Jack...before you could say 'hello'."

"Why did he do that? That's stupid."

"Well, I suppose because... wait a minute!" Dr. Silva puckered his chin. "Are you trying to change the subject?"

"Is it working?"

"No! Now, Max, the point is, we will always have a plan as long as you're willing to help us help you."

"Okay." Max nodded, but the trace of a smile lingered. "How long?"

"You mean how long would you be there? Well, it's hard to say exactly, but probably at least six months, maybe a year."

Max's smile morphed to a frown.

Maggie knew he was worried, and her heart wanted to draw him close to her, but it remained stoic.

Max worked his eyebrows, trying to comprehend it all, maybe trying to figure out how his life would change, how he could live on his own. "Then what?" he asked.

"Well...then...I guess then we'll see. Depends on how well you do there." He paused a moment before he went on. "Look, Max, I'm not sure what will happen after that, but we would never release you without a plan. There are other programs, other things we can do... to... transition you...to help you become..." Dr. Silva worried his eyebrows. "Well..." he finally said, "to help you become a viable part of society. We just need to take it one step at a time."

One step at a time. Maggie liked the sound of that. It echoed her mantra and gave her encouragement. "I can help, too, Max," she said. "But I don't think living with me is the answer. I worry that it would make you more dependent."

A pall settled over Max's face. He leaned his elbows on his knees and studied his hands dangling between them.

Maggie wanted to jump in and reassure him.

Please, please don't cry. Please, please, please, don't. Be strong, Maggie. Don't give in, don't give in.

Max skewed his face to hers, eyes searching for answers. "Will I ever be able to come home again?" he mumbled.

Maggie swallowed hard, and her icy resolve seemed to melt and pool at her feet. She felt herself slipping—being pulled into that puddle of uncertainty. No words felt adequate.

Dr. Silva glanced at Maggie and once again saved her. "Let's think about that a minute, Max. Has your mom ever turned her back on you?

When Max didn't answer, Maggie's head wheeled toward him. "Excuse me?" she said, having suddenly lost her motherly instinct of empathy. "Maxim Timothy Axline!" It wasn't exactly a shout, but it was definitely more than a loud rebuke. "Have I ever once, in your entire life, ever not helped you in any way I could?".

Max seemed to be thinking this over. "Well, there was that time you wouldn't get me that leather jacket..." his voice trailed off. Maggie knew he didn't have a leg to stand on. He was grasping at memories as watery and thin as Oliver Twist's porridge. And he knew it.

"Oh, please," Maggie huffed and crossed her arms.

Max shrugged one shoulder. "Okay. Guess I can do it."

Maggie tempered her voice. "Anyway, Max, of course you'll be able to come home. Like, oh, I don't know. Like, for visits," she said. "You know, on holidays. Maybe stay for a little while at Christmas. Stuff like that."

Max nodded half-heartedly.

"Max," Dr. Silva went on, "it's important that you learn how to live on your own, that you know how vital it is to continue your medications and your appointments even when no one is there to tell you to. How vital it is to not drink or drug. Not even a toke. But," he stared hard at Max, "you also need to know there will be a support system in place to help you, in case you..."

"Get weird again?" Max finished for him.

Doctor Silva relaxed his shoulders a little and tweaked one side of his mouth. "Yeah," he said. "In case you get 'weird' again."

CHAPTER 52

And so, Max went to court. They released him from involuntary commitment as long as he went to the PALS unit, and Max's life began a period of stabilization. So did Maggie's. She still went to visit Max every two weeks, but now they could go for walks, or go get a pizza, or enjoy the freedom of sitting outside to smoke.

Five months passed. The end of the school year, summer, and fall slid by without incident. They were on the cusp of Christmas again, and Maggie knew Max would want to come home for a few days. Yes, she knew it, but trepidation was creeping back in, and the closer it got to Christmas, the more skittish she felt.

She told herself it would be fun. She told herself it would be good for Max. She told herself they would all enjoy it. She told herself all the correct things, but she didn't really believe them.

Maggie arranged to pick up Max on December 23rd, have him stay three nights, and return him on December 26th. And everything went fine...for a while.

She had invited her dad to dinner, but as usual he had declined. Maggie was sure Miss Mountains had something in store for him, and if her radar was on target, it was probably Wild Turkey... and a little something more for dessert. She thought about inviting a few singles stragglers but decided maybe this first year with Max home, the less confusion, the better. But Clive was a different story. It was certain both Max and Braxton would miss him if he didn't come, and Maggie knew in her heart she needed him there most of all.

"Hey, anybody home?" Clive hollered as he knocked once and came in the front door.

Max looked up from the ridiculous mounds of tissue, ribbons, bags, and gift wrap Maggie was struggling to stuff into garbage bags. "Would it kill you to help me here, mister?" she said as she pulled a curly ribbon from under Max's foot.

"Hey, dummy, help your mother!" Clive yelled as he took a mincemeat pie to the kitchen.

"Huh?" Max seemed oblivious to Maggie even being in the same room, let alone lifting his feet so she could get bits and scraps off the floor. "Oh, yeah, sure," he mumbled and picked up a couple of bows and tags that were within effortless reach and handed them to her.

Hearing his grandfather, Braxton ambled out droopy-eyed from his after-opening- presents-and-before-dinner nap. Maggie knew he was catching up on his sleep after finals at Wazzu, but she also knew that he, too, had some angst about Max being home. And how could she blame him? His experiences with Max the last few years were a tangled mess, just as his brother's life had been.

It was a bit like Pavlov's dog...with a twist. The minute he heard Max's voice, instead of salivating, he ran in the other direction. It was a classic case of conditioning, beyond his control. Maggie knew he would get over it...eventually. But it could take years. If only they could keep Max stable for that long a stretch.

Dinner was pleasant enough but a little edgy. Most of the conversation was between Braxton and Clive. Max sat at the table sullen and drawn into himself. Both she and Clive tried to pull him into the conversation, but he dug his heels in and wouldn't budge from his non-verbal pout. Finally, Maggie gave up and concentrated on trying to make the day as normal as she could for Clive and Braxton. Mostly the three of them made small talk. Maggie showed interest in what Clive would plant in the spring, laughed in all the right places when they talked about reruns of *The Carol Burnett Show*, and showed proper concern when they discussed the genocide in Cambodia. But her heart wasn't in it, and although she tried to focus, her mind strayed.

After dinner, she waved away help with the dishes, Clive excused himself and went home, and Braxton excused himself and went to his room. Max shuffled into the living room and flipped on the end of the George C. Scott version of *A Christmas Carol*.

Maggie put the turkey pan to soak and plunged her hands into a sink full of hot, therapeutic suds. She fished around for silverware and ran her fingers along the tines of a fork, exfoliating layers of dried gravy and sweet potatoes until it was smooth, trying to will her mind far away from the enigma that sat in the other room watching television. But after a few unsuccessful minutes, she snapped her red hands out of the water. "This is ridiculous," she groused, shaking them and reaching for a towel.

She stood for a few seconds staring out the window over the sink, then thwacked the towel against the counter and stomped into the living room. At first she stood with her elbows akimbo and stared at Max as she tried to figure out where to begin.

Be firm but compassionate, Maggie.

She dropped to the sofa and looked at the TV.

Dang! I love this part! Scrooge was sticking his head out the window and exclaiming the boy below was a delightful fellow, an intelligent fellow. Max snickered but didn't seem to even know Maggie was sitting next to him.

No, don't wait until it's over. You'll lose your nerve. We've both seen this movie a hundred times. And this won't be the last.

She cleared her throat and postured herself toward him. "Max," she ventured. "Max!" she said sternly when his eyes didn't leave the set.

"Huh? Oh, hi, Mom." His gaze flicked to her then back to the TV.

"Max, I need to talk to you."

When Max still didn't look at her, Maggie reached for the remote and clicked it off.

248

If looks could have killed, Maggie would have already been laid out in her finest, but she did her best to ignore the black eyes staring her down with daggers and continued in her well-practiced, firm but compassionate, I-love-you-but-I-mean-business voice.

"I need to know how you're feeling right now."

When Max continued to scowl, she went on. "Max, I know you don't want to go back tomorrow, but—"

"Hell no, I don't want to go back!" Max burst out.

Maggie immediately thought of Braxton in his bedroom. She lowered her voice almost to a whisper, hoping Max would follow suit. "Of course you don't. Don't you think I know that?" Oh, how she hated this conversation. "But, Max, you know you have to."

"But I don't want to." Max muted his voice to the crestfallen whine of a child who has been told to go pick up his toys. "Why?"

She couldn't bring herself to say, "Because this isn't your home anymore," so she opted for the strategy she used when the boys were young: give him a choice. "Well," Maggie measured her words carefully, "you do have a choice, Max. You can either go back, or I will take you to a homeless shelter in Vancouver tomorrow. But that would only be for a few days. After that, when they kick you out..."

Maggie trailed off and lifted her shoulders and brows, leaving the possibilities of the consequences up to Max's imagination. Her body tensed as she waited for his reaction.

Max stared at the blank screen so long Maggie wondered if he thought it was still on. She waited...and waited. She let her shoulders ease down and folded her hands in her lap. One minute passed. Two minutes. A lifetime.

Wait him out. Don't say anything. Wait.

Finally, Max turned his dark gaze back to her. "'kay," he mumbled.

Maggie released a very quiet, very slow, drawn-out breath of air, patted Max on the knee, and returned to the dishes.

Before they left the next morning, Maggie called the hospital and made an appointment to talk to Dr. Silva after she dropped Max off. Although he wasn't Max's supervisor in the PALS unit, he had kept track of his progress and, after all, he was the keeper of "the plan." Maggie figured it was time to explore that plan a little further. She didn't know exactly when Max would be released from his current situation, but she did know that one day soon it would be upon her. She'd had enough surprises. Surprises no longer brought the wonders of Christmas morning, the delights of childhood. Surprises were the enemy.

They drove around to the back side of the hospital to the PALS entry. Maggie gave Max a hug, being careful not to let her emotions get out of hand. *Matter of fact, Maggie. This is not a sad situation.* Or, at least if it was, she didn't want it to show. She couldn't see any reason that Max needed to know about her meeting with Dr. Silva. She didn't want him to get his hopes up or worry about what they might discuss, so she said her goodbyes, drove back around to the far end of the building, and went up to the fourth floor.

In a pink and gray argyle tie, Dr. Silva looked almost...normal, Maggie thought as she sat across from him. "Well, it's been almost...what...six months now?" he said, fingering the file in front of him.

"Yep." Maggie knew what she wanted to ask, but didn't quite know how to do it without sounding like a meddlesome, nosy mom who really didn't have a say in her grown son's business. Or without whining. She paused and went over the questions in her mind: shouldn't we be thinking about "the plan"? Is there really a place for him to go after PALS? Finally, she settled for, "So, how's he doing?"

"You know, he's doing fine. We've had a couple of small set-backs, but they didn't really amount to much."

Maggie raised her brows until Dr. Silva continued.

"Well, you know, some pretty normal stuff for a kid his age...well, young adult, I guess. Apparently he decided one day he was going home. We found him sitting at the bus stop a couple of blocks away." Dr. Silva grinned. "One of the unit nurses spotted him on her way to work. I don't think she would have even noticed him if he hadn't been sitting with another client who had no pants on. That's what caught her attention."

He put his hand on the file, still amused by the story that must have been played back several times in the staff room since then. "But, you know, we talked to him and got him back on track. Anyway, that was six or eight weeks after he went to PALS. I imagine it had to do with the adjustment he was going through."

Maggie smiled politely. She could see the humor in it, but it also said something about the state of mind Max must have been in. He hadn't been keen on staying there in the first place. Was this going to become a recurring problem? "So, do you think he's improving? I mean, what comes next?"

Dr. Silva thumbed through the file. "I think he's going to be ready to move on in a couple of months, and I have an idea for the next step if we can talk him into it. Again, it's a volunteer program, so..."

"So, it might work if I still won't let him come home," Maggie finished.

"Exactly. But it's a good program. It's kind of a Job Corps type deal for people with mental diagnoses, and I think Max will be ready for it in a month or two."

"Is it here at the hospital?" Maggie asked. She was hoping the next step in "the plan" would be a little closer to home.

"No, actually it's in Sedro-Woolley; ever hear of it?" When Maggie shook her head, Dr. Silva went on. "Sedro-Woolley is a town up north of here, past Seattle, closer to the Canadian border." When Maggie frowned, he added, "But it's a good program, Mrs. Axline, and I think Max could get a lot out of it."

"Oh, no, I'm sure it is. I was trying to calculate the trips in my mind. Might have to modify how often I see him. So, what's it like, this program?"

"It's called PORTAL. To tell you the truth I don't remember what it stands for. But the clients actually try out some different types of on-site jobs and even get paid a little bit. I think they put it away in a savings account for them, so they can have a little something when they get out...or at least that's the idea."

"Sounds good," Maggie said, although the calculator in her brain was still trying to figure out how far away it was, how long

251

it would take to get there, and how often she would be able to visit. "So, how long do you think he'll be there? I mean, is there anything in the plan for after that?"

"Well, I do have some ideas, but I think we need to get through it one step at a time. We may have to adjust our strategies if this doesn't work."

CHAPTER 53

But it did work.

Two months later Max went to PORTAL in Sedro-Woolley, and Maggie changed her 130-mile-every-other-week visits to 250-mile-every-three weeks visits.Yes, the trip was long, but she found the small town, when she finally arrived after a tedious five-hour drive, was a distinctive little place steeped in a vibrant past—from Tusko, the circus elephant that ran rampant through the settlement in 1922, demolishing fences, Model Ts, and anything else that got in its way, to Bottomless Lake, or the notably historic Stumphouse Man. Sedro-Woolley did not exactly flourish, yet somehow maintained a tranquil and unruffled existence twenty-five or so miles east of the San Juan Islands in Puget Sound.

At one time it also boasted of Washington's Northern State Mental Hospital which, when it closed in the 70s, was archived into the town's intriguing past and became fodder for imaginative ghost stories. And next to this hulking stone and brick monument, now as quiet as a church graveyard, sat PORTAL, newer, shinier, and not nearly as thought-provoking as a creepy abandoned hospital, but functional nevertheless.

As Maggie approached the anodized aluminum doors at the end of one of four long, narrow units, she was once again caught off guard by the characteristic aroma. While it was clean and tidy, the unit had a slightly medicinal smell to it, not unlike that of a nursing home. It made sense. Being a life-skills center for people with "dual-diagnoses," she imagined most, if not all, clients—at least twenty in each of the four buildings—were on prescribed drugs of some sort.

They had identified Max as paranoid-schizophrenic/alcoholic. And, although he was more stable now than he had been for a while, she knew that one day off his medications, one drink, one trauma could send him right back to "start" in this baffling game of Psychological Life.

Did Max know that? Oh, there was no doubt he had been told many times. She, Dr. Silva, and a plethora of other doctors, nurses, and caregivers had stressed it, and she was sure it was an integral part of his on-going rehabilitation here, but did he actually grasp its import?

Maggie was glad she no longer had to wait outside to be admitted; it was more normal and less "hospitally" she decided as she walked to the lobby to sign in. This was her third visit since Max had come, and it was his twenty-second birthday. She wasn't sure what their protocol was for birthday cakes, so she left it in the car for the time being.

She spotted Max on the far side of the commons area shooting pool with a wisp of a young man as skinny as a linguini noodle and with features as delicate at a gnat's eyebrow. Max waved and finished his corner shot, but the noodle crossed the room in a fleet series of hops and dodges, and even before he opened his mouth, Maggie knew that fragile façade was a smokescreen for the churning mass of molten lava camouflaged beneath it.

He extended a twig with a bird-bone hand attached to the end of it. "Hi," he squeaked, "I'm Harold, but Max calls me Art because he says I remind him of some guy they called the Artful Dodger in some book he read once, but my real name is Harold, so you can call me that or you can call me Art I don't really care I'll answer to almost anything I guess you're Maggie."

"Uh...yes," Maggie stammered as she gently shook the end of the spindle.

Max sauntered over and gave his mother a cursory hug. He flicked his head toward his friend. "This is Art," he said.

Harold did a scrawny leprechaun's version of Lord of the Dance, then flopped grandly onto a sagging, faded green chenille sofa.

Maggie watched him for a moment, fascinated, then turned back to Max. "Well, okay then," she murmured. "Oh, and happy birthday, Max!" She gave him a hug warmer than the one she received. "Hey, I've got a cake out in the car and some other stuff. Do you know if it's okay to bring it in? I made an extra big one so we can share."

Max shrugged but was clearly pleased, and Maggie was pleased that he was pleased. "Hey, Dakota!" he hollered across the room at a staff member, "Okay if my mom brings in my birthday cake?"

"What kind?" he hollered back.

Max glanced at Maggie who joined them by hollering, "Devil's Food!"

"I like German Chocolate!"

"I'll remember that next time!" Maggie grinned. The lighter atmosphere here was comforting. "Come on, Max. You and, ah, Harold, can help me."

The rest of the visit was casual and relaxed, or at least as relaxed as it could be with a pint-sized Whirling Dervish tagging along. Max had already shown her the work stations on a previous visit. He had tried working in the silk screening department and the upholstering department, but had settled in the sewing shop where he kept track of and recorded the hours of others that worked there. No, it wasn't much, but Maggie figured it gave him a sense of purpose and being needed.

As the three of them went back down the hall to take a walk around the grounds, one of the clients working on the janitorial unit push-broomed his way toward them. As he passed, Harold did a half huff, half high-pitched giggle, and Maggie caught him giving Max a devilish glance.

"So, Max," she said nonchalantly, did you ever do janitorial work here?

Harold giggled again, and Max said, "Kind of," and shot a warning glance back to him.

Maggie left it at that. She was pretty sure these two often shared in mischief. Max always could find creative ways to get into trouble, and she was positive Harold was a leading architect in this capacity.

255

The grounds were expansive. The old hospital lay between the four PORTAL buildings that stretched out several hundred feet on the south end and another building on the north end that housed the "real Job Corps," as Max put it. A walkway ran beside the hospital and linked the two areas with a common cafeteria that served both organizations.

But the fascination for Maggie, and certainly anyone else who had not seen it, was the derelict, deserted hospital that loomed between them. While they strolled around the old building peeking in broken windows, Maggie ran her hand along the massive, eroding facade and examined broken tiles that spoke of the one-time grandeur and pride that now stood crumbling in decay. It was no wonder it was ingrained in the imaginations of the locals and the tomes of historians.

Max walked next to Maggie, pointing out curiosities that had been passed down from ear to ear for years, while Harold flitted in and out of alcoves, jumped up on ledges, and swung from branches of gigantic oaks that now intruded into the once-empty space along the outer walls.

"Hey! There's one!" he yelled, and jumped off a deep windowsill and ran with arms flailing in the direction of a streak of black and orange fur headed for asylum. But Harold's pursuit was no match for a feral cat running for its life from a maniacal lunatic. It ducked into a chink in the foundation before he could even get close.

The show took only five seconds, but it was bizarre enough that it stopped Maggie dead in her tracks. "What in the heck's he doing?" she asked as Harold flew head first toward the getaway hole.

"He's kitty-rustlin'," Max said, then yelled, "You'll get him next time, Artie!"

"Next time?"

"Yeah, we come out here at night sometimes and try to catch 'em."

At night?

Did she dare ask? "And the staff doesn't care if you do this?"

Max looked at her like her question rated right up there with "Do you like liver?"

"Well, yeah they care."

She knew better than to delve too deeply into the impracticality of doing something against the rules. This was, after all, Max's gig, not hers. Instead, she asked, "Ever catch any?"

Max's mouth spread to an impish grin. "Once," he said. Then his face turned sober and the smile vanished. "Scratched me so bad, I had to go to the infirmary." He frowned. "They gave me a shot."

"It was that bad?" Maggie pictured a crisscrossed mass of bloody streaks.

"For cat scratch fever," Max said, still watching Harold as he reconnaissance belly-crawled over to where the cat had disappeared. "It's not just a song, ya know."

It was true a riff from Ted Nugent's song did flit through her mind, but she rolled her eyes and again let it drop. She could only hope Max had enough intelligence and common sense to blaze a few trails that didn't involve another cat scratch fever shot or a cohort that was clearly headed in the direction of entanglements.

But by the time she left PORTAL that day, Maggie was feeling better about Max's stability. They had lit the candles on his cake and sat talking with counselors and clients who had strolled out to the lounge when word got out of an impromptu birthday party. A few of the residents even rummaged around their rooms and found suitable gifts they no longer had use for to give Max: a couple of well-used guitar picks, a chipped mug with the "Denny's" logo on it, a mostly-used jar of freeze-dried coffee, and a half-dozen cigarettes. In exchange, they ate cake and enjoyed the privilege of forgetting for a while the reason they were at a "dual-diagnosis" work center.

As for Maggie, nobody asked her for a smoke, nobody regaled her with farfetched stories of being a secret agent assassin, and best of all, nobody asked her to clip their toenails.

She drove back to Vancouver that afternoon with a lighter heart and buoyed hope.

It wasn't until two weeks later Maggie got the phone call.

257

CHAPTER 54

Maggie turned the clock toward her. The red digital numbers glared "5:02 a.m." She fumbled for the phone.

"Hi, Mom."

"Max?" Why was Max calling that time of day?

"What? Where are you? What do you want?" She fumbled for the clock and groaned. "It's five o'clock, Max."

"I'm here."

"You're where?" Maggie bolted up in bed as if she half expected to see Max standing outside the window.

"I'm here," he said again.

Maggie had gotten used to Max repeating himself if he couldn't think of a quick, plausible explanation. "And where is 'here'?"

"I'm here!"

Maggie took a deep breath. "Max. Think for a minute. Exactly where are you? In Vancouver? In Sedro-Woolley? In Kathmandu?" She knew her voice was edgy with frustration, but she didn't care.

"In Vancouver," came the also edgy voice on the other end.

"Okay...where in Vancouver?"

"Here. At some motel."

Maggie heaved a sigh. "Max, I'm going to need more to go on. Do you know the name of the motel?" When there was no answer, she said. "Look, try to find matches or something in the room with the name of the motel on it. If you can't find that, go outside and look at the sign."

"Hold on a minute." It sounded like Max put the phone down; there were muffled words as he apparently tried to find a clue as to where he was. All Maggie heard was, "What's the ...wants to know...hell, I don't...go out..." and then she heard the squeak of a door, a slam, and a shuffling as he picked up the phone. "It's called the "Shangra-la-di-da Motel. Do you know where it is?"

Maggie knew exactly where it was. Close to the freeway, the Shangra-la-di-da Motel often made the five o'clock news for all the wrong reasons. Usually it was something to do with a drug bust or prostitution, but occasionally a shooting or stabbing was thrown in to keep it lively. She assumed it was cheap, and she could only hope that was Max's reason for choosing such stellar accommodations.

"So who's with you Max?"

There was a brief pause before he said, "Art."

Maggie closed her eyes. "And what plans do the two of you have? Are you going back to PORTAL?"

"Naw, we decided that place is a drag. We weren't getting anywhere there."

"What? You mean like they were holding you back?" Maggie tried her best to keep the eye-roll tone out of her voice while all the fears, the doubts, the panic came tumbling back.

She was on the verge of losing her composure when Max said, "I thought you could pick us up and we could stay with you...you know, only 'til we find someplace else."

And in that split-second Maggie made up her mind. She knew what she had to do. "Nope," she said.

There was a long silence, then, "Whadda ya mean?"

"What I mean, Max, is that you may not stay with me. You chose to leave PORTAL, you chose to come to Vancouver, you chose to make a stupid-ass decision, Max. You chose those without giving any thought as to how it would work out."

"Yeah, but what am I supposed to do now? I'm almost out of money."

Maggie's shoulders sagged. As resolute as she was about Max not staying with her, she simply could not let him live on the streets...or at least she hoped it wouldn't come to that. "Well, one thing you did not choose, Max, was to have a mental illness, so what I will do, and the *only thing I will do*," she emphasized, "is help you get back to PORTAL."

Max didn't answer immediately, but she could hear a muffled one-sided conversation again. "She won't... don't know why...no, she won't let...no, not even if you pay...she said... I don't know if they'll ..." Then, to Maggie he said, "Okay, I'll try, but I'll have to call them. I don't know if they'll take us back." Maggie found the number of PORTAL so Max could call them and charge her telephone account. Two hours later, as Maggie sat hovering over the phone, Max called her.

"They don't know if they'll let us come back," he said. "They're going to meet on Monday to decide. Can I stay there until then?"

He sounded so pitiful Maggie considered it for a moment. After all, it was only until he could go back.

But what if they won't let him go back? What if he's stuck here? What's he going to do then? What am I going to do then?

Maggie swallowed hard and said, "No."

She knew Max had no idea how hard that was for her to say. She knew he had no idea how easily, with just a little more effort, he could have pushed her to reverse her decision. She was teetering on a dilemma strung as tight as a fiddler's bowstring. But an idea came to her that would buy her a little time.

"Okay, Max. I am willing to help you a little until they decide. I'll pay for your room there until Monday when you find out. But only 'til then!" she added quickly. "How much money do you have right now?"

She waited while he and Harold counted their pooled funds. "Almost thirteen dollars," he said.

"Good, that will be enough for you both to eat for two days if you're careful."

"But how—?"

"I don't know how, Max. You'll have to figure that out." She drew in a deep breath. "I'll be over within an hour to pay for two more nights."

Maggie pulled herself from bed, leaving behind her hopes crumpled among tangled sheets. It took her only forty-six minutes to throw on jeans, sweatshirt, and tennis shoes and high-tail it to the Shangra-la-di-da Motel. She wanted to get this over with before she caved.

Perpetual wind from I-5 traffic had blown years of litter up against a rickety chain-link fence that led to the entrance. As she drove around the end of it, it was obvious the motel was in worse shape than she remembered when she'd been by it two years ago. Yellow paint peeled from the stucco, the parking lot was strewn with cans and broken bottles, and paper, cigarettes, and gum were ground into the asphalt by incessant ne'er-do-well traffic. To add to the ambiance, some of the bulbs on the motel sign were burnt out so it read, "The Sha g-la-da Mote."

She paid a questionable proprietor for two nights of "luxury living," and went to see Max in "suite twelve," which, Maggie noted, was no more a suite than her home was the Hearst Castle. She told Max she would be home all day on Monday and suggested he call PORTAL by check-out time to see if they had made their decision.

Saturday and Sunday he phoned her several times, but she knew it would have been even more if the noodle had not been with him to keep him occupied.

It was a long two days.

On Monday, Maggie took a personal leave day from work and hung around the house until she heard from him. The waiting was torturous, but she maintained her "one-step-at-a-time" stance, trying not to dwell on what would happen to Max if PORTAL would not let him back in the program.

He called at 11:30 with an answer.

It was not the one she wanted to hear.

"You're kidding me!" Maggie thunked down on a kitchen bar stool and let her head drop to the counter. When she raised it after a few moments, she sucked in a big draft of air with renewed determination. "Okay, then. You will do what you have to do to get back."

"But I..." Max started.

"Yes, Max, you can do it. I'll help you, and we'll just...get it done."

Max had called PORTAL, all right. And, in fact, Maggie knew the outcome could have been worse. They told him they

261

had serious reservations about allowing him to come back, but they had talked it over and decided their conditions. If he wrote a five-hundred-word essay telling them why he left and how he planned to use the program to improve himself if he came back, they would consider it, and if they approved the essay and felt he was sincere, they would allow him to return. If he decided to leave again, they would wash their hands of him entirely.

"And what about Harold? Does he have to do the same thing?" Maggie was dreading the thought of helping with one essay, let alone two.

"Oh, well, he doesn't need one," Max said. "They won't let him go back so he took off a few minutes ago. I think he has some relatives in Ashland or something like that."

"Oh?" Maggie tried to keep the delight out of her voice. She didn't ask why; she didn't want to know. She simply said, "Well good for you for not going with him, Max," and dove in. "Okay then, here's what we're going to do." And Maggie laid out a spur-of-the-moment plan. She didn't ask Max for his approval. She figured if he didn't like it, he could go it alone, and she would have to hope for the best.

Maggie told him she would pick him up in an hour and they would go to a coffee shop and write the essay while they had lunch. But now, since she needed to pay for food as well as somewhere for him to stay, she hoped to find a place that was even cheaper than the Sha g-la-da Mote until he heard from PORTAL again.

Max did not exactly greet the plan with enthusiasm, but at least he didn't argue with her about it.

Maggie grabbed a legal pad, some pencils, and an envelope. At the last minute, she snatched the newspaper from the couch and headed again to the seedy side of the world.

It had started to rain, and by the time she got there, the clouds were having their way with the ground and pelting it with a typical, cold June deluge. "Drismal" Max used to call it when he couldn't remember if it was "drizzly" or "dismal" outside.

She found Max already checked out and shivering next to the building under the cover of a doubtful awning that looked as though it could never "awn" anything. He clambered in and flashed a meek smile as she rolled to a stop.

Although shabby, the restaurant was clean, dry, and warm, and the coffee was strong and hot. She waited until they ordered before she shoved the tablet and pencil across the table to Max. "Might as well get started," she said.

Max picked up the pencil but sat staring at the paper. His eyes drifted up to his mother's. "Can't you write it for me?"

Maggie had been expecting this. She knew that since his first psychotic break, Max had trouble organizing his thoughts on paper. It didn't help that his handwriting had become deplorable. More like cat scratches from "kitty rustlin'" than penmanship.

"No, honey. You can do this. I'll help you get started. Let's begin with who you are writing to. You know, like a letter." Max stared at her as if she had asked him to name all nine Supreme Court justices.

"Okay, who did you talk to this morning?" she coaxed.

"Dakota."

"Do you know his last name?"

"No."

"Okay, why don't you start, 'Dear Dakota and PORTAL Staff.'"

To watch Max write even that much, tested Maggie's patience. She had to still her hand from snatching the pencil from him and writing it herself. But she sat patiently and kept her expression positive even though behind it she felt like an exposed mass of nerve endings.

When he had finally scribbled the salutation, one by one Maggie fed him a series of questions he could answer in his essay.

"Why did you decide to leave?"

"Do you think your decision to leave was good or bad?"

"Why?"

"Why do you want to go back?"

"What will you do differently if they let you come back?"

"Are you sorry you left?"

"Why?"

When they finished two hours later, Maggie read his essay. It wasn't bad. Sincere. Fairly legible. And the best thing was that Max seemed genuinely pleased with himself.

Before they left the restaurant, they looked in the newspaper and picked out possible places with rooms to rent. Maggie left a generous tip for the extra time and multiple cups of coffee, and they went in search of somewhere for Max to stay for a few days. They found three affordable places. All downtown. All in sleazebag hotels.

They chose the least disturbing of them, and Maggie helped Max carry his few belongings up one flight of stairs to an eight-by-ten room that was void of character or even a hint of cordiality. No warmth or tenderness could be detected in the austere furnishings or the picture on the wall of a crow with boots on, huddled against the sleet. The entire room was yellowing and smelled of hard drink and hard times, and it was all Maggie could do to leave Max there. But she knew she had to so she gave him a long embrace and walked back down the steps and out into the biting rain.

CHAPTER 55

On her way home, Maggie took the letter to a Mailbox Plus to send it overnight delivery. With luck, the staff at PORTAL would make its determination the next day, and she could at least plan the next step. Max's immediate future weighed in the balance. If he was allowed back, it would feasibly buy a few more months of stability for both of them. If not...well, Maggie would deal with it then.

Yet, despite her one-step-at-a-time credo, options for that next step crept surreptitiously into the fringes of her thoughts. She even went so far as to look up the numbers of the social workers she had met when Max was at Vancouver Memorial. She also kept Dr. Silva's number close at hand...just in case, Maggie told herself.

She took another personal leave day from work. She asked Max to call Sedro-Woolley early and let her know what he found out. So he tried in the morning, in the afternoon, and in the evening, but still had no answer.

The next day, and yet another day off work, Max finally called her with their answer.

Midway through the first ring, she grabbed the phone. "Well?"

"They'll take me back, but I have to get there myself by tomorrow afternoon."

"Okay, good."

Steady as she goes, Maggie girl.

"Okay, this is good," she repeated as her mind did flip-flops trying to gauge the effects of several options for returning the escapee. It was already eleven in the morning. Even with a good run, if she left now, it would be midnight before she got home, one o'clock before she got to sleep if she was lucky, and up at four-thirty the next morning for work. She could take him the next day, but she had maxed-out her personal leave days so it would be a day without pay.

The other option was to put Max on a bus. If she went with that one, he'd probably get in about eleven or twelve that night, at the earliest. Then there was the problem of getting a ride from the bus depot to PORTAL. She crossed that one off the list.

"Listen, Max, I really don't want you staying in that dump another night. I'm going to pick you up right away so we can get up there as soon as possible."

Before she left home, she called Sedro-Woolley to let them know Max was on his way. She thanked them profusely and told them, yes, she did know it would be his only chance to come back, and no, she had no idea if it would happen again, but yes, she also certainly hoped it wouldn't, and WHAT? HE HAS TO GET HIS HAIR CUT?

"Is there something you forgot to tell me?" Maggie asked as Max slipped into the car.

The look she got was of pure innocence.

"Never mind," she said. "There's a barber shop one block over. That's our first stop."

The look of innocence changed to one of disbelief. Maggie didn't know if it was disbelief that she was making him get his hair cut or disbelief that she had found out. But as soon as they pulled up to the barber shop, his expression changed again to disgruntled resignation.

With torn emotions Maggie watched the long, dark hair float to the worn, black-and-white linoleum tiles. Once silky and fluid from careful grooming, now dull and stringy from rain and neglect, his hair symbolized the change in him over the last few years. Max had always prided himself on maintaining a full mane of thick hair, even after many rock stars had modernized their images by cutting theirs. And while Maggie was never particularly fond of it, she always believed it was one

266

aspect of his life he should have control over. Besides, a good rubber band was always an option for keeping it off his face if it got too unruly.

Maggie was also aware cutting his hair represented another hard lesson: life is not always fair, but sometimes hard choices have to be made to get on with it. Maggie knew those choices all too well. She'd been making them for years.

They hit the Seattle rush traffic, and from Tacoma through Everett, they crawled. It wasn't until Maggie got home at one-forty-five the next morning and flopped into bed, that she allowed herself a rush of relief. And the tears broke through the stoic facade, giving some relief to her stored-up anguish.

CHAPTER 56

According to Will Rogers, "There are three kinds of men. The ones that learn by readin'. The few who learn by observation. The rest of them have to pee on the electric fence (to find out for) themselves." Max had peed on the electric fence, survived, and come out a wiser man.

Of course, Maggie knew most of his choices were not voluntary. She knew the illness, the breaks, many of the bad decisions were not of his choosing. No one chooses to be mentally ill, to be in a hospital, to be thought of as a social pariah. But it happens. And Max had learned there were certain things he could control and certain things he could not.

He stayed at PORTAL another eight months where he learned better coping strategies, and that life is sometimes a crap-shoot so you might as well take what the dice rolls and make the most of it. Whether he learned skills there, Maggie couldn't say, but he did learn another life lesson that became his model for the way he treated others. In doing so he changed his thinking and how he interacted with people and was rewarded with a room of his own, more respect from the staff, and occasionally an extra helping or cookie when he visited the mess hall.

He even coined a phrase he was fond of repeating to Maggie: "Being nice will get you a bigger sandwich," he'd tell her when she spoke curtly to someone in the heat of the moment.

At first, she wanted to wring his neck, then she accepted it as just an ego-centric conviction and tried to slough it off. But by the time he left PORTAL Max had become a genuinely kind, soft-hearted man, whether or not he got a bigger sandwich.

And Maggie's life became...well, perhaps not what she would call "routine," but at least less like a rollercoaster and more like a merry-go-round that, for the most part, glided smoothly with some ups and downs that usually didn't throw her completely off track.

Max moved back to Vancouver to a halfway house with thirty or so other residents under the supervision of the mental health program. There, although they monitored his medications, helped him keep track of his appointments, and had therapy sessions with counselors, it was a step closer to independent living. It was the year 2000, and Maggie hoped the new millennium would bring a rebirth to their tired lives.

One day in April when Maggie went to visit him, he was sitting outside on the front steps. His hair was growing long again. But it was his huddled posture that caught her attention. It was a cool spring day; the temperature was in the fifties. So, why was he hunched on cold concrete steps with no coat on?

A lump formed in her stomach and worked its way up to her throat. "Max?" she said as she approached him.

His head bent almost to his knees, Max raised damp eyes to her. Then she saw the source of his anxiety. In his arms, he cradled a small kitten, mostly black with white splotches.

"I think it lost its mother," he said and rounded his shoulders toward the kitten to afford it the most protection possible.

She was so relieved, she could have done a happy-dance right there on the sidewalk. "Oh! That's...," she began, then corrected herself. "I mean, awwww, that's too bad."

She sat next to Max and peered at the ball of fur nestled against his chest. "What're you going to do?"

"I'm going to name it 'Oreo'," Max said.

"Okay, but then what are you going to do with it?"

He didn't have an answer for that, but the look of determination told her no one was going to take that cat away from him.

269

When she saw Max a week later, there was a cardboard box at the end of the long, covered porch. A flannel shirt had been stuffed inside it, and the two pickle jar lids sitting next to it offered table scraps and milk.

By the time he moved to a group home five months later, the half-way house had added another member. Oreo, approaching kitty adolescence, was a permanent petted, pampered, and over-fed part of the diverse collection of occupants there.

Max struggled with leaving him behind, but by then Oreo belonged to everyone. Maggie assured him there would be plenty of opportunities to have other pets, and Max wasted no time in adopting another cat as soon as his bags were unpacked and his part of the refrigerator was established. He named it "Snow." It was mostly grey so Maggie was never quite sure why other than there was an unseasonably early dusting of snow that October.

The share-house lodged six or seven adult males of varying ages. There, they did their own shopping, own cooking, renewed their own medications, and basically controlled their own lives. However, being under the umbrella of the mental health system, they had a visiting counselor/overseer to help the living arrangements run efficiently and harmoniously. And, for the most part, despite a conglomeration of temperaments and personalities, it did.

Max took on some interests, appointing himself the social director of the house and organizing potluck parties they could invite their families to. He also started his own non-profit enterprise by taking donated run-down bicycles and refurbishing them to give to children of low-income families.

Maggie was pleased, but not everything was smooth sailing. Now that he was doing so well, his counselors often pushed him to get at least part-time work. And Maggie understood why. He was on Social Security Disability, and any opportunity for him to make money of his own would ease the financial burden on the state, as well as make him more independent. But she also saw the torment every time he went to a new work location. He tried his hand at several jobs, but each ended in disappointment and left him a quivering bundle of nerves and frustration.

When she could, Maggie would pick him up and drop him off at a restaurant, a warehouse, a grocery store, or wherever he was trying to work that month. During these times he was always anxious, and when he became anxious, he became silent.

But it was an icy Tuesday in December when she noticed a more disturbing change. She was taking him to a grocery store chain where he was supposed to try his hand at bagging. He was silent as usual, but kept rolling his window down, gulping air, then rolling it back up. Maggie kept an eye on him, but said nothing, hoping it would pass.

But a block away from the store, Max grabbed his head with both hands and rocked back and forth. Maggie swerved to the shoulder of the road and slammed on her brakes. "Max?" she said.

But Max didn't hear her. "Ohhh. Ohhh." He moaned, still rocking, still clutching his head.

"Max!" Maggie said firmly. "Max. You need to talk to me."

When Max stopped rocking she said more softly, "Max, can you tell me what's the matter?"

The confusion in his face was heart-wrenching. "It's going to be okay, Max. You can tell me. We'll take care of it."

"I don't know what's the matter with me. I think..." his eyes scanned the inside of the car, then he looked out the window as if the answer might be there. "I think..." he started again.

"What, Max? What do you think?"

"I think I need to go to the hospital," he finally said.

Maggie's body buckled.

Think Maggie. Think!

After a moment, she drew in a breath. "Good, Max. I think it's wonderful that you can tell when you need to go to the hospital. We're going to go there right now." She did an illegal U-turn right there in the middle of Fourth Plain Boulevard and headed to Vancouver Memorial.

That Max was enough in touch with his illness he knew he needed help was, without a doubt, incredible in itself, but what happened over the next few months truly amazed Maggie.

271

CHAPTER 57

Maggie sat in the cramped waiting room at Vancouver Memorial. Same yellow plastic sofa. Same Van Gogh sunflowers.

A nurse had taken Max into an examination room until he could be evaluated by the doctor on call that day. It turned out to be Dr. Friedberg again.

The doctor came to the waiting room two hours later, smiled pleasantly, sat on the laminated coffee table in front of Maggie, and extended his hand. "Good to see you, Mrs. Axline."

"Good to see you, too...and it's Maggie," she said out of habit.

She filled Dr. Friedberg in on what Max had been doing and where he had been since the last time he was at Vancouver Memorial. She wasn't sure what medications he was on right then, but she did know he was taking antipsychotics, something for depression, and others that were for side effects of the ones he was taking. "Sorry," she finished, "He's changed meds so many times. I know Columbia River Health Center can tell you exactly what he's on right now."

"Of course." Pause. "We'll give them a call." Pause. "But for right now, Mrs. Axline, I'd like Max to stay here a few days for observation." Dr. Friedberg took off his glasses and cleaned them with a loose shirt tail, held them up to the light, and perched them back on his nose. "And, I'd like Dr. Perrin from Columbia River to come here for a consultation."

Maggie must have looked dubious, because with an uncharacteristic spurt of enthusiasm Dr. Friedberg said, "I think Max will be fine, but we need to take a look at those meds. I think he needs a," pause, "tune-up."

"We want to try something new, Max."

After two days at Vancouver Memorial, they met with a doctor again. This time it was Dr. Perrin. It had been years since Maggie had seen him. She didn't know if he remembered her, but if he did, she hoped it wasn't because she had pushed him to make a correct diagnosis the last time he saw Max.

Maggie had asked if she could sit in. She didn't go to most of Max's meetings, but she still wanted to keep track of his progress, or his lack of it, if it came to that. After ten months of Max being back in Vancouver with no incident, her anxiety was beginning to ebb. Then this last episode.

Was he backsliding? Would he get worse? End up in Steilacoom?

She'd been there before, and she wasn't about to let a sneaker wave throw her off balance again, or worse yet, be hit by an unexpected tsunami and have to start building their lives from scratch once more.

She sat next to Max in one of the conference rooms on the second floor of Vancouver Memorial, holding her questions in check. But try as she would, she could not completely hide her reactions. Smiles, shrugs, eyebrow gestures, and her mouth opening and closing like a fish gulping for air, were a dead giveaway that she was a tacit part of the conversation. Still, she knew she was a guest observer, and perhaps to Dr. Perrin, an unwelcome one at that. So if she stayed quiet, and if she listened closely, sooner or later, her questions would be answered.

The "something different" Dr. Perrin was talking about was a medication that was fairly new on the market.

"Clozaril," he told Max, "is called a 'last resort' drug for people with schizophrenia. But it's shown excellent results for reducing the risk of suicidal and delusional behavior." He let this information seep in before he went on. "Now you know there are always possible side effects like everything else we've tried, but we're going to keep an extra close eye on you this time."

273

Dr. Perrin explained the side effects to Max, the least of which were hypersalivation and weight gain. It wasn't those Maggie was concerned about. Diabetes and agranulocytosis were another matter altogether. Agranulocytosis, Dr. Perrin said, was a rare blood disorder characterized by a severe loss of white blood cells making those who had it susceptible to bacterial infection. A much more serious consideration.

She knew that schizophrenia was not considered curable, and over the years it had become clear no drug or combination of drugs was completely effective for Max. And now, another glimmer of hope. Even with dangerous side effects, could this be the one?

They kept Max at Vancouver Memorial for two more weeks so they could get him started on Clozaril and monitor him closely for side effects.

The medical staff was on top of it. After the hospital, they had him go back to the half-way house where they could still keep a vigilant eye on him for a few more weeks before they let him return to the group home. And after weekly, then bi-weekly, and finally, monthly blood-draws, Max's life became almost predictable, and that, to Maggie, was amazing.

CHAPTER 58

December was sloppy. Sloppy and bone-chilling. But it was the first Christmas in a long time Maggie had really looked forward to. And that made all the difference. That made it a Norman Rockwell, Cricket on the Hearth Christmas. Well, maybe not quite. But the lawsuits had finally been settled, and as Bernie had predicted, Maggie no longer had to worry about losing her home. And this Christmas Max was more stable than he had been in years, Braxton would soon have his degree in Structural Engineering, James Parker hadn't fallen in the river lately, and Clive was...well, as rock-solid as ever.

After dinner that year, no one went to his room and no one went home. In other words, no one tried to escape. The sloppy rain turned into fat white flakes falling softly on the cedars, the dirty dishes sat soaking in the sink, and the fire cracked and popped its pitchy tamarack song. And Maggie sat in the living room with Max, Braxton, and Clive.

"So, did you see that game last week?" Clive didn't have to say which one. He and Braxton spoke the same language.

"Yeah, Pittsburgh might make it to the Super Bowl." Braxton sank further into the red, over-stuffed armchair and put his feet up. "They have a shot at it, but my bet's on the Patriots."

"Maybe. And the Rams?"

"Maybe."

The conversation was languid and comfortable.

"What about you, turkey? What do you think?" Clive nudged Max's foot with his.

"I think it's snowing," Max said.

Clive and Braxton tracked his gaze outside the bay window to the white accumulation on the trees. "Huh," they said at the same time.

"Probably should be heading home before I get snowed in." Clive yawned, but didn't move a muscle.

The fire sizzled and spit as Maggie put another log on it and sat back down.

"Hey, isn't there a game on today?" Clive asked.

"Yeah, I think Blue and Gray are playing right now." Braxton reached for the TV remote. But he didn't turn it on.

And still, the four of them sat, content and warm.

That evening, after Braxton had gone to bed, after Clive had gone home, and after the last of the pots and pans had been scrubbed and put away, Maggie and Max sat at the kitchen counter sipping hot-buttered-rum, minus the rum for Max, extra rum for Maggie.

"You know," Max said, "I think this is the best Christmas ever."

It had been a long time since she had heard those words. They felt almost tangible. She sighed. "What was your favorite part?"

"Oh, let's see..." Max looked at his gifts piled in a corner, at the white lights of the tree reflected in the window, and at the candles sputtering to an end. "All of it, I guess."

"Yeah," Maggie said, "it feels good, doesn't it?"

Max nodded. "For me," he started, then stopped short. He worked his eyebrows as he tried to put his thoughts into words. "For me," he started again, "well, it makes me feel like...well, like my pants are lined with fleece."

Yes, she thought, that's exactly how it feels.

Before she went to bed that night, Maggie stepped out on the porch. The snow arched indiscrimately in soft, luminous lumps over tree stumps, old bicycles, and a forgotten lawn mower. She breathed in air as crisp and clean as she had ever known. "Tomorrow," she whispered to herself, "is going to be a good day."

Bon Jovi said, "Miracles happen every day; change your perspective of what a miracle is and you'll see them all around you." Maggie had changed her perspective of what a miracle is. It was simple, really. A miracle is a crackling fire, an almost-normal family, and once in a while, if you're lucky, some fleece-lined pants.

THE TRANSLATION OF MAX

Printed in the USA
CPSIA information can be obtained
at www.ICGtesting.com
LVHW021917281223
767684LV00010B/453

9 781494 992774